CHARLIE'S LITTLE SECRET

GERRY DUFFY

Charlie's Little Secret by Gerry Duffy

Note to the reader: This novel is set in London in 1963 and many of the characters use racist and homophobic terms common at that time.

ISBN: 978-1-7392461-0-5

For Christine, Thomas and Stephen

CONTENTS

Chapter 1 9

Chapter 2 28

Chapter 3 48

Chapter 4 81

Chapter 5 93

Chapter 6 104

Chapter 7 126

Chapter 8 159

Chapter 9 168

Chapter 10 187

Chapter 11 207

Chapter 12 219

Chapter 13 249

Chapter 14 278

Chapter 15 292

Chapter 16 296

Chapter 17 305

Chapter 18 307

BRITAIN IN THE 1960'S – FROM DARKNESS TOWARDS THE LIGHT

In 1963, when this novel is set, Britain was still very much in the dark ages. Capital punishment was still in use, it was still completely legal to discriminate on grounds of race but illegal to engage in homosexual activity. Divorce was expensive, rare and required a guilty party.

But things were changing fast. The Britain we know today was invented in the 60's.

1961 – The Contraceptive Pill made available on the NHS – for married women only

1963 – The Profumo Affair involving John Profumo and Christine Keeler
– The Great Train Robbery
– President Kennedy assassinated

1965 – Death Penalty suspended – finally made permanent in 1969

1965 – First Race Relations Act – outlawing racial discrimination for the first time

1967 – Sexual Offences Act – Homosexuality decriminalised

1967 – The Abortion Act – legalising abortion for the first time

1967 – The Contraceptive Pill made available on the NHS to all women

1969 – Divorce Reform Act – introducing 'no fault' divorce for the first time

'So on the nights they're here, after lights out, make sure you face the wall. When he comes in just lie dead still. Close your eyes and don't move. Don't even breathe and hope he passes you by. But if you feel his hand on you, it's your turn.'

CHAPTER 1

He stood in the dim room staring out at the darkness. Rain danced against the window, smearing his reflection, running down the glass and blurring the twinkling lights in the streets way down below. It was a penthouse view up here in these new high rises, a rich man's view. Out there, the bombed-out buildings and slums were disappearing under the wrecking ball. Maybe everyone in London would be living in the sky soon. It felt good up here, looking down on things. It felt right, or as right as anything ever could after what had happened.

Behind him a clink of glass as Maggie poured herself another drink.

'Come over and sit down,' she said, her soft Irish lilt coaxing. Ken roused himself, watched her watching him in the reflection, and walked over to sit with her on the settee, him at one end, her at the other. The only light in the room that altar of hers on the wall with the big glowing statue of the Virgin Mary and the Christmas lights around it. Christmas lights all year round.

The wreck of the day lay about them, empty bottles and glasses scattered like an exhausted army. He felt her move on the settee and glanced over. She was lying back looking at him over her glass. The glow from the altar behind gave her a halo like some picture of a saint he'd once seen. With her long black hair and blue eyes she could have been one.

'Been a long day,' he said.

'Don't remind me. I haven't slept for two nights. I'm dead.' She dipped her head, rubbed a palm slowly across her forehead, and gave a short, bitter laugh. 'That makes two of us.' She glanced towards the bedroom door.

He forced a smile to show he got the joke. 'Why d'you do that anyway – keep the body at home?'

'Tradition.' She took a swig of her drink. A big one. 'Us Irish are great ones for tradition. You darkies wouldn't know anything about that.' Her voice was teasing now.

To Ken it seemed the Irish had some pretty strange traditions. Charlie lying in his box in the bedroom and the flat full of people drinking all day at this thing; this party they throw when you're dead – The Wake. There must have been forty people in the little flat for a while. People from Charlie's place; black, white, flush, skint – people who never mixed except at Charlie's. Outside, they'd cross the road to avoid each other. Inside, it was different. It was always different when Charlie was around. Now with everyone gone, his widow sat a couple of feet away, her legs crossed, one foot in its black stiletto-heeled shoe, moving up and down; up and down. He wondered if there might be any other traditions he didn't know about. She had that look in her eyes.

'What are you looking at?' Her voice was soft again, inviting.

'Just you.'

'And what do you see? '

He met her eye. Even with the strain of the last couple of days showing in her face, it was beautiful. 'I see a lovely lady in need of some sleep.'

She closed her eyes and took a sip from the glass. 'It's hard to sleep after what's happened,' she said. 'I need a little comfort.'

'Don't take it from a bottle.'

She opened her eyes again and let them rest on him. 'Where should I take it from?'

He said nothing.

Earlier, people had gone in to the bedroom and looked at him, a whole crowd of them. A mark of respect, they said. He hadn't. He didn't want to see all those drunks gawping and gaping, treating the sight of Charlie as something to tell their friends about in the pub. But after they'd all left, he went and stood with Maggie, looking down on Charlie lying there in the suit he'd only had made for him a couple of months ago. It was strange, the coffin at the foot of the bed; Maggie's clothes on a chair; the bedside table. Had she slept in here last night? Someone had laid a half bottle of whiskey in with Charlie. His thick frame looked too big for the box, as if he'd been squashed into it and could split the whole thing apart if he just drew one more breath. But he never would. And Ken wondered how he could keep the sky from falling without Charlie there to hold it up.

'Tell me about your Ma,' she said, the tease back in her voice.

He wondered why she asked. 'You already know.'

'Tell me anyway.'

'I don't remember her. All I got is the one photo.'

'What does she look like?'

She knew that too.

'She looks like you.'

Charlie shouldn't have died like that – in his sleep. It was all wrong. He should have gone out with fists flying and all guns blazing, the way he'd lived. Not choking on his own puke. Undignified. The drink had done for him, the doctors said – two of them, according to Maggie. Charlie always liked his booze, even back at the home where he got into trouble for it. But he knew how to take it too – could out-drink most men. So how does an ox like Charlie die at the age of twenty-nine?

Then there was that look she was giving him. He knew all about it. When he met her eyes across the top of her glass it took him back to all the other times he'd seen it in a woman's eye. It must be ten years since the first time, with Ann. When he was fourteen and still at the home – Charlie grown up and gone, not around to watch out for him anymore. Ann in her blue cardigan, his Houseparent, his stand-in mother, told him to come and sit beside her in the dark. So he did. She lit a cigarette and gave it to him – strictly against house rules. They'd sat there in the glow of the electric fire, sharing the cigarette and listening to the sounds the other kids made when they were asleep; the heavy breathing of a dozen heads on a dozen pillows through a thin ceiling. He'd started to wonder why he and Ann were doing this, but then her hand was on his thigh and her lips were at his ear whispering the same words he was hearing now.

'Kiss me.'

He leaned further back into his end of the settee. 'Maggie, you're all burnt out. You don't know what you're saying.'

'Try me.'

'I'd be taking advantage.'

'Tonight, I want to be taken advantage of.' Her voice was weary, almost a sigh. This woman, with plenty in her eyes but no tears, wanted him too – like so many others, so many who wanted a piece of his golden body. At night he was golden. By day he was just half-caste.

He'd have to decide whether to slide across the settee and take her in his arms. He didn't like to turn down an invitation from a lady. It felt unprofessional. But right now there was something about that couple of feet of settee. Charlie had been the nearest he'd ever had to family, and he was lying dead in the next room. It wasn't right. And there was that look. He knew it alright, but there was something else going on in those blue eyes too. Something most men sitting where he was wouldn't waste their time on. But he saw it. He didn't know what it was. But when he caught it, a little chill ran down his spine.

* * *

Last night's rain had given way to a bright blue sky. With the funeral scheduled for ten thirty, he'd been out of his bedsit at a godforsaken hour to grab the bathroom before the Italian woman upstairs got there for her long soak. Now he walked up the street towards the tower block and it was barely nine thirty. That must be some kind of record.

Cars lined both sides of the street and a big hearse was backed up against the entrance to the block. He didn't realise Charlie knew so many people with cars. Some were good ones too; Consuls, Corsairs, Humbers. Charlie's crowd liked to spend and didn't mind where the money came from. And the never-never was a way of life around here.

Above him the neighbours were out on their balconies, leaning over, shouting to each other, cockney accents ringing across the street. Everyone had a view from the gallery for today's show.

The men hung about in groups, talking and smoking. There were others who looked more like professional mourners from that Catholic church of Maggie's. He could tell from the way they dressed – dark Sunday best – a string of rosary beads in the hands of a woman. Charlie's friends were the kind of people who came to wakes more than funerals, but a lot of the white ones had made the bleary-eyed effort. Their suits were a bit too flash for the occasion, but you had to make do with what you had. Some he knew. One or two nodded to him, others didn't. He was used to it. Not everyone wanted to know the darkie in daylight – if that's what he was. His colour threw them a little. If his skin had just been black then their instincts would know where to take them. But it wasn't, and that left them pausing to think about what to make of him. He'd lived his life working that pause.

It seemed none of them were the kind of personal friend that went up to the flat at a time like this. He was, but he drew some looks from the neighbours in this white part of town. The East End didn't take to outsiders, especially those who didn't even have the decency to have the same colour skin. Dressed in his sharpest blue sharktooth suit and a thin black tie set against his mustard silk shirt, he could guess what the old women on the balconies were muttering to each other. Pimp. What's that pimp doing in our block of flats? Fuck them. He took the lift up. The door was on the latch so he pushed it open, walking in on a busy scene.

Maggie looked good in black. She had on a wide-brimmed hat with a little lace veil. It suited her, made her look mysterious. She gave him a hug, but not too close, so it didn't spoil her appearance. That couple were here, the ones he didn't know, who were leaving as he arrived yesterday. They were putting their coats on, and were well-dressed in a conservative way that said they had money. She was maybe mid-twenties, not good-looking but with strength in her face. Not his style. He preferred a little more fun in his women. The man was much older, with black hair, thick black eyebrows and a serious look that hadn't changed since yesterday – and probably for a good while before that. The undertaker, face pulled long for the occasion, was getting his two pallbearers to pick up the coffin. The lid was screwed down now. Ernie, the red haired old boy Ken recognised from Charlie's place, held open the door while he directed the traffic. Charlie had introduced him to Ken once while ordering up the drinks, calling him 'my associate' – whatever that meant.

* * *

The hearse took it pretty fast to the crematorium. When you're dead you're expected to show up on time. Ken sat next to Ernie as the old man's Rover followed on behind the rest of the cortege. He'd taken the opportunity to scrounge a lift as they'd waited for the bearers to load Charlie into the hearse. Maggie and the couple he didn't know were up ahead in the black limo.

'Who're those in the car with Maggie?'

'I only met them meself this morning,' said Ernie, his voice deep and rasping. 'Turns out they're relations of Charlie's. The woman's a cousin or something. Her name's Hazel Dolman. Her man's a doctor. They live north London somewhere.'

'I didn't know Charlie had any relatives.'

'Funerals have a way of flushing out the long lost relations. There's always a chance of a few bob from the will.'

'Not from Charlie.'

'They don't know that. Charlie was a businessman.'

Ken had never heard Charlie called that before. Ernie was surprisingly talkative with someone he only knew as a barman at the club. He was old, sixties maybe, with a leathery hangdog face and big, thick hands.

'Not exactly the upright kind of businessman, though,' said Ken.

Charlie's business was a little club – his shebeen, he called it – that did a good trade from midnight until six most nights. The location had to change from time to time, due to the unlicensed nature of its activities, but people always knew where to find it. It had started out as just a drinking den. There were Dockers and labourers plus a few black and brown faces – seamen off the cargo ships. Charlie didn't operate a colour bar – about the only place that didn't in this part of town. All that mattered was the colour of their money, he said. The setup suited Charlie – brought him most of the things he seemed to want from life; booze, fights and the respect of his customers.

'So?' said Ernie. 'You start a business in the East End you can't be too choosey. Not many silver spoons round here, are there?'

Following the cortege down the Mile End Road, they passed the run-down little shops, the tired pubs, the hunched grey people who called these shabby streets home.

'No, not many,' said Ken. 'What'll happen to the club?'

'Who knows? It's Maggie's now.'

'I suppose it is.' The thought hadn't come to him before. 'Think she'll keep it?'

Ernie gave a little twist of the head. 'Not that simple. She'll need advice. I hope she's good at taking it.'

Ken didn't know Maggie well, but from what he'd seen he had a feeling Ernie was going to be out of luck on that one. He shook his head. 'If it goes, I don't know what I'll do without the place.'

After he left the home, Charlie started him off behind the bar. The shebeen had moved on, specialising in Calypso, Ska, Bluebeat – the new sounds from the Caribbean that the seamen brought over with them. The local Jamaican population – the Rude Boys – loved it, coming in to show off their sharp suits, their white girlfriends, their switchblade knives. The raucous nights, the dancing and the music was something new, something happening, and it didn't take long for Beatniks, Mods and Chelsea fashion-chasers to find their way there too, all melding together in the heat and the sweat and the beat of the little club.

The place had a pretty rough edge to it, and at times there'd be disagreements; switchblades facing off against broken bottles. But Charlie was always there, a sawn-off shotgun clamped in his big fists, smacking heads. He never had to do much else, because everyone knew Charlie never backed down from a fight and everyone knew the gun was loaded.

'Dolmans ain't interested in Charlie's business,' said Ken. 'They're Mr and Mrs Doctor – straight as they come. Not their style.'

Ernie shrugged. 'Maybe,' he said. 'But they've hardly been out of Maggie's hair since Charlie died. They're here for something.'

* * *

They followed the drive of the crematorium and Ernie pulled into a bay outside the grey, windowless building. They climbed out and walked quickly to the entrance. Ernie was a slow driver. Everyone else had already gone inside except for a little group huddled in a circle in the car park.

'Well, well,' said Ernie, nodding in their direction.

Ken recognised the Dolmans standing with the priest in his robes and four big white men in Mackintosh's he'd never seen before. One of the four was doing the talking. Whatever he was saying seemed pretty interesting because the rest stared at him while he spoke in a low, intense voice. But as Ken and Ernie walked by, he stopped, starting up again once they'd moved on.

Inside, the big chapel was nearly full. There were a lot more here than outside the flat and the lively hum of conversation told Ken several had primed themselves in the pub beforehand. The coffin was laid on the track to the furnace. A shiny pink curtain separated the chapel from the machinery behind it. Maggie was sitting at the front on her own. He and Ernie shuffled into a pew behind her.

There was a long wait. The Dolmans didn't appear, or any of the others Ken had seen outside. Conversation started to run out amongst the mourners. When the priest finally came in, he walked up the aisle from the back of the chapel, which struck Ken as odd. He went straight to the pulpit. His face was as grey as the building.

'I am sorry but there will be no funeral today. These gentlemen are policemen.' He gestured to the back and everybody turned round to look at the four big men marching up the aisle. 'And they have come to remove the body.'

The priest disappeared through a door without another word and the men began lifting the coffin. The shocked silence that followed the priest's words gave way to angry mutters from the congregation. Then Maggie sprang to her feet. 'You can't do that!' she yelled. 'Get your hands off my Charlie!' She shuffled out of the pew and made a grab at one of the men, who put out an arm and pushed her away. A sudden roar of anger went up from the mourners behind Ken. The police had no friends amongst this crowd. The aisle started to fill with people. Ken pushed his way amongst them and got himself next to Maggie. He put an arm around her, supporting her as the throng surged forward. They became part of a wall of people pressing in on the policemen, blocking their movement down the aisle.

'Get out of our way!' shouted the one in charge – the one he'd seen talking outside. They tried to move, but the crowd heaved and jostled around them. The cop reached into his inside pocket and pulled out a piece of paper. He waved it in the faces of the people in front of him.

'This is a court order,' he yelled. 'We have to take the body away.' They were trying to shove their way down the aisle, force their way through, but the harder they tried the more determined the resistance became. The aisle was packed now and the crowd had them surrounded. They weren't going anywhere. Then the same cop pulled out a whistle and blew it, its sharp screech echoing off the high ceiling. The chapel doors were flung open and half a dozen uniformed men appeared. Ken waited for them to draw their truncheons and wade into people, but they didn't. Instead, they formed themselves into a wedge and slowly forced a gap in the crowd until they got to the others with the coffin and helped them out. The crowd shoved them around as they went, but during the whole thing nobody had thrown anything as inconsiderate as a punch. This was some kind of church after all. By the time he and Maggie got outside the cops were closing the doors of a van. Two of them climbed into it, and the others got into police cars that had appeared from somewhere. The driver of the van hit the accelerator too hard, spraying gravel up at the mourners who gathered to watch them go and give them a jeering send-off. Ken watched the Dolmans climbing into a taxi. They seemed in a hurry to leave.

* * *

Back at the flat Maggie held together better than he expected. She didn't cry or break down. Instead she just sat looking dazed. He stayed with her while people arrived, made their sympathetic noises, and sat around for a while in awkward silence. Everyone acted like it was a normal funeral – as if they'd buried Charlie instead of seeing his coffin carried off by the police. There weren't any rules for that, so the women busied themselves making tea and washing up, and the men drifted out onto the balcony to smoke. After a while, Ernie took charge again and started sending them on their way; polite but firm. When he'd herded the last of them out of the flat he looked like he was going to move Ken on too but Maggie stopped him. Ernie made tea for Maggie and poured a hit of whiskey into it, then took her into the kitchen for a long conversation behind the closed door while Ken sat it out on the settee. He wondered what they were talking about. Ernie was a bit of a mystery to him, involved somehow with Charlie but not in any way he could fathom, nor any way Charlie had ever explained. When they finally came back, things between them looked a little troubled. Ken felt the need to find something uncontroversial to say.

'Who are those Dolmans?' he asked.

Maggie sighed. 'Hazel's his sister. Two or three years younger than him,' she said. 'Charlie always knew about her but she was adopted when she was young – didn't even have the same surname. He never saw her much – maybe the odd note now and then.'

Charlie never told Ken about this sister. But then Charlie was very good at keeping secrets. Like where he got the money to start the shebeen. Not from the labouring jobs he used to do, that's for sure. Not by the time he'd drunk it all away on a Friday and Saturday night. And like that diary he used to keep at the home. Once he'd got Ken to hide it for him for a couple of days, but only after getting him to swear he wouldn't look at what he'd written in it.

'So what're they up to?' said Ernie. 'Why cause trouble at a time like this?'

Maggie sighed again and shrugged her shoulders. Ken wondered if Ernie was going to ask the big question: why did those coppers take Charlie's body away? Ernie said nothing and Ken took his lead from him. This wasn't the moment.

Maggie stood up. 'Ernie,' she said, 'I hope you don't mind, but I'd prefer to be on my own a while.' Maggie had a way about her. Ken had seen it before, a way of saying things that didn't invite argument. So Ernie got up and started putting on his coat.

'Right you are, Maggie.' He didn't sound too put out. It had been a tiring day. It was already nearly three. Ken wondered whether he should reach for his coat too. She wanted to be alone, but it was Ernie she was talking to.

'Call on me soon and let's talk again,' Ernie was saying. 'Charlie was a fine man. More than most people knew. If the law come back I'll arrange some help.'

'You're a diamond, Ernie,' said Maggie. She followed him to the door and Ken heard her gently closing it behind him. When she came back into the living room she sat down next to him on the settee where they'd sat apart last night. They stayed like that for a minute, not speaking. Then she leaned slowly over to him, took hold of his thin black tie and pulled him close.

'This time, Kenny boy, I'm not taking 'no' for an answer.'

He didn't say anything, just put his arms around her and

gave her a long and tender kiss. He felt the tension drain from her as he held her. He kissed his way down her neck, ran his fingers through her dark hair. She took his hand and put it to her breast. He felt her heartbeat, it was beating fast. She slid his tie off whilst he worked at her clothes. He could do the right things – make the actions seem smooth, practised – like they had been lovers a long time. She slipped out of her dress. He pulled it from beneath her and dropped it on the floor so it wouldn't get creased. Her hands were on his mustard silk shirt, tearing at it, and he was afraid she might rip it. He took her hands and smiled.

'Maggie, we can burn a little slower. There's no hurry.' He bent his head and kissed each breast. She slowly unbuttoned the shirt and peeled it off him. They helped each other unzip and unfasten until they were naked. He let his head slide back down between her breasts and smelt her body. She drew him onto her. He was slow, calm, in control. This was the thing he knew how to do. And he was good – as good as always. She gripped his shoulders, her fingers like steel. He took charge of her with his weight and his rhythm, feeling her react to him. Then they moved as one, and all he had to do was adjust the pace and keep the long ride going until she got there with a cry so raw it seemed to have nothing to do with the sex.

Afterwards he held her, her body curled around his. She was rested, peaceful – until she started crying. 'Poor Charlie,' she sobbed, 'poor Charlie.' As if the grief had had to wait until now. As if she'd needed this act to break the dam.

She kept on crying while Ken lay holding her and whispering all the words of comfort he could think of. Her tears on his chest. The November sky darkened and the light began to fade. It made the glow from the altar seem stronger. He ran his fingers slowly down her back, and counted the big dark bruises he could see there. Eleven, twelve, thirteen.

* * *

It was a policeman's knock – loud, determined, a knock that meant business. He'd know it anywhere. Ken pulled on vest and trousers and checked his watch before opening up. Eight o'clock – early, but could be worse. The two standing there were from the Crematorium yesterday.

'Detective Inspector Davis.' He was the cop who'd been waving the piece of paper in the chapel. The stare Ken got told him everything he needed to know about Detective Inspector Davis's feelings on the subject of dark-skinned men opening doors belonging to white women. Opening any kind of doors come to that.

'Is Mrs Ward at home?' Davis said it like he didn't need to ask.

'You couldn't get Charlie to talk?'

'Don't try my patience. He's going to be telling us plenty. Go and get the lady.'

'Right with you,' said Ken, closing the door. Davis's foot stopped him. The door banged back into his face sending him reeling backwards. Davis and his sidekick walked in.

'It's cold out there. We'll wait in here,' he said, coming up close to Ken and giving him an eyeballing. 'If that's all right with you, boy.' He emphasised the 'boy'. They always did. Davis took a step back and looked Ken over in that way cops like to. Like you're guilty of something, but he hasn't worked out what just yet. 'Don't I know you from somewhere?'

Ken got asked that question a lot. It didn't mean anything. Davis and all the other cops didn't know him from anybody else whose skin wasn't as white as theirs. But he knew Davis. He didn't notice it yesterday during all the action, but now it hit him. He couldn't get a hold on where from, but he had that face in his head somewhere.

'She's not up yet,' said Ken.

'Oh?' Davis threw a look to his sidekick. 'Active night was it?' The sidekick sniggered.

'What you did to Charlie yesterday, to her, right there in the chapel, it was disgusting, man. It destroyed her. It would anybody. She needs to rest.'

'I'm not the only one who's been doing things to Charlie.' Davis's voice was a low growl now – the serious heavy cop. 'Get her up.'

* * *

Maggie seemed to be expecting it. Or maybe after yesterday nothing was ever going to surprise her again. She got dressed and stood in the kitchen gulping down the cup of tea Ken made for her. Davis and his sidekick sat quietly watching and practising their sneers on Ken.

'Where're we going?' she said to Davis.

He looked at her and seemed to decide against one of his sarcastic remarks.

'Stepney Green.'

She turned to Ken. 'Call Ernie. Got his number?'

'No.'

She rummaged in her bag and pulled out a small diary. Tearing a page from it, she scribbled a number on it and handed it to Ken. Then she reached into the bag again, pulled out a key and tossed it to him.

'Make sure everything's ok, will you?' she said and walked out without waiting for the two cops to catch up. They got up quickly and followed her out of the flat. Ken shut the door behind them and stood listening to the sound of the lift coming up, the rumble of the door opening, then closing. Then the lift took them all away.

He went back to the kitchen and turned on the transistor radio. They were still talking about President Kennedy being shot dead in America last week. He wasn't sure why it mattered to anyone over here. It didn't seem as important as what happened to Charlie, but that wasn't news. After he'd washed up, tidied the flat and got dressed, he checked his watch. He needed to find a phone box to call Ernie, find a barber shop to buy some rubbers. Then he just had nice time to get across town to meet Betty.

CHAPTER 2

Betty Blake was beautiful, rich and married – Ken's favourite kind of woman. Small, dark-haired and intense, she must have been really something when she married Thick Rick – the name she liked to call her husband when he wasn't around. Rick might not have had too much between the ears but he knew how to make money. It was the one thing he was good at, according to Betty. That was pretty much the whole story of how he came to meet a gorgeous girl like her. She'd decided a long time ago that she was going to leave behind the two rooms in the East End tenement where her mother, father, and four younger brothers still lived, and find a better way of living. She moved to West London, bought some nice clothes and hung around in a lot of chic little cocktail bars until she bumped into Rick.

The problem with Rick was that he was like a lot of those rich men, he worked so hard making himself a millionaire that he'd forgotten how to have fun – especially with his wife. Betty hadn't forgotten how to have fun, though. She and Ken usually had fun once or twice a week.

According to Betty, Rick didn't really expect her to be happy because he wasn't that happy himself. He seemed to think that if he gave Betty enough money she'd just forget that she was unhappy and so could he. So he gave her plenty of his money. He gave Ken quite a bit of it too. He just didn't realise it. It went to Betty and Betty spent it on Ken. Like that sharktooth suit he was still wearing. She liked to buy him suits. There were other people in his life who liked to buy him shirts or shoes. It was a cool arrangement as far as he was concerned. He gave them the pleasure they weren't getting anywhere else, and they gave him things in return. Betty had even found him the place he was living. Thick Rick made his money renting out places to what Betty called 'lowlife', and she'd worked something out for him. It was an arrangement that helped remind Ken of his status in the relationship.

Today she was smoking. She sat outside the coffee bar in the chilly sun looking Italian. She had on one of those dresses that kept a tight hold of her body all the way down to where her legs were crossed at the knee, and a silk headscarf wrapped around her head and thrown over her shoulder. She looked like Sophia Loren. She wore a pair of big dark glasses, and held one of those long American cigarettes out in front of her so the smoke didn't get in her eyes. He didn't like her smoking. It made her breath taste raw, but she always smoked when she was worked up about something. He sat down beside her and put his arm around her waist.

'Hey baby, you're looking good today,' his usual greeting. She blew out a long jet of smoke – like steam, and pressed her lips together. This was a bad sign. He ordered two coffees then put on a hurt look.

'What's the matter baby – ain't you glad to see me?'

'We're in bother, Ken.' She might have looked like she stepped out of a magazine, but her voice was pure Bethnal Green. 'He's found out.'

Ken let that sink in for a minute.

'How?'

'I told him.'

He flung himself back in his chair. 'You did what! Why'd you do that?'

'We were having an argument. It came out.'

'What were you arguin' about?'

She put the cigarette to her lips and took a slow drag, then reached over to the ashtray and tapped it with a long manicured finger.

'If you really want to know, it was about some shoes I bought him.'

'Shoes?'

'He said they pinched.'

'Really? Pretty serious stuff, then. So you let him have it right between the eyes.'

'Something like that. You've got to be married to him to understand.'

'Sounds like he was sparring and you were fighting for the title. So how'd he take it?'

She slid the glasses down her nose so Ken could glimpse the black eye. 'Gave me this, then walked out.' She slid the glasses back into place.

Ken whistled. 'Looks like he was in for the title too. When was this?'

'Yesterday.'

Their coffees arrived, frothy in small white cups.

'So what did he say?'

'He was mad. Did a lot of shouting, said he was going to do the pair of us.' She stubbed out the cigarette. 'Never thought he had enough interest in me to bother.'

This was bad news. Her old man had been throwing his money around for a long time to show what a great guy he was and it had worked out well for Betty and him. But that was all going to stop now. Instead it looked like he might throw Betty around a little more. Him too, maybe. He knew where Ken lived. That big lump of lard, Meatball, who came round every fortnight for the rent, didn't he used to be a wrestler or something? It was hard not to feel concerned about this turn of events.

'What d'you think he'll do?' He tried to sound more relaxed than he felt.

'Who knows? Kill us both probably.' Betty looked across at Ken and gave him a little smile. 'That'd be a good way to go, wouldn't it – murdered in each other's arms?'

Ken stopped blowing on his coffee. She reached out and patted his leg.

'Don't worry, sweetheart. I ain't got no plans to die young. We'll just stay out of his way for a while, 'til he cools off.'

'Maybe we better not see too much of each other for a

while.' Ken couldn't help glancing around, just in case Rick was lurking somewhere in the shadows with a meat cleaver. He tried to stay calm.

'Not afraid of him, are you?' Betty's face gave nothing away. Her dark glasses weren't giving him any help either.

'I'd climb any mountain for you Betty baby, you know that. But mixing it with your old man?' he shook his head slowly. 'I don't know about that. I don't like to interfere between a man and his wife.'

* * *

It was Friday, and nearly one o'clock – an important time for him. It meant the bowler hats in Whitehall would be making their way out to their clubs in Pall Mall for that extra-long lunch they needed to get the weekend off to a good start. It meant Ken was heading in that direction too. He took a tube ride from where he'd met Betty in Chelsea, got out at Green Park station and made his way down the steps to Saint James's Park. The weak November sunshine lit the autumn leaves, turning their brown to gold. It was amazing what a bit of sunshine could do at this time of year. People strolled, making the most of the brightness. He turned a corner and walked to a long line of benches. Already several were occupied by young, hungry-looking men like himself. He exchanged nods with one he recognised. Finding a vacant bench, he sat down to wait.

This was how he liked to live, everything in its little compartment. He didn't try and hide his life with the women too much, because it gave him a kind of status among the punters at the shebeen, but this part he kept to himself. So long as he was careful, there wasn't much risk. He could easily spot the cops from the Vice Squad with their regulation short-back-and-sides, but getting caught meant a prison sentence, so the fewer people who knew about it the better.

He tried not to worry too much about Betty and Thick Rick. The thing was complicated, and it made him weary to contemplate. He'd never been any good at dealing with problems. He'd have to think about it sometime, but not now. Instead he took out the key that Maggie had thrown him and held it up. It wasn't the sort to fit the door of a flat or a house. This was for a big padlock. It was Charlie's key to the shebeen. She was asking him to go round and check it out for her. It had been locked up since Charlie died. He felt the weight of it in his hand. It was a useless piece of junk without Charlie, unless Maggie was going to take it on. Maybe that's what she intended. She used to be at home in the place, enjoyed being queen of the bar, until she gave it up a couple of years ago. But would she want to run it? Still, everything that used to be Charlie's was hers now, and that seemed to include him. He wondered what was happening at the police station – what she was telling the cops. If Charlie didn't die the way Maggie said, then what did happen?

Someone came and sat down on the bench. In his off the peg grey pinstriped suit and pearl tie, he was just one more invisible from the army of pen-pushers Ken saw swarming onto the evening tube trains. He could have passed for middle aged, but when Ken looked closer he could see he was younger, maybe thirty or so. He was on edge and Ken could smell the drink on him. Dutch courage. For a minute the man stared across the park. Then he turned and looked at Ken.

'Come here often?' he said.

'Most Fridays.'

The man relaxed a little and smiled. 'How much for a hand job?' he said.

'Three,' said Ken.

The man raised an eyebrow in surprise. 'I understood two was more like the usual rate.'

'Two and a half then.'

The man nodded. 'I'm Larry.' Larry smiled again and got up from the bench. He walked off in the direction of the park café. After a minute Ken got up and followed him. The man eventually disappeared into the toilets behind the café. Ken went in. There was a stranger at the urinals. He and Ken looked at each other, instant hostility on the face of the stranger. Ken went back outside and waited. The stranger emerged.

'Queer cunt,' he muttered as he passed.

Ken re-entered the toilets.

'Larry?' he said in a low voice.

The door to one of the cubicles opened a little. Ken pushed it and went inside.

* * *

At the end of the day he took the District Line going east, back to the poor side of town. It had been a busy afternoon and he didn't have time to tot up his earnings until he was at the station; another tired commuter on his way home. Five visits to the toilets and he'd made nearly as much as a factory worker did in a week. It was easy work, and gave him plenty to get by on – though he might have to do a bit more now he wasn't working at the shebeen.

He sometimes wondered how these men lived the rest of the time. Just like the women he knew in West London, they weren't getting the right kind of sex. So they went looking for young studs like him, taking big risks for a few minutes of freedom. But the women seemed happier. They might be spending their husbands' money, but they were in control. These guys often seemed as twitchy and miserable after the sex as they were before. Maybe the thought of ending up in prison did that to them. He imagined them going home to respectable houses and maybe even respectable wives somewhere. Leading lives so different from his, in places so far away they might as well be distant stars. He had never been out of London. The outer limits of his universe were the ends of the tube lines; Epping, Uxbridge, High Barnet. Even these were exotic places he'd never been to. As for the places these men sometimes mentioned; Reading, Luton, Watford, he could summon only the vaguest idea of them. If he really put his mind to it, he could conjure little villages, an easy horse and cart ride from each other, with churches and old pubs and flowers. But what kind of lives they lived in these places; whether they took any more pleasure with their wives than they did with him, that was where his imagination ran out.

He sighed, looking around at all the weary faces on their way home. People could find all kind of ways to make themselves unhappy, but not him. He just went with the flow. Thinking was hard work and he preferred not to do too much of it. He'd had things worked out pretty well until Charlie died: these Fridays in the park; the work in the shebeen; his women. But everything was different now. He felt numb when he contemplated life without Charlie. He'd have to make a new one for himself now. It wasn't something he was looking forward to.

* * *

As the District Line train wound its way east, he remembered the key in his pocket that Maggie had given him. He could get off a stop later and wouldn't be far from the shebeen. Might as well go down and take a look – a good excuse to go back to Maggie's and see her again. Find out what had been happening with the law, see what kind of state she was in. He needed to know.

He remembered that first moment when she'd walked into the shebeen. It was still early, the pubs only just closing for the night, and almost nobody in yet. She had on a gabardine overcoat that hadn't been in fashion for a few years, and a little black hat with a small red feather stuck in the side of it. Charlie didn't even notice her, but he did. There was something about her – the hair, the eyes – that reminded him of the picture he carried in his wallet, and he felt a small disturbance ripple through him while he told himself it was impossible. She couldn't be the right age.

She walked over to where Charlie was leaning on the bar. 'Are you Charlie?' she said, her voice clear and sure.

He looked at her for a few seconds, taking in the details of her face, before asking her name.

'Maggie,' she said, smiling warmly.

'What can you do for me Maggie,' said Charlie.

'Bar work. I'm strong. I can heft the cases by myself.'

Charlie gave her an amused look. 'You sure?'

'Try me,' she said, and put an elbow on the counter, hand up, as if inviting him to arm-wrestle.

He laughed then, and put his thick arm against her skinny one, his big paw curling around her fingers.

They gave it a go, Charlie bending her arm down to the counter, but with a little look of surprise on his face that said it took more effort than he'd expected. Ken didn't know it then, but that was the moment Charlie was smitten.

He'd been a little chilly around her himself though. Things were different between him and Charlie after she came on the scene. He didn't blame her exactly, just kept out of her way. He didn't have much contact with her, except in Charlie's company. So she must be pretty messed up and lonely right now to want him in her bed all of a sudden. He could understand it, but it didn't feel too good to be giving that kind of comfort. He owed Charlie. Charlie had been his protector since he was nine, in the home and in the world. He felt like he'd lost a brother – more than a brother. But since yesterday she was on his mind. Somehow she had found a way across the distance he liked to keep between himself and other people. When he thought about her sitting on that settee with the light behind her; her black hair; her blue eyes, he just wanted to keep on holding that picture in his head. Reaching into his inside pocket, he took out his wallet and opened it, looking at the photo of his mother. The black and white picture couldn't tell him the colour of her eyes. But the black wavy hair, and that wide, fun-loving smile – they were a lot like Maggie's. Only he hadn't seen Maggie smile like that since Charlie died. A long time before that come to think of it.

* * *

It was dark and quiet when Ken walked down the narrow lane that led to the railway arches. The shebeen was under one of them. Charlie never liked to draw too much attention to his business so he tried to find places that weren't going to get the neighbours complaining. Down here there was nothing but deserted streets of condemned houses boarded up for slum clearance; a few little workshops; a scrap yard. He passed some teenagers trying out their motor scooters; their green parkas done up tight, making them look like Eskimos. Two, cooler than the rest, had no parkas. They stood under a streetlamp, smoking, the light shining down on their tight Italian suits and pork pie hats. They checked him as he went by. Checking his clothes; the way he walked; white kids looking for the cool.

As he got closer to Charlie's place he noticed movement outside. It was open for business. And as he got nearer, the sound of Ska floated out from it – The Upsetters, 'OK Skank'. A black man was doing door duty. Ken went up to him. He was tall and strong-looking, with a suit a bit like his own – well cut, tailored, with the lapels and trouser legs fashionably narrow. Even in the bad light Ken could see the shirt was expensive too. He was a real elegant guy.

'What da fuck you doin' here, white boy?' His accent was real Jamaican. He hadn't been off the boat long. Just long enough to buy himself a nice suit.

'I ain't no white boy.'

'You ain't no black boy neither. Which side of the fence you belong?'

'The wrong side,' said Ken.

The big man smiled. 'You fuckin' bet you do,' he said. 'What you want, man?'

'I'm here looking out for Charlie's place – see its O.K,' Ken said. Behind Mr Elegant he could see half a dozen people standing by the bar.

'Charlie's place's doin' fine, and it ain't none of your fuckin' business, man.'

'Charlie was a good friend of mine. I'm here to respect his memory.'

'You're here to stick your nose in where it don't belong and you're goin' get it sliced off if you don't ride into the sunset.' A smaller man wearing a leather trilby had come out of the bar and was standing close by the side of him, and Ken could feel the heat from his stare. He had a hand round behind him by his back pocket. Ken guessed there was a switchblade there, ready in case the discussion took a serious turn.

'Charlie's gone,' said Mr Elegant. 'We claim it now.'

'Claim it?'

Mr Elegant let out a deep, harsh laugh. 'On your way, boy.'

'This is still Charlie's place,' said Ken, trying to step past him.

Mr Elegant snapped out a hand and grabbed a fistful of Ken's mustard shirt. 'Fuck off, white boy,' he said and sent Ken staggering backwards with a shove. Trilby stepped closer, the long blade of a knife glinting in his hand. It was time for Ken to do what the man said. He took a few steps backwards, keeping his eyes on the blade until he was out of reach, then turned and walked. Behind him, above the sound of the music, he heard a voice calling from inside the shebeen.

'Who was that?'

'Nobody,' came Elegant's voice. 'Just some half-nigger.'

* * *

When she opened the door to him he could see she'd been drinking again. The clothes she'd been wearing this morning looked creased and a thick strand of hair hung down over her face.

'Come in,' she said, letting the door swing open as she turned back into the flat. 'I could do with some different company.'

He followed her into the living room and found Ernie sitting in one of the armchairs. The look he gave Ken said he wasn't glad to see him. Maggie slumped onto the settee and took a swig from a glass. There were two whiskey bottles on the coffee table, one full, one nearly empty. Ken carried on standing. No-one invited him to sit down.

'I been down to Charlie's place,' he said, by way of filling the silence.

'And?' said Ernie. It was a sharp, unfriendly question.

He hesitated before answering. 'You ain't goin' to like it. You sure you want to hear it?'

'I'm in the mood for bad news,' said Maggie.

'The place was open; doin' business. Bunch of people there – Rudies – taken it over.'

'Jesus Christ,' said Maggie, jumping to her feet. 'The bastards. They didn't waste any time.' She began pacing the floor, agitated and angry.

'Who did you see?' said Ernie.

'I didn't recognise nobody 'cept a couple of regulars at the bar. I talked to a big Jamaican bloke in a snappy suit.'

'Real big fella, well dressed?' Ernie leaned forward in his chair, inquisitive now. 'Did he have a tough-looking little friend?'

'Sounds like 'em.'

'Screw Face's crowd. The big fella's his strong-arm. Winston is it?' said Ernie. 'His little friend's got a fancy name like

Alphonso or something. Mean little bastard.'

'I wouldn't want to cross him,' said Ken.

'Well, I'll cross him,' said Maggie. 'That place is mine now, and all that goes with it. Isn't that right Ernie?' She looked meaningfully in Ernie's direction.

Ernie scratched his chin thoughtfully. 'That makes things complicated,' he said.

'One bloody thing after another,' said Maggie. She sat back down on the settee and reached for the whiskey bottle but knocked it off the table. She left it lying on the floor, opened the new one and topped up her glass. Holding it up, she looked at them both.

'To my inheritance.' She took a swig.

The atmosphere was still tense.

'I'd better be going,' said Ernie, suddenly standing.

'Don't let me keep you,' said Maggie.

They exchanged looks again.

'Look Maggie, I'm trying to help,' said Ernie, 'We'll see this through together. We can talk again tomorrow when you're – when you're feeling better.'

Maggie said nothing. Ernie pulled on his overcoat and without acknowledging Ken, left the room.

They waited for the slam of the front door.

'What was all that about?' said Ken, sitting down in the armchair vacated by Ernie.

'Business,' said Maggie, waving a hand dismissively. 'So those Jamaican bastards have got Charlie's place open?' It seemed Maggie wasn't ready to take him into her confidence just yet.

'Act like they own it,' he said.

'They've got a bloody cheek. What did this Winston say?'

'Charlie ain't around, so they've claimed it.'

Maggie was silent for a minute. Her face caught the light from the altar and the soft yellow glow of her skin gave her a dreamy look.

'Screw Face. Fucking bastard,' she said with sudden vehemence.

'Who is he?'

'Jumped up little arsehole off the boat looking for easy money. God knows what his real name is. He tried to muscle in once before. Charlie saw him off. Now he thinks he's seen another chance so the bastard's back. Didn't take him long.' She let out a long sigh and laid back on the settee.

Ken remembered some trouble, maybe a year or so before. Charlie'd shrugged his shoulders like it was nothing, but he did it while he was reloading the shotgun.

Maggie was tired as well as drunk, he could see that. But he had to find out what was going on. He moved over and sat next to her.

'So what happened with the police?' he said.

'Well now, there's a tale,' said Maggie, livening up and taking another sip of whiskey. She held the glass up in front of him. 'D'you want one?'

'No, Maggie. And you don't either.' He reached for the

glass, but she pulled it away.

'Yes I do, Kenny boy, yes I do.' She took a deep swallow. 'Do you know what they think I did?

'What?'

'They think I killed Charlie.'

He was surprised, but not sure why. Maggie was telling him something he hadn't thought about, but only because he'd decided not to think it. The cops don't stop a cremation for no reason.

'Who said he was killed?' he said.

Maggie took another slug of the whiskey. 'His sister did.'

'His sister? Hazel Dolman? Where does she come into it?'

'How do I know? Maybe she's making up for all the time she never gave a toss about him.'

'So why'd the coppers pick on you?'

'I was the last to see him alive. That's what they said.' Maggie poured herself another glassful. 'And they think they're going to find something in his blood.'

'Something? What?'

'Poison.'

He was shocked, baffled. None of this made sense. Maggie and Charlie were good together. He could be pretty wild sometimes, especially when he had drink in him, but she'd always seemed able to handle that side of him. And Charlie loved her. Ken knew that – everyone knew it.

'But the docs said it was drink. Isn't that what you said?'

'Yep, both of them. Signed the death certificate and all.'

Ken shook his head, trying to clear it, work it out. 'So what did they do? Arrest you?'

'No. I'd be sitting in a cell if they did. They say they haven't enough to go on yet. They're waiting for the results of the tests on Charlie's body.'

Ken relaxed. 'So they were just fishing. They don't know nothing, Maggie. It's all crap.'

'Don't they? They act like they know everything.'

'They always do that. It's all lies. How did that sister Hazel get involved in the first place?'

'I wrote to her about the funeral. Charlie had an old tin where he kept papers and the like. I found some letters from her in it. She came down with her man – the Doctor. They asked a lot of questions. Where did I find him? How long was he dead? How much did he drink? Next thing they've got the police over at the chapel grabbing Charlie.' Maggie rubbed a hand across her face.

Why was this secret sister suddenly on the scene? Charlie never talked about her and as far as Ken knew he never saw her. People die by accident sometimes. What made Hazel Dolman think different?

'So then the coppers are at me,' said Maggie, 'hours of it – asking the same questions over and over and writing everything down. On and on. Then Ernie got some old solicitor with dandruff to come in and he finally got me out of there.'

He was looking at her face. The strain of the day was showing. She noticed and smiled.

'Don't worry about me, Kenny boy. I can look after myself. They can ask me all they want. I've nothing to say.' She was shrugging it off, like the day had been no big deal. But the cops must have thought they were onto something and they were good at interrogation – even when they weren't kicking it out of you. She was tough to get through it. He could see it. Anybody in Charlie's life needed to be tough.

'But if they think they're going to find something...?' Ken let it drift out, unfinished. He wasn't even sure exactly how to finish it.

Suddenly the bravado in her dropped. She put her head in her hands and rocked to and fro. 'I don't know. I'm too tired to think about it.'

He put his arm around her shoulder and she leaned into him. They stayed like that for a while. Then she put her lips against his cheek and her hand on his thigh.

'Maggie, baby, you've had a long day. You should just take it easy.'

'I don't want to take it easy,' she said, pulling him to her. They kissed. She was full of fire now. She fell backwards on the settee taking him with her. They manoeuvred awkwardly until they were lying side by side, his arm around her waist, his leg between hers. She closed her eyes and worked her groin slowly, lazily against his thigh. He wished she'd stop – half-wished anyway. He put his lips to her ear and, in a voice barely above a whisper, began to sing an old Bluebeat love song.

'If love's the answer to your prayers then I'm right here to

sooth your cares,'

She smiled and kept her eyes closed, her body relaxing.

'Let your love combine with mine and we'll go on 'til the end of time.'

They stayed like that for a while, then he raised his head to see her reaction. She was asleep.

He climbed carefully off the settee so he didn't wake her. Gathering up the glass and the two bottles, he went first to the kitchen and dropped them off, then to the bedroom and took a blanket from the bed. Gently, he put it over her, tucked it in, and switched off the light, so only the altar continued to cast its yellow glow. It lit her face again, now without the cares of the day etched so heavily into it. On an impulse, he reached for his wallet and took out the picture of his mother. In this light, the resemblance was so strong it unsettled him. He put the picture away and let himself quietly out of the flat.

CHAPTER 3

He sat at the curved white vinyl cocktail bar that doubled as a table for his little galley kitchen, and sipped a mug of tea as he looked through the local paper while his supper cooked. It had been a busy few days. He wasn't big on staying in, but once in a while it was good to relax and recharge. He wondered if there was anything about Charlie's death in the paper. It didn't take much to make the East London Advertiser. On one of the inside pages a piece caught his eye.

'POLICE INVESTIGATION AT BARTLETT HOUSE.' His old home. It came up now and then, usually when one of the kids got done for burglary or joyriding.

'*A police investigation has been launched into allegations concerning staff at Bartlett House children's home in Forest Gate - .*'

There was knocking – pounding – on his door. He put down the paper, got up and opened it. Filling the doorway was the hulking form of Meatball.

'Hullo Kenneth.' He was only inches away, looking down on him. Ken could smell his sour breath and stepped back to put some distance between them. Meatball took that as an invitation to walk in.

'You're in a spot of bother ain't you?' said Meatball. He looked around and, noticing the tea Ken was drinking, reached a long arm over the counter to a spare mug on a shelf. Taking it down, he poured himself one from the teapot. He splashed milk into it and added three sugars, stirring it for a long time while fixing Ken with a stony glare, then sipped it.

'This tea's cold,' he said. 'Put the kettle on and make us a fresh brew'.

Ken's heart thumped as he moved round to the sink and filled the kettle, keeping an eye on Meatball. He put it on the little two-ring stove, struck a match and lit the gas.

'You seem to have fallen foul of Mr Blake. Terrible temper on him these last couple of days.'

Meatball sat down on one of the stools at the cocktail bar. It creaked under his bulk. Ken stood where he was and picked up his mug. His hand shook so he put it down again before Meatball noticed.

'How come? I ain't even seen him for months.'

'That's not the problem now, is it Kenneth? You don't need to see him to upset him, do you? Seeing and upsetting, they're different things. In fact he was just saying to me yesterday 'I never want to see that black bastard again.' No, you've upset him, even though you ain't seen him.'

'I ain't done nothin.'

Meatball shook his head sadly. 'Kenneth, Kenneth, Kenneth. You've been looking down Mrs Blake's blouse, and she don't like it.' His watery green eyes looked straight into Ken's.

Ken thought this over. 'Is that what Rick's been telling you?'

'You mean *Mr Blake,* don't you? That's right. That's what

he's been telling me. And what have you got to tell me?'

Ken picked up his mug again and took a sip. His hand was a little steadier now. 'That ain't the real story.'

'Yeh?' Meatball leaned forward, elbows on the counter. 'So what is the real story?'

'There was nothin' serious goin' on.' Ken didn't know where he was going with this. It just felt like a good idea to keep talking. But he had to watch himself. He could let his mouth run away when he was nervous. 'Betty – Mrs Blake – she likes to get what she wants and she's a very generous woman.'

Meatball nodded sagely. 'It has been said.'

'Like most of them rich women, she has a lot of time on her hands.'

'Mr Blake takes care of her every need.'

Ken shrugged. 'You might say.'

Meatball made a pantomime of slowly understanding. 'I s'pose she must get a bit bored from time to time.'

'I guess she does, living in that big place they got in Chelsea.'

'Nice place.'

'I've never been in it.'

''Course not. Who'd want you in there?' said Meatball 'Unless they wanted a toilet cleaner.'

Ken made himself smile.

'Still,' said Meatball, 'she's got no housekeeping to do – in fact she's got fuck all to do most of the time.'

'Exactly,' said Ken. 'So she needs to find some ways to pass the time, don't she?'

Meatball's watery eye was on him again while he gave this question some thought. 'I expect she does. When you put it like that, goin' off and fucking the nearest darkie makes a bit of sense.'

Ken didn't like the way the conversation came back to him. 'Whatever she does, it's like I said, she's jus' passin' the time. Nothin' serious.'

'Way of the world among them rich types, I expect.'

'There you go. Anyway, anythin' between me and her was started by her.'

'So that's your story?' said Meatball slowly raising his eyebrows. 'Well, ain't you the little tell-tale. Mr Blake would be most displeased to hear his Betty's good name besmirched like that.'

'I'm just relatin' the facts. Your boss ain't goin' to tell you everythin' about his business. He don't want to be embarrassed in front of his staff.'

The long watery look again. Ken wondered if he'd pushed it too far. Meatball got off his stool and walked round to where he was standing in the narrow kitchen, opened a cupboard and looked inside.

'Ain't you got any biscuits?'

Ken reached up and pulled down a tin, conscious of Meatball's closeness. He opened it. Meatball took a packet of digestives, pulled out two and began to eat them both together.

'So you've just been doing the lady a favour by helping relieve her boredom?'

'That kind of thing.'

'Providing a service.'

'I didn't do nothin' she didn't want me to do.'

'But you did do something Mr Blake didn't want you to.' Meatball reached out one of his big hands. Ken saw it coming but Meatball was fast. He caught Ken by the neck then slammed his head sideways down hard on the bar, pulled him up, and slammed him down again, holding him there.

Ken could feel blood tricking out of his ear, the side of his face hot and sore where Meatball pressed it against the bar, his throat aching from the grip of Meatballs thick fingers. He struggled to breathe. 'What you doin' this for?' His words came out thin and croaky through his twisted lips.

Meatball leaned down until his mouth was next to Ken's good ear, the stench of his breath again. Meatball's voice was low and calm. 'Mr Blake told me to. He's very, very angry you see. It's one thing for his missus to do what she likes behind his back, but it's another to have it rubbed in his face. See? So he told me to hurt you and make you disappear.' He let go of Ken. Ken straightened up, holding a hand to his ear.

'What do you make of that, now?' said Meatball

'What?'

"Make you disappear.' I wonder what he meant by that. He was so mad he just turned around and walked away without explainin' himself. What d'you think he means?'

Ken looked at Meatball. He was standing watching him, trapping him in the narrow space of the galley kitchen, and reaching for some more biscuits. He was relaxed, enjoying himself.

'I can't say,' said Ken.

'Can't you? What about 'hurt you' then?'

'You've done that already.'

'Have I? I don't think so. That's not what I'd call hurt. Barely a mark on you. No, Mr Blake wouldn't be very happy with that. He'd call that a very poor job.'

Ken saw Meatball's body tense up, ready to spring again.

'That ain't hurt at all.' Meatball lunged at him. Ken tried to side-step but there was no room in the tiny space. Meatball got one big hand on his throat again and the other on his arm, pushing him backwards until the back of his head smacked hard against a cupboard. Then Meatball got both hands on his arm and twisted it until it was stretched out straight and taut, and Ken was kneeling to stop it breaking.

'Stop! Please!'

'Did I ever tell you about the time I broke Iron Ken Castle's arm? Top of the bill we were, giving it a good old heave-ho and sending the punters wild. Then he belted me a real one. Knocked me clean out of the ring. Never saw fit to ask first. Thoughtless. Downright thoughtless.'

Ken could barely hear the words through the pain in his own arm but Meatball seemed not to notice as he continued his reverie. 'So I jumped straight back in and went for him. Soon as he saw me coming he took off. Out of the ring and off. I chased him up the aisle and caught him. They still had the spotlight on us. I got 'im just like I got you and – snap.' He twisted Kens arm tighter. 'Broke it in two places. Got six months and me licence suspended for that. Learned me a lesson. I won't be doin' that again. Broken arms – thing of the past.'

Meatball grabbed the sleeve of Ken's shirt and ripped it until it dangled from his arm. Then he reached over to where the kettle was coming to a boil on the gas ring, picked it up and slowly poured the hot water down onto Ken's bare arm. As the pain bit into him Ken tried to scream but nothing would come. He felt sick. He retched, his body jerking and twitching. He screwed his eyes tight closed.

Meatball stopped pouring, leaned down and held the hot bottom of the kettle to Ken's face. He tried to pull his head away, tried not to think about what his face would look like with the flesh scorched off it.

'Now you know what 'hurt' means, you'd better work out what 'disappear' means.' He let go of Ken and stood up. Helping himself to two more biscuits, he walked out.

* * *

Under the bandages the flesh of his arm screamed with every movement, but he couldn't let that stand in his way. Meatball had delivered the message and it wouldn't be long until he was back to deliver another. Two battered brown suitcases lay open on the bed. Anything that didn't fit into them would have to go to the pawn shop. He looked at the pile of clothes he'd set aside. Some good gear there. He'd get next to nothing for them, but he couldn't take them. He took care to pack the most recent presents from his women – the things they'd notice most if he wasn't wearing them. After those it was down to a few favourites and forget the rest. Anyway, it felt good to lose a few things – travel light.

Emptying the final drawer of the cheap dressing table, he picked up the bunch of letters held together with an elastic band. He hadn't looked at these since before Charlie died. Charlie had sent them to him after he'd left the home but Ken was still living there. He held them for a moment, before sitting on the bed, peeling off the elastic band and taking the top one from its envelope. Charlie's big, uneven handwriting sprawled across the page.

'Dear Ken,
I can not believe how good it is out here. I am earning money and getting drunk and showing everyone that us kids from the home can take it because we are hard. We really are compared to this lot out here. Even the girls could beat them in a fight. I am going to win all before me because no one is going to stop me.

You might see some strange things go on in there now I am gone. They will have read this letter before you get it for sure. But if there is anything happening you do not like you let me know when I see you and I will sort it out. Tell them to remember Charlie's diary.

Stick it out little man. I will look after you when you are old enough to get away.
Best Wishes,
Charlie.'

Charlie. Always ready to take on all comers. He stood up for himself, and for Ken too, even after they left the home. He was brave, and never counted the cost. How would he have survived in that place without Charlie?

He remembered the time when he was ten years old and Trevor, the Head of home had him and his friend Sally standing in that room – that same room where Ann turned the lights down years later. There was a problem, a very big problem.

He and Sally had been out shoplifting at the newsagents a few streets away. The owner's son caught them with Milky Bars in their pockets. All they got from the police was a telling off then shoved into a police car to deliver them back to the home. But he knew the real trouble would start once they were inside. In the back of the car he pulled Sally close and whispered to her.

'Say it's all my fault – that you didn't do nothing'.'

Sally flicked her terrified nine-year-old eyes in his direction and nodded dumbly.

Trevor was waiting for them, holding a brief, grim-faced conversation with one of the policemen before ordering them into the room. They stood to attention with their arms by their sides, the way Trevor had taught them to whenever they were in his presence. He shut the door.

This was a grave matter, Trevor said. He was going to see to it that this kind of behaviour stopped right now. So he was going to be tough with them. Very tough. Ken elbowed Sally but she said nothing, just stared down at the floor. They were going on report to the Council, Trevor continued. They would of course be getting a beating. He might even have to consider expelling them from the home. That meant going to an Approved School instead, where they locked you up and beat you every day. And Trevor knew all this because he used to be in charge of an Approved School.

Ken had heard all this before. Trevor went through the same speech every time, no matter what the transgression. There was a long list of things you could be punished for since Trevor arrived. Approved School was a real threat. He had seen an older boy taken away to one just a couple of months ago. But there were even worse things. Sometimes, if you were bad enough they sent you to a mental home. You mixed with all the loonies until you went mad yourself. Either way, they locked you up, only with the Looney Bin you never came out. They threw away the key. They could do it whenever they wanted. They just had to say the word and you were gone, and nobody was going to care or listen to anything you had to say, because you were mad.

That's what Trevor was telling them now, walking round them, bending down to talk right into their faces, like some Sergeant Major.

'It was me,' said Ken, his voice wavering. 'I did the nickin'. She didn't do nothin'.'

Trevor straightened up, his dead eye resting on Ken for a long time before moving on to Sally.

'Is this true?' he said to her. She hesitated before slowly nodding, still looking at the floor.

Trevor pursed his lips for a moment. 'Then it's a three for you, Sally,' he said, 'just to teach you not to hang around with little thieves like him. I'll get the Strop.'

They stood waiting while Trevor went down the corridor to the office. Sally began to whimper. Ken took her small hand in his. It was hot and damp and he held it tight. 'It's OK,' he said gently, 'three's not so bad.' But she'd never had it before, and he felt her trembling from the fear of it.

They had been introduced to the Strop on Trevor's first day, three years ago.

'This used to belong to my father,' said Trevor. He held up the length of thick leather so the children, sitting cross-legged on the floor after supper, could get a good look. It was like a belt but fatter and wider with a handle like a cricket bat at one end. 'It's called the Strop' went on Trevor. 'My Dad was a barber, and this is what he used to sharpen his razors on. It's also what he used to beat me with when I'd done something wrong. He gave up the barbering game a few years back and he didn't need it any more. So he gave it to me as a present. Something to remember him by, he said. And ever since, I've found it very handy when it comes to keeping discipline!' He suddenly swung it through the air and brought it down on the table in front of him with a deafening crack. Ken, like all the other kids in the room, jumped, and went to bed afterwards with the sound of it ringing in his ears.

So now they were waiting. At these times word got around the home quickly, and the place went quiet as everyone held their breath and waited too, listening for the punishment to be dished out. Since Trevor's arrival punishment had become part of their lives. For Sally it would be a three. That was the minimum, then six, then ten. If you were older the minimum was six, then twelve, then twenty. You didn't have to do much to earn the maximum, and Ken knew he had earned a ten today.

Trevor reappeared at the doorway. He beckoned to Sally.

'Come.'

Her fingers tightened around Ken's, but he nudged her forward and she took a reluctant step. She walked to Trevor and he reached out for her hand. They turned and left the room as if they were going on an outing. Ken heard the door to the next room close. Trevor always made sure no-one else was watching when he used the Strop. A few seconds later the first sharp smack sang through the wall, followed instantly by Sally's scream – shrill with the shock of the pain. Then another smack, and another, Sally screaming louder with each one. Then it was just the sound of her sobbing. It was his turn next.

Trevor was back in the room, the Strop dangling by his side. He closed the door.

'So Ken, you were a bit naughty down at the shops today.'

Trevor's mood seemed to have improved. His voice was lighter, almost friendly, even a little smile. But Ken knew this was when Trevor was at his most dangerous, getting people's guard down, looking for weaknesses, trying to wheedle little bits of information out of them he could use against them later.

Trevor was circling him now, the leather Strop swinging against his leg as he walked. 'And leading poor little Sally astray as well. She's not going to be going on any more shopping trips with you, I'd say. Not for while anyway.' He bent down until his face was level with Ken's. 'Is she?'

'No.'

Trevor circled him again, casting an examining eye over him.

'You're a good looking lad, aren't you Ken?'

'I'm not.'

'You are. Everyone says it. I expect you'll be quite a hit with the girls when you're older.'

'I don't know,' said Ken.

Trevor stopped in front of him.

'How old are you now?'

'Ten.'

'Well, well. Double figures. So you're one of the older ones now.'

'I'm not,' said Ken again, his voice rising in panic.

Trevor leant down to face him again, all friendliness gone. 'Yes you are!' he snarled. He straightened up again. 'So you know what that means don't you?'

Ken said nothing, his mouth dry.

'It means you're going to get a twenty.'

A jolt ran through Ken at the word. He'd never even done a ten before. A six had left him barely able to walk.

Trevor turned away from him, walked over to the sofa against the wall and sat down. He stared at Ken for a moment, a strange look, like a hungry animal. Ken did his best not to look away, but the stare bored into him, making him squirm inside.

'Unless.'

Trevor let the word hang in the air as he lay back on the sofa and stretched an arm along its length, all the time holding Ken in his gaze.

'What?'

'Unless you come over here and do exactly what I tell you.'

Ken hesitated. He knew. Everybody did. Not exactly what, just that something – something bad and frightening went on. And he knew his turn would come sometime. He took a step towards the sofa.

The door suddenly opened and Charlie walked in.

'Hello Trev,' said Charlie, just as calmly as Trevor had been speaking to him. But Trevor sprang from the sofa, his face twisted with rage.

'What – !' He got no more words out. Charlie had grabbed him around the throat with one big, beefy hand. He was still only fifteen, but he was already bigger and stronger than most of the adults. He pushed Trevor's bony frame up against the wall.

'What did I fucking tell you, eh?'

Ken watched, frozen with shock. He was afraid for Charlie

– the amount of trouble he was getting himself into. Afraid for himself, because he was there too, part of it. He felt sick as his head spun with consequences. Nobody ever did this, least of all with Trevor. This wasn't going to end with the Strop; this was the Approved School, the Looney Bin. Charlie had to stop. But he wasn't stopping. He was still talking to Trevor, swearing at him again.

'When I tell you something, you fucking well pay attention. You got that?'

Trevor's eyes bulged, his face red and contorted as he fought for air. He reached up, trying to loosen Charlie's grip on his throat. Charlie slapped his hand away, then head-butted him on the nose. Bright red blood gushed from it, running down around Trevor's mouth and dribbling onto his clean white shirt. Ken's stomach was tight with fear. He desperately wanted Charlie to stop because if he didn't Trevor would make it bad for everyone. It was already bad now.

Charlie steered Trevor back to the sofa and dropped him into it. He turned and held out one of his big hands to Ken. 'Come on,' he said, 'we're going.'

Ken took his hand but his feet remained locked to the floor. He couldn't leave. Trevor hadn't given him permission. He looked wretchedly from Charlie to Trevor, who was lying across the sofa holding his nose, blood oozing between his fingers. Trevor's eyes shone with hate and humiliation.

'Get out of my sight!'

For the next few days Ken waited for the place to explode.

But everything stayed quiet. Nobody went on report; nobody got a beating; nobody got kicked out or sent away to Approved School. It was like the whole thing had never happened.

* * *

He stared at the letter and felt tears well up in his eyes before he could stop them. He'd forgotten so much. So much of that time – that place where he'd spent more than half his life. It was so long ago. Fourteen years on from that strange day and Charlie hadn't won; he'd lost. Lying dead in a police morgue, waiting to be buried, he wasn't going to be there for Ken any more. Life had been a safe and hopeful place when Charlie was around. But now, suddenly, he was gone, and everything that held Ken to the ground was gone too. He was floating on the breeze. That breeze blew cold and comfortless right now. Where would he land? Maybe people like him and Charlie just never belonged anywhere. Never found any space in the world that could be theirs. And the only thing to do was keep moving, make the most of what little they had while they had it, and never think about the past or the future or anything beyond today.

He wiped his eyes with his hand. Then he put the letter back in its envelope, retied the elastic band round the bundle and threw it into the suitcase.

* * *

The lift opened and Ken stepped out with the small suitcase, put it on the landing and then used his good arm to drag the big case out as well. He paused, took a deep breath, and knocked on Maggie's door. She opened it, took one look at Ken, another at his cases and said 'No, Ken, no,' and started closing the door.

'Wait, Maggie. This ain't what you think. I'm just looking for a floor to sleep on.'

'What's wrong with your own?'

'I had to go. I need to explain the situation. Let me in.'

She stood thinking about it, weighing things up.

'Please Maggie.'

She caught sight of the bandaged arm. 'What happened to that?'

'Someone thought it needed warming up.'

'What with?'

'Boilin' water.'

'Jesus Christ, Ken.' Her voice softened a little. She opened the door. He stepped in with both cases and put them down. She helped him ease his coat off and he went into the living room and sat down on the settee while she made them some tea. It was good to see her sober. There was no sign of the whiskey bottle.

Once the cups were in front of them, she settled on the settee beside him.

'So tell me what happened,' she said.

Ken sighed. He knew he was going to have to explain to her, but had kept away from thinking too much about it.

'It's like my rent collector came round to see me.'

'You must be a long way behind with the rent.'

'He didn't want to talk to me about that.' Ken sat forward and took another deep breath.

'What have you been up to?' she said suspiciously.

'Things have been gettin' pretty complicated.'

'Have they? Well confession is good for the soul, Ken, so why don't you tell me all about it.' Maggie sat back; getting comfortable. 'Take your time.'

He felt nervous. He wasn't normally shy about his activities – with the women at least – but here, next to Maggie, he struggled to find the right words to start. She sat with her legs crossed, rocking her foot up and down like she did so often. It was the first time he'd seen her sober since Charlie died.

'Us Catholics do it all the time,' she said.

'What?'

'Confess.'

'Why's that?'

'So God'll forgive us our sins and wash them away.' She was watching him, enjoying his discomfort. It looked like she was taking some time off from her grief, from worrying about the police or the shebeen.

'And does he?' he said.

'If we ask him to he does.'

'Where do they go to, these sins?'

'God just washes them away.'

'Like they never happened?'

She nodded.

'Maybe I should confess to him,' said Ken.

'Confess to me first.'

He drew a deep breath. 'Well, you see there's this lady called Betty,' he said. 'She's a pretty nice married lady but her old man, he don't always understand what she needs.'

Maggie pursed her lips. 'And you do, I suppose.'

'She just likes to take a little consolation from me now and then. Helps oil the wheels of the day to day livin'. Nothin' serious.'

'So you've been oiling her wheels.'

Was she joking or sarcastic? He wasn't sure how she was taking it. There was something teasing about her again.

'Anyways, her man gets to hear about this little thing that me an' hers got. He don't like it. Furthermore he's my landlord. So he sends this big bloke round to do me harm an' explain that it's time for me to find someplace else to live.'

'I see. Persuasive was he?'

'You bet he was, Maggie.' He held up his bandaged arm. 'I ain't no coward, but I didn't feel like sticking around to see how much more serious he wanted to get.'

Maggie was silent for a while, thinking it all over. 'I thought you'd be used to running away from angry husbands,' she said.

'This one means business.' As he said it, he realised she'd known about his women all along, probably through Charlie. She'd just been playing with him. He waited in silence for her verdict.

'You can stay for a few days,' she spoke crisply now, decision made. 'But you'll have to keep a low profile. They don't let blacks live in these flats. The neighbours will be on the warpath.'

'I've been here plenty of times an' people seen me around.'

'Yes, and I've been warned about it already. They hate them round here. Some of them'd drop dead before they'd talk to one.'

'The whites don't like to see their women running around with coloureds do they?' said Ken. He leaned over, putting his arm around her waist. She slapped his hand away and got up.

'Let's just get the situation understood first, Kenny boy.' She stood in front of him with her hands on her hips. He smiled up at her, but got only an angry glare in return. 'You sleep on the settee and you move out as soon as you've found something else. And no night-time visits.'

That was a surprise. He'd worried about telling his story to her, but he hadn't thought much about what would happen after that. He had assumed once he'd had a chance to explain himself and Maggie understood the situation, she'd be glad to have him in her bed – for a while at least. After all, she'd made the running up to now. That's why he'd come. But new rules applied, and he had no choice in the matter until he found a new place to live.

'I'll just have to dream about you instead,' he said, smiling at her.

'Well don't start dreaming yet. You're going to be helping me out while you're here, so you'll be earning your keep.'

* * *

A thin fog hung under the street lamps as Ken and Maggie walked down the cobbled lane to the shebeen. Beyond the dimmed lights, the darkness was so thick no sound seemed to penetrate it. They had nothing but the echo of their own footsteps for company until they turned into the alley by the railway arches where the distant light of the shebeen cast a feeble glow into the night.

He wasn't sure what Maggie was doing with this visit. It didn't seem like a good idea, walking into the lion's den like this. She'd talked about her right to be there but who was interested in that? Not the Jamaican heavies he'd met the last time he was here. But she was determined to come, and he'd started to realise that when Maggie decided something, nothing was going to stop her. He couldn't let her go alone. But he was nervous.

A Ska beat drifted towards them that Ken knew straight away – Derrick Morgan singing 'Blazing Fire' – a favourite on the dance floor that summer. Ska was the music people came for, the coolest thing around and it was playing right here in a little backstreet in the East End of London.

The sound mingled with the voices of people lounging outside. The same big Jamaican in the same suit was on the door – Mr Elegant. He didn't seem to recognise Ken. All his attention was on Maggie in her short dress, her legs making his brow furrow in concentration.

Inside, beneath the big arch, the club was dark, loud and

smoky – like any night when Charlie had stood behind the bar. Against one wall was a homemade sound system, two big speakers enclosed in rough plywood. Between them a middle-aged black man in a fedora sat next to a small box record player. It was The Duke, a famous face on the Ska scene and here he was in Charlie's place. These people had connections. There was something else different about the vibe tonight. The gangs of Rude Boys in pork pie hats and dark glasses still talked and shouted and drank, but now some of them drew on thick reefers as well. Out on the dance floor their girlfriends danced around their handbags and chatted. Beyond them, away from the lights, a bunch of Mods gathered around two black men, who were exchanging uppers for cash, making no effort to disguise what they were doing. The reefers had always been a feature of the place, but Charlie had insisted on discretion. The pills were new – in here anyway. Up West they were everywhere. The new operators of Charlie's place were making sure they cashed in. What had gone missing were the white men in working clothes sipping pints of Guinness. Dockers, or friends of Charlie's from his building site days – men who came to Charlie's to enjoy the vibe, and step outside the confines of the narrow white lives they lived most of the time. They were gone. The place had taken on a sharper edge.

Maybe only he noticed. A lot of the faces were the same, with the same tight suits and Fred Perry shirts, holding court, checking each other out, swaying and dipping to the music. These were people who would never care too much about who was laying on the entertainment, so long as it was late and the scene was cool. And all the while, the Ska beat bounced off the arches, boomed in their ears, worked into their bones.

A small ripple of recognition from the regulars greeted Maggie, heads turning to catch sight of the widow. She smiled, looking relaxed. Turning to Ken, she took both his hands and pulled him towards the little dance floor. They squeezed between the groups of girls and swaying couples. Monday was lovers' night, so the Ska sounds ran a little slower, and the rhythms pulsed to the heartbeats of couples. They pressed close together and started moving to the music. His arms around her, he felt her smooth curves under the tight dress as she writhed gently, gracefully to the beat, her body hugged in tight to his. With Maggie in his arms, he forgot the unease he felt about coming here, almost forgot the pain in his arm. She moved well – nearly as well as a black girl. She had the beat inside her. And she let it out through her hips and her thighs, through her belly and her breasts. The whites, with their Cliff Richard and Frank Ifield, were only just starting to get what music was really about – what Ska was about. Ska was sex. And as their bodies moved as one, something seemed to give inside him, as if the rhythm locked him to her in some way that could never be dissolved, and the sound entered them and flowed through them, carrying them on its wave. He wanted her then, more than he had ever wanted any woman. He put his face in her hair and drew in her smell – her scent, her sweat, every last element of her. He felt the heat of her body and the rhythm passing through her, every touch, every contact. Every particle of skin where his body touched hers was on fire with longing at that moment, and he wanted it all to go on, to be wrapped in this embrace with her forever.

The number finished – too soon for him, and she took his head in her hands, kissed him briefly and said 'Come on, let's say hello to the new boss.'

His nervousness returned as they crossed the dance floor to the bar. A lone barman lounged at the end of it, smoking and talking to a customer. He came over.

'What can I get you?' he said.

'You can get me Screw Face,' said Maggie.

The barman smiled half a smile. 'Can I?' he said. 'What makes you think that?'

Ken noticed the big scar all the way down the side of the barman's face that made the corner of his mouth turn up, giving the impression he was smiling all the time. The barman noticed him looking.

'You should watch it when you're shaving, man,' said Ken.

'You should watch it when you're talking,' the barman replied.

Ken felt Maggie's eyes on him and didn't say anything back.

'Tell him Charlie's widow wants to see him,' said Maggie.

The barman gave Ken a long cool stare then glanced back to Maggie. 'Charlie's widow, eh?' He looked her over. 'You a good looking chick. What you hanging round with a deadbeat like this for?' He gave Ken another glance and moved away to the end of the bar. Beyond it hung a length of brown curtain that Charlie had put up to keep his stock out of sight. The barman went behind it. After a minute he lifted the curtain and gestured for them to step through.

They walked between tall stacks of cases towards the back of the arch. An ancient desk had been placed there now, with a lamp on it. Sitting behind it was a small black man with a shiny bald head, wearing an African-style shirt in a lot of bright colours that had Ken wondering where the man had left his sense of taste. On the wall behind him was a big flag in green, red and gold, with a face printed on it - a bearded man with a high forehead. The words 'EMPEROR HAILE SELASSIE' ran above the head. Ken had never heard of this emperor. The man at the desk was copying details from a stack of bills into a big ledger. He worked quickly and methodically, completing his entry before sitting back and looking at the two of them. His face lit up with a big smile.

'Welcome,' said Shiny Head 'I believe I know you Maggie, but I don't know your friend.' If he still had any Jamaican left amongst the clipped English accent it was hard to spot.

'I'm Ken – a friend of the family.'

'A friend of the family,' repeated Shiny Head slowly, mulling that over. He was smoking one of those gold-banded cigarettes that were supposed to keep your fingers from being stained by the nicotine. Who would even notice on this shiny black man's fingers? 'What kind of friend?'

'Charlie was like my brother.'

'And Maggie is like your sister?'

'We ain't here to discuss the family ties.'

'What have you come to discuss with Screw Face?' He carefully stubbed out his cigarette in a big metal ashtray already brimming with dog-ends.

'What are you doing in this place?' said Maggie. 'You've no right to be here.'

He made a show of mock surprise. 'It belongs to Screw Face,' he said.

'It's Charlie's.'

For a moment he said nothing, instead just leaned back in his chair, his eyes drifting away from them. Behind him, off to one side, almost invisible in the shadows cast by the desk lamp was an armchair in which sat, Ken could now see, a much taller, thinner man with a long grey goatee beard protruding from his chin and a fez resting upon curly grey hair. He was holding a newspaper in one hand, while the other leant on an old-fashioned silver-topped cane. He leaned forward and whispered in Shiny Head's ear, feeding him his lines.

'Charlie doesn't need it anymore,' said Shiny Head.

'Then it's mine,' said Maggie. She spoke calmly, but Ken noticed her hands, rolled into tight little fists.

'Well now,' said Shiny Head slowly, 'that just isn't the way in these matters. You see, white sister, it belongs to whoever takes it.'

'Then you're robbing me.'

'Not so, white sister. Your man Charlie looked after this place, that's true. He can't do that anymore, so we must.'

'This club is nothing to do with you.'

He leaned back again.

'Why don't he talk for himself,' said Ken, nodding at the man in the shadows.

'Screw Face does not speak with those who are not of the same understanding.'

'What understanding is that?' said Ken.

'Those who know not of it shall hear not of it.' Shiny Head was still smiling, but he seemed serious. Screw Face was whispering. Shiny Head spoke.

'Charlie feared no evil,' said Shiny Head, 'but he's gone, and – ,' he shrugs, 'we are here now.' He stared at Maggie.

'This place is mine, you thieving bastards!'

Ken put a steadying hand on her arm. He'd been afraid she might blow up while she was here – afraid that any trouble she started would end up coming his way.

Once more, Shiny Head leaned back to receive words in his ear. He nodded slowly, smiling all the while, then leaned forward, clasping his hands and resting them on the desk. He might have been a bank manager delivering the verdict on their loan application.

'Screw Face is a poor black man who must make his way in the white man's world. He's taken something back for his people. You say you have been robbed, but we have been robbed too. Robbery has existed since the time of Creation. The black man once ruled the world and owned all its gold. White people stole the gold. Screw Face does what he can to help the black nation regain its lost treasure. Screw Face's path is a righteous path.' He was still smiling, dismissing them with this little sermon; feeding them words that made no sense, because it just didn't matter.

'This place belongs to me and I'll get it back.' Maggie's voice was rising. Ken could see she was losing her temper but this wasn't the place to do it. That barman was still behind them, and probably others too. He took her arm and tried to whisper to her, but she pulled it away. Shiny Head was still smiling.

'Well that's more like it,' he said. 'You're beginning to understand now. You want it? Take it from us – if you can. Then it's yours. Maybe you can get your man here to blow us away with his six-gun.' He reached for his cigarettes. 'Or maybe you should talk to the police.' He pulled out another gold-banded cigarette, tapped it on the box and stuck it between his lips. He looked back at Maggie. 'But maybe you've talked to them enough already.'

Maggie spoke, her words slow and angry. 'You fucking pair of pricks. You're not going to walk all over me. You didn't try it with Charlie because he'd take your head off. Well I'm better than Charlie –' she suddenly slammed a fist down on the desk, 'and I'll do the fucking same. I won't let you beat me.'

Shiny Head's face lost its smile and instead took on another look of surprise – this one genuine.

'Baby, you got some bad language on you, you know that?' His accent had slipped, along with his cool. He leaned forward and jabbed a finger at Ken. 'You wanna get this chick under control, man. Slap her around a little before I get someone to do it for you.'

Ken put his arm around Maggie's waist. 'Maybe we should be moving,' he said, but she didn't budge. She and Shiny Head stared at each other, her face set in grim fury.

It was Shiny Head who broke the angry spell. 'I don't know what you got in mind, white sister, but if you've come here looking for trouble, you're gonna find it.' He glanced at Ken, his expression changing again, an effort made to recover his earlier cool. 'Now,' he said, his accent back in place, 'you'd better get your bitch out of here before I take further offence.' He reached for his lighter, flicked it on and lit his cigarette. He leaned back in his chair and slowly blew out two perfect smoke rings. Ken watched them rise for a moment. He gently tugged Maggie's arm and this time she yielded. They turned away from Shiny Head and Screw Face. The barman was still standing by the curtain and he held it open for them.

He could feel her trembling with anger as they walked back to the bar. He wondered if he'd ever seen this much rage in a woman before.

'Take it easy, baby. There's nothing to be done here and now,' he said. He took her arm. 'The best thing we can do is get out of here.'

'No.' She jerked her arm away from him. 'This is my place and I'll leave when I want to.'

As she spoke the record changed and instead of another lover's number, an upbeat sound came on – 'The Fits is on me Now' by Owen and Leon

'Let's dance,' said Maggie firmly.

He didn't like this situation, the tension crackling in the air, but Maggie was already pulling him onto the crowded floor, determined to make a statement and hold her ground. As they danced he once more pulled her close to him.

'You sure this is a good idea?'

She ignored him, deliberately concentrating on the rhythm. His eye caught the barman talking to the little guy with the leather trilby he'd seen the other night. They were both looking over at them. Trilby broke away and moved over to talk to a group of Rude Boys standing by the dance floor. He had his back to Ken now, but as he spoke he jerked his head over his shoulder in their direction and the Rudies started staring at them too. The temperature was rising.

'Let's go, Maggie. We need to be out of here.'

'We'll stay a bit longer.'

'We've already outstayed our welcome. Things are about to get heavy.'

Maggie looked around and picked up on the stares, Ken looked over her shoulder. The Rudies were still in the same place.

'They're rubbing my face in their shit, Ken. I won't let them.'

'They'll do it for real if we stick around. Save it.'

Her mouth was set thin and straight. For a minute he thought she was going stay – start a fight. He tried to quell his rising sense of panic.

'Then we'd better go.' She said it grudgingly, as if it was somehow his fault.

'We can still walk out, but after that we might be running.'

'I can't, not in these heels.'

'Take 'em off outside.' Ken hooked his arm into Maggie's and started a slow, but accelerating walk towards the door. As they saw the two of them on the move, the Rudies and Trilby began to cut across the dance floor, trying to cut them off. The floor was crowded, but Ken and Maggie's line to the door was clear. Then a few feet from it, Trilby was suddenly in front of them, a twisted smile on his face as his hand reached for his switchblade. In one fast movement Maggie bent to the table next to her, snatched up a glass and jabbed it hard at Trilby. He leapt back, avoiding the glass in his face only by jerking his head aside. For a brief second the shock froze him. Ken grabbed Maggie's hand and they ran.

* * *

As they burst into the night, they slammed into Mr Elegant, sending him stumbling and cursing. But they were already leaving him behind. The fog had thickened and they could barely see their way. Maggie stopped and took off her shoes. Ken waited, heart pounding. They could hear the Rudies piling out of the shebeen, yelling at the bouncer.

'Which way, man? Which fuckin' way?'

Then they were coming – fast, the sound of their feet echoing like thunder off the high walls of the railway arches. He and

Maggie ran on until they came to a crossroads. To the left was a lane with no street lights. They took it. On either side were boarded up houses – another condemned slum waiting to be cleared. At the end of the terrace they came to a row of derelict shops. The doorways were deep and shadowy. He pulled Maggie into one of them. It was pitch-dark. He held her as they tried to catch their breath silently. Back up the lane there was the sound of the Rudies reaching the junction. A voice said 'Split up' – the sound flat, dying quickly in the fog. Seconds later a lone figure ran past. They pressed themselves further into the blackness of the doorway. Ken glimpsed the figure, tall and skinny, holding something in his fist. A blade maybe.

Just the one, he thought. He considered running after him and surprising him, but jumping a man with a blade in his hand wasn't always a good idea. His thoughts were interrupted by the sound of footsteps coming back towards them, eerie through the fog. He eased Maggie in behind him. He wanted to stop her doing something crazy like she'd just done in the club. But he also knew he had to be strong, had to be protective, show her he was man enough to live in her world.

They waited while the footsteps stopped a couple of times, then the figure came to the doorway where they were trying to make themselves invisible in the shadows. The man stopped, turned to face the road and looked up and down. He couldn't be more than five feet away, but in the thickness of the fog his outline was hazy and indistinct. He folded away his switchblade, slipped it into his pocket, and took out a packet of cigarettes. Putting one between his lips, he began searching his pockets for a light. Then he turned around and walked straight into their doorway. Unzipping his flies, he took out his dick and started pissing into the opposite corner from where they were standing. As he finished, he found his lighter and flicked it on, lighting up Ken's face inches from his own. He was a boy of about eighteen and he jumped like he'd been electrocuted. Ken grabbed his shirt, pulled him close and sent a knee hard into the kid's balls, doubling him over. Forcing the boy's head down, he used the knee again, smashing it into his face. There was the kind of crunch Ken had only ever heard in Westerns as the kid's nose broke. He grabbed Maggie's hand and they ran and kept on running.

CHAPTER 4

Back at the flat he pushed the front door shut and stood in the hallway with her, kissing, their bodies still pumping from the action of the night. They wrestled, pulling at each other's clothes, trying to get naked fast. He seized her body, his bandaged arm suddenly immune from pain. Every muscle in her was tensed. She felt firm, hot, ripe. She leant back in his arms and he let her down onto the floor, lowered himself on top of her and pushed inside. No wasted time. They fucked – fast and hard and furious. When it was over they lay together on the floor, getting their breath back, feeling the release of the tensions of the night and basking in the moment. It felt like new territory with her, some barrier broken, a meeting of their two animal natures and a fresh intimacy formed. Something had moved, and it felt good.

'How're your feet?' he said eventually, suddenly remembering their run through the streets.

'No bother,' she said. 'When I was young we were so poor we had to go to school without any shoes, come hail or shine.'

'Wow,' said Ken. He couldn't imagine such a thing. But probably she couldn't imagine his childhood either. Not that she ever seemed curious. And when he had told her things, she never responded with something of her own. So this small splinter of her past was a special moment.

'You grew up tough where I came from,' she added, 'had to fight for everything. So I'll get those bastards back if it kills me.'

He didn't respond, afraid it would wind her up.

'Did you see what they had in the back?' she said.

'What?'

'All that stock. There must be hundreds of quid's worth. Fucking bastards.'

'What about it? They've got it now.'

'It's mine. I'm going to get it.'

'How're you goin' to do that?'

'You mean how are *we* going to do it, Ken.' She rolled away and got up off the floor. 'I'm going to bed.'

Ken turned over onto his stomach and put his head on his hands. 'Can I come too?'

She remained with her back to him. 'No. Not tonight.' She walked into her bedroom and closed the door.

He rolled back over and lay on the floor, staring at the ceiling, trying to work out what kind of woman Maggie was. Not like any kind he'd known before. Sometimes she was just another one lapping up his charm. Other times she walked all over him. He wasn't used to the kind of brush-off she was so good at giving him. He'd spent most of his years since leaving the home living off women, getting them to like him so they would give him things. He knew about them, and what they wanted. It was an exchange, where everyone knew the value of what they were giving. Maggie was different. There was a big part of her that he never even got close to; that was always in control. Except for the anger he'd seen back there in the shebeen. That was something else.

His mind went back again to when he'd first met her. For the first two or three years after he'd left the home, he and Charlie hung around together all the time. Charlie was building up the shebeen and Ken worked the bar, cleared tables, did whatever. In daytime he was up West, drifting about looking for chances, watching the money walk by until someone answered his smile. The life they were living was so light, so free – nobody giving orders or laying down the law, no-one in charge or telling them to stop. They were outlaws, living in the spaces between the rules. Then came that night when Maggie walked into the shebeen looking for bar work. A few months later she and Charlie got engaged.

There was a little engagement party in a pub. As well as Maggie and Ken, Charlie had a few drinking pals along, and a couple of their girlfriends. No relatives or friends of Maggie's. She said she'd run away from 'the middle of nowhere' in Ireland and didn't want her family to find her. So they were all from the same mould – all orphans of a kind. She had a big smile, an easy laugh and a teasing way not just with Charlie but with all the men around her. He imagined her growing up amongst a lot of brothers and giving them all hell. But she seemed head over heels with Charlie. And they made a handsome couple. Charlie's shoulders had grown even broader from the labouring jobs he'd had before opening the club. In his new suit he looked like a successful gangster, and with Maggie, sparky and eye-catching by his side, they looked glamorous against the bomb craters and tower blocks, boarded up streets and building sites of the East End.

But it had all left Ken spinning. They married and found the flat, and Ken worried that Charlie was disappearing from his life. Because suddenly he was different. On the surface he was the same towards Ken as he had always been – giving him work at the club whenever he wanted it, helping him out with money. But the easy intimacy between them that they used to have was gone. When people marry you expect them to change somehow, but it was as if Charlie was trying to become someone new and that involved putting a distance between the two of them – at least that's how it felt. But there was still the same devil in Charlie that made him fun and dangerous at the same time. It was what made his club worth going to. There might be a free drink or a fight – maybe both. The wildness never went away. And Maggie never seemed to want it any other way.

He could see why now. That same wildness was in her too. The way she came on to him when Charlie died; the way she'd handled herself in the club. She'd even got him fighting tonight, and he wasn't a fighting man – didn't used to be anyway. Life was going to be a lot livelier around Maggie. She lived by her own rules, just like Charlie did. But Ken knew Charlie. He still didn't know Maggie at all.

* * *

When he came to on the settee in the morning he had an ache in his neck and his arm was burning with a fierceness that made up for the night before. The sound of Maggie going out had stirred him earlier than he was used to. He preferred to ease slowly into the day. Heaving himself up, he got to his feet and made for the bathroom. Catching sight of himself in the mirror he grinned, threw some punches at his reflection then winced at the pain in his arm again. Maybe he wasn't Sonny Liston, but he wondered how the kid with the broken nose was doing.

After freshening up, he turned on the transistor radio. 'Housewives Choice' was just finishing, and he turned it off again before the boring band on 'Music While You Work' got going. He wondered if there would ever come a day when his kind of music would be on the radio like it was in America. He doubted it. This country was an old place, run by old people with old ideas. Nothing was ever going to change here.

He sat down with a cup of tea to read the East London Advertiser. As he turned the pages his eye caught a small headline on an inside page – 'BARTLETT HOUSE – INVESTIGATION CONTINUES.' The article was short. '*Police began taking statements yesterday in what a spokesman described as a complex investigation which was likely to continue for some weeks. He confirmed that no charges had been laid and that all those alleged to have been involved were continuing in their posts pending further enquiries. He issued a further appeal for ex-residents to come forward.'* His thoughts jerked back to the paper he'd been reading when Meatball paid him a visit. There was a story about the home in that too. He hadn't read the whole thing. He began to think back, working out which edition it might have been. It only came out twice a week. As his mind worked he got up and wandered round the flat looking for old copies. The place was a mess. It needed some real attention. Maggie was in no shape to look after the place lately. He'd have to get to it himself. He liked things neat and orderly – something he'd carried with him from the home. He began to tidy up a bit. There was so much stuff on the coffee table and the floor. He found a paper – the wrong one. After ten minutes of serious tidying, the place was already looking better. The carpet was nearly clear enough to get the sweeper to it. Picking up a cushion from the floor he saw another paper there. Flicking through it, he found the article. There was something to be said for untidiness after all. Sitting down at the kitchen table again, he began to read.

'POLICE INVESTIGATION AT BARTLETT HOUSE. *A police investigation has been launched into allegations concerning staff at Bartlett House children's home in Forest Gate. A police spokesman said that the matters under investigation went back a number of years, but declined to give any details. However this paper can exclusively reveal that enquiries centre on the activities of a group of staff as well as local community representatives – some of whom remain in office today – involving a number of children from the home. The spokesman said that an appeal was being issued for ex-residents to come forward and make statements. The investigation is likely to take several weeks to complete.'*

Well, well. Something big was happening. They were asking people to come forward. Ken was one of those they were appealing to. They wanted his statement. What did he have to tell them? What everyone knew about Trevor? But all he had was second hand stories. Charlie had seen to it that he was left alone. What else? There were some strange things. The people who came to inspect and stayed long into the night; the sounds of a party drifting up through the thin ceiling to where he lay in bed awake – afraid but not knowing why. There were the runaways – the kids who vanished and never came back. Sally was one. He supposed every home had a few of those, but there seemed to be a lot at Bartlett House. But why wouldn't they, with Trevor around? If it hadn't been for Charlie he'd have run away himself. The man was pure scum. Charlie would have things to say, if he hadn't been dead. He could have told them things – made statements. He could have told them plenty probably. He wouldn't tell Ken anything, but he was there – at all those parties. Now he couldn't say anything to anybody. Or then again, maybe he could. There was his diary. The one Ken had only ever seen that once. He recalled the line from Charlie's letter; 'tell them to remember Charlie's diary.' Whatever was in it had made them sweat.

There was that night, just before Charlie left the home for good, when they searched the place. Charlie had crept out to go drinking. He often did it then. He was only just sixteen but with his size he could get away with it. They knew he did it, but had given up trying to stop him. That night they came up – Trevor, Anne, and that little guy who didn't last long – Ian. Ken was in bed listening as they went into Charlie's room, bangs and thumps coming from the other side of the wall. Then suddenly the light came on in their own room. Anne stood in the doorway looking like he'd never seen her before – drunk, angry. His guts churned at the memory. She shouted to everyone to get out of bed. The four of them crawled out of their bunks and stood around in their pyjamas, blinking and shivering even though it wasn't cold. Trevor and Ian came in and started turning the room over, pulling books off the shelves and boxes from under the beds, searching everywhere. Ian looked scared shitless. There was sweat on his stupid little beard. The noise they made woke the others and a couple of the girls stuck their heads around the door to watch.

A sleepy Sheila said 'What's going on?'

Anne, still standing at the door, yelled at them. 'Get back to bed and mind your own business.' They went. Dave, the youngest in the room, started to cry. Then Trevor turned to Anne.

'This is your problem too.'

Anne started helping in the search. They tore into everything; the cupboards, the shelves, the toys. They took all the bedclothes off the beds, then the mattresses. They hardly said a word. Ken watched them working. He was afraid again. Afraid that they'd find whatever they were looking for and it would be his, and he would be to blame for all this shouting, all this damage. He tried to think of things he had they might want. Trevor was looking at the books on the shelf. He took one down at a time, flicked through it and tossed it on the floor. Ian was going through the clothes in the wardrobe, feeling them all and pulling stuff out to look at. Anne even pulled the beds away from the wall and picked up the lino in the corner to look under it. Ken wanted it all to stop, but it went on, the three adults so wrapped up in their search, the children ignored. Trevor pulled Ken's shoebox from under the bed – the box where he kept his model soldiers and his photographs – emptied the contents onto the floor and began rummaging through it. He picked up the thin bundle of photos Ken kept carefully tied with string – the ones of his mother and some relatives he didn't know – and started looking through them.

'Put them down!' Ken yelled as he flew at Trevor. He tried to snatch the photos away but Trevor held them up out of his reach and pushed Ken's head down, spinning him round until he fell over. He got back up and jumped at Trevor again. It took him by surprise and this time Ken got an arm around Trevor's neck. Trevor shouted out and Anne and Ian pulled him off, holding him by his arms as he panted and struggled. Trevor took a step over, clenched his fist and swung it hard into Ken's face. The blow stunned him. Anne and Ian let him drop to the floor as he sobbed with the pain and the shock. He kept on crying, his hands over his face where he'd taken the blow. Through his fingers he watched Trevor tear up his photos and fling them on the floor. Then it went on. The searching. On and on until the three had worn themselves out with the effort of it. Trevor sat down on the springs of Ken's bunk. He looked over at Ken and the others, like he wanted to start a fight.

'It's not here either,' he said.

Anne gave a big sigh. 'He must have it with him,' she said. 'Or he's got somewhere else to hide it.' She looked tired and beaten. Everybody was silent except Ken, crying quietly as he lay on the floor, his eyes on the photo that had fallen under the bed where Trevor was sitting. The only one left.

* * *

He hadn't thought about these things for a long time. Why would he? He could feel the tight knot in his stomach, just like he had that night. He'd blanked it from his mind. Even now, he was conscious of the way he could make himself empty of all feeling when he thought about it. He used to do it deliberately at the home – stop any thought that would let the bad feelings out. It had become a habit, a good one as far as he was concerned. Some things – a lot of things – were best pushed down and forgotten.

So all he had left of the photos was the one he kept in his wallet. But maybe now there was a chance to get back at Trevor and the rest of them. Did it matter? Charlie must have thought it worth the trouble of keeping the diary and hiding it away. The least Ken could do was find it and see what was in it. He looked at the living room. Maggie's living room.

Charlie's living room. The diary must be somewhere right here in the flat. It was Charlie's place, but when he looked around there wasn't much of Charlie in it. Everything was Maggie's – the furniture and the pictures; the glasses and the whiskey bottles. That was only to be expected. Charlie never spent much time here. He was a man of the street, a talker and a dealer, a drinker and a fighter. He was never going to be interested in the colour of the curtains.

Ken was seeing the room the way Anne and Trevor had been looking at his bedroom. Where could things be hidden? Where could secrets be kept? He gazed around until his eye fell on the altar in the corner. Beneath the figures, forming part of the altar was a small drawer. He looked up at the glowing statue of the Virgin Mary, her head bent, her plastic stare aimed at a little lamb, her arms reaching out to him. The lamb was snuggled up around her feet gazing up at her. To the other side of Mary knelt a little angel, hands together in prayer. Around the angel's neck was a small chain with a key on it.

Reaching up, he hooked the chain over the angel's head and took the key between his fingers. He hesitated, feeling suddenly guilty about this act of prying. Shouldn't he wait for Maggie to get back and ask her about it? He knew the answer was no even though he couldn't say why. Slipping the key into the lock, he turned it. Pulling the drawer out, he lifted it down to see inside.

It brimmed with Catholic stuff. Tiny statues of Mary and Jesus; little medals – one of them a Saint Christopher on a chain, 'To Charlie love Maggie' engraved on the back; some strings of beads with crucifixes on the end; cards with printed prayers; two rolled up pieces of paper with red ribbon round them; some candles; a prayer book. Then, a small square packet with a picture of a rat on it. He held it up. 'Redinox – Effective against rats. Caution: Poison. Not to be taken.' Ken read the words slowly, twice. He opened the packet and looked inside. Nearly empty. He sat down on the settee and stared at it for a long time. It didn't mean anything. The drawer was full of junk. Maggie put all kinds of things in there. She might have used that stuff for anything. Maybe even killing rats.

He thought about the look he'd caught in her eye that night, here in this room, with Charlie laid out in the bedroom. Had he seen something then, in amongst the come-on? Whatever it was he couldn't decipher it. Maybe it had something to do with those bruises on her back.

He went back to the drawer to see if he'd missed anything. He didn't know what he expected to find: more packets of rat poison or suspicious bottles, or maybe a confession or something. There was nothing. He was glad. He needed doubts. He wanted reasons not to see everything cold and clear. Collecting up the items, he put them back in the drawer, shoved it back into its place beneath the altar and locked it. Finally he carefully hung the key back around the angel's neck. That drawer had given him something to think about, but nothing to convince him of anything. And no diary either.

CHAPTER 5

The key rasped in the lock of the front door signalling Maggie's return. She entered the living room followed by Ernie. For a second she seemed surprised Ken was there.

'Make us some tea will you Ken,' she said, slipping her coat off. It sounded like an order.

Ernie was silent, his eyes unfriendly. Ken went into the kitchen and started making tea. After few minutes they followed him in and sat at the kitchen table.

'Ken, you should hear this, so sit down with us,' said Maggie.

His immediate thought was that she was kicking him out of the flat. He put the teas in front of them, passed the sugar around and sat down, waiting for the blow to fall.

Maggie took a deep breath. 'Tell him the story, Ernie.'

Ernie's face was a picture of misery. He turned to face Ken.

'When I met Charlie he didn't have a penny to his name.' Ernie's gruff voice ground out the words. 'But he was all for getting this club goin' an' I could see he was a man who'd make a good fist of things if he had half a chance.' He paused, summoning his thoughts. 'He had a plan in his head, he just needed some start-up. I know a lot of people. So I talked to a couple of them and the long and short is they bunged us a monkey and me an' Charlie went into business together.'

He glanced at Ken, seeing his puzzled expression. 'Five hundred quid.'

Ken nodded. Five hundred pounds was a lot of money. He was starting to get the picture. 'These people...'

'They're business associates, local lads made good,' said Ernie, 'operate a lot of clubs themselves – up West. We go back a long way – I knew their Mum when she was just a girl.' His face turned darker. 'But business is business and they want their money back.'

Ken looked at Ernie and then at Maggie. Ernie was still glum, Maggie had her jaw set. He decided to ask the question.

'What happens if they don't get it?'

Ernie's face was suddenly red with fury. He lunged at Ken until his face was inches away, making Ken draw back. 'They're going to fucking kill us of course!' He flung himself back in his chair, a look of mock surprise on his face. 'What did you think? They're going to lay on a fucking party for us? They have one simple rule – you don't pay, you're dead.' He jabbed his temple with his finger, his eyes bulging. 'Really fucking simple, see?'

There was silence for a few seconds. He'd never seen Ernie drop his man-of-the-world air before, and the fear pouring out of him was infectious.

'That's what I inherited from Charlie,' said Maggie. She took a sip from her tea. She seemed eerily unruffled by Ernie's outburst. 'So let's talk about what we're going to do about it.'

Ken wondered how she could stay so cool with something

like this on her plate. She hadn't been calm last night. Ernie's face lost a bit of its colour and as he looked at Maggie it seemed to take on a little glow of hope. This old man with his experience, his cigars and his connections, was waiting for Maggie to take charge of the situation.

'We've been round Charlie's pals and drummed up forty pounds,' she began.

'Hardly worth the bother,' chipped in Ernie.

'But the stock down at the shebeen's got to be worth a good bit,' she continued. 'If we got hold of it, would it clear the debt?'

'Not what Charlie used to keep,' said Ernie.

'There's a lot more,' said Maggie. She looked at Ken for confirmation.

He nodded. 'Maybe twice as much.'

Ernie pulled a face. 'Maybe.'

There was a sudden hammering at the front door, making them all start.

Ken recognised it immediately. 'Police.'

Maggie gave an exasperated sigh. 'Dear God in heaven, haven't I enough to think about without them.'

They got to their feet and Ken went to the door. Outside stood Detective Inspector Davis and his sidekick, behind them half a dozen others in uniform.

'Remember us?' said Davis.

And in that moment Ken did remember – a younger, thinner face, more hair, less sneer, and a very new raincoat the older men made fun of. Must be a present from his Mum for becoming a detective, they said, as they gathered in one of the sitting rooms at the home.

'Maggie's not in,' he said automatically, but he could already hear her behind him.

'It's ok Ken,' she said, stepping past him.

'Well she can take her coat off,' said Davis, 'because she's staying here for the search. It's you we want.' He reached out and Ken winced as Davis grabbed him by his bad arm.

* * *

He juddered down the steps of the police station, his head buzzing with everything that had happened. It felt like a tidal wave had hit him and dragged him under. It was just last night he and Maggie were walking down the alley to the shebeen; only a couple of hours ago that Ernie yelled in his face. And now this. Without thinking, he turned and started walking. His legs carried him fast, but he willed them to go faster still. He wanted to run, but his throat was tight and his breathing hard. His hurry to get away from the police station propelled him along the pavement. He needed to be somewhere – anywhere that was a long way away. But he also needed to slow down, to think. There was so much, so much stuff flowing through his mind he couldn't get any of it straight. It boiled inside his head. He had to force himself to stop so he could look at it all and see how it made sense.

There was a small park on the opposite side of the street.

He crossed and went through the gates. Dossers and tramps sprawled on several of the benches, but he found an empty one and sat down. He pulled hard at his face, hoping the stretched skin would sharpen his mind. He had to think. He had to get it straight.

As soon as they started asking him about his 'relationship' with Maggie – in that ham-fisted, police way – he knew where they were going. Charlie was dead and suddenly he was on the scene. Davis's sidekick had spoken to the neighbours and knew he was living in the flat now – knew that he'd been staying over before that. The neighbours, it seemed, kept a pretty close eye on him. He explained as best he could that nothing started until after Charlie died. But then the question of how soon after came up. The truth wasn't going to help him. He'd hedged, not knowing what Maggie had already said or what they might get out of her, today, tomorrow, whenever. But it didn't matter much. Suddenly they had found their motive for Charlie's murder, and all their questions were around how to tie the story up. Was it just her or both of them? Who planned it and who executed it? Then a grim smile from Davis as he produced his killer punch. The search of the flat had turned up the rat poison. Whose prints would they find on the packet?

'Just that Irish bitch, or yours as well?'

That was when he knew they had him – he'd held that packet between his fingers while he tried to work out what it meant. As he sat silently staring at them, unable to think of anything to say that might help him, he abruptly realised how much he had been kidding himself. The idea that Maggie hadn't killed Charlie suddenly looked completely stupid, and he couldn't even see why he'd believed it for so long. Of course she'd done it – though he couldn't say why. He felt himself in freefall. He had been sucked in. Was this what she'd planned all along? Setting him up to take the fall? No, that couldn't be right, she was on the hook too. But what had she been saying to the police? He didn't know. He only had her version. Just as the cops only had her version. And even if he'd had a better story to tell, he could see they could pin it on him if they wanted – set him up and make it easy for themselves. The voice of one black man would count for nothing against the police. They had him.

But then, a halt to the proceedings. Davis and his sidekick disappeared, leaving Ken in the company of a silent young copper in uniform for a long time. When Davis finally came back into the room, it was with a blue file tucked under his arm, and minus the sidekick. He instructed the young cop to leave and carefully closed, then locked the door. He and Davis were alone together. Ken's heart beat faster as he felt panic rising in his chest. A black man and a white detective locked in an interview room with no witnesses. What 'statement' was Davis going to beat out of him? Was he suddenly going to be confessing to Charlie's murder here and now? No time wasted in hanging it round the coon's neck and tidying it away.

Davis pulled back the chair and sat down in front of him. Sitting was good. The table was between them. You needed to stand to hand out a serious beating, do some hard kicking. But then Davis took out a packet of cigarettes and offered him one. He declined. Davis stuck one between his lips and lit it with a flashy gold lighter. He leaned back in his chair, taking his time.

'Charlie grew up in Bartlett House didn't he?'

Ken nodded, unsure where this new line was going to lead him.

'You as well.'

He nodded again, remembering the young Davis in his new raincoat, earnest and fresh-faced – a long way from the dead-eyed thug sitting opposite him now. How long ago – twelve years? Fourteen?

Davis opened the file and took a sheaf of photographs from it. Picking one out, he put it on the table and slid it over until it was in front of Ken. The bland-looking middle aged man pictured could have been anyone.

'Know him?'

'No.'

Another photograph.

'No.'

Davis tried a couple more with the same result, before smiling to himself as he chose the next one.

'You know him though, don't you?'

The man in the picture was Trevor. Ken nodded.

'We've heard a lot about him. Want to tell us more?'

'Why're you askin' me about this? I got nothin' to tell you.'

'You don't know why? The local paper's full of it. You can read, can't you?'

'Must've missed it.'

'You were there, weren't you? Saw what was going on? Didn't you go to any of those parties?'

This was the thing he'd thought about doing – walking into a police station and telling them about Trevor. Get some revenge. But sitting here in front of Davis he knew what a mistake it would have been. A man who'd been there himself was doing the investigating.

'I didn't see nothin' much.'

Davis studied him. A long, hostile stare. Ken felt moved to break the silence.

'What's this got to do with Charlie?'

'Now that's a very good question. You're brighter than you look.' Davis reached into the folder again, this time pulling from it some typed pages. He cast his eye over them until he found what he wanted. 'It says here in this statement from one of your fellow 'inmates', if that's the word, that Charlie used to keep a diary when he was there.' Davis gave him the stare again. 'Is that true?'

So that's what they were after.

'I never saw one.'

'Didn't you?' Davis looked down at the typed sheets again. 'But it says here that you and Charlie were best buddies.' He looked up, the dead eyes on Ken once more. 'You might've thought he'd at least mention it – being big pals an' all.'

Ken shook his head, maybe a bit too quickly. 'He never said nothin' to me.'

'Nothing?' Davis leaned forward, and rested his elbows on the table between them. 'You wouldn't be giving me the coon's run-around would you? Telling me porkies?'

'No.' Ken kept his head still and tried to stare out Davis.

Davis held his stare, but seemed lost in thought for a moment. 'Doesn't look too good for you, does it?' he said.

'What don't?'

'They're talking about getting rid of the death penalty. You might not hang – might just get life.' said Davis, looking down and picking at something on his hand, as if making chit-chat. He took another drag on his cigarette, stubbed it out on the pockmarked table and turned his eyes back to Ken. 'I mean, all we need are the toxicology report and the prints on the packet and we're finished, aren't we?'

'I didn't do it. Charlie looked out for me. He was like a brother.'

'Yeah, but that missus of his, she's something isn't she? Couldn't resist, could you? You coloureds are like that, aren't you, always trying to fuck our women. Streets aren't safe to walk.' He leaned in to Ken, a confidential pose. 'And I bet you give her plenty, don't you? Got a nice big length on you, I'll bet.'

Ken looked at Davis, again remembering his visits to the home. What was he doing there? Apart from seeing him hanging about in the hall he couldn't remember anything about him. Davis's face was only inches away, full of the dishonest friendliness of cops and nothing else.

'One of you or both of you are going to take the drop for this. I'm the one who decides what happens. So if you help me out, I can help you out.'

He couldn't answer. What could he say that wouldn't dig him or Maggie further into the hole?

'So what about it then?' said Davis, suddenly leaning back in his chair and returning to the interrogation.

'What?'

'Charlie's diary. Where could it be, d'you suppose?'

'How would I know?'

Davis sighed impatiently. 'Look, if I thought some black bastard was holding out on me – .' He suddenly kicked back the chair and grabbed Ken by his lapels, hauling him halfway across the table. He put his face close to Ken's. 'I know that fucking diary exists and I want it. My lads didn't turn it up in the search of the flat. So if you don't want to go down for Charlie's murder you'd better get out there and fucking find it for me.'

* * *

The light in the park was already starting to fade. It was only about two in the afternoon, but the sky was grey and this late in November the days were short. Some dirty sparrows danced at his feet, throwing up dust. His breathing was back to normal now but he could still feel his heart beating in his chest. He didn't like the spinning, babbling confusion in his head. It made him ill.

Since leaving the home, he'd made an orderly life for himself. His appointments with his women, his meetings in the park, his work in the shebeen, there had been a neat rhythm to it all – and always Charlie behind him, watching over him. It sustained him through the years. But now, suddenly, he was in a world of threats and violence. It was like being sucked back into the past, back to the home. He should never have taken up with Maggie – got clear after Charlie died, cut his ties. But he knew he couldn't have done that either. Charlie mattered too much, and Maggie – he just couldn't think straight about her. She pulled him towards her in so many different ways, even while she left him hanging. And what was he to make of her now he knew her secret? He pushed the thought away.

He needed a plan and didn't have one. He wanted to disappear, find somewhere far away and start a new life – a simple life like his old one. But he had nowhere to go. All he knew of the world was within a tube ride. Anywhere else and he wouldn't even know how to communicate, let alone survive. So he was beaten before he started – trapped by everything that was happening around him.

CHAPTER 6

He was sitting in the nearly empty tube carriage on his way back to the flat, travelling back into Maggie's world. Thoughts of escape still drifted through his head – just to get away from the whole thing for a while, try and think things through. His only real option was his list of girlfriends. He got out his wallet and extracted a neatly folded handwritten list. Running his finger down the names and phone numbers on it, he stopped at Lucy. He hadn't seen her for a long time. She was a little old for him, but she had no husband to chase him around and was always grateful for his attentions. She wouldn't be sober, she never was these days, but she might do. Could he just keep hiding away – use his little list of contacts and keep moving around them? No. They'd no more welcome him turning up on their doorstep looking for shelter than their hairdresser or their cleaner. He had no status beyond the service he provided. Could he just find somewhere of his own in a new part of town? He could earn as much as he needed to survive from cottaging until he got things sorted. He had options. If he had a place, maybe he could find a way to get free of Davis and stay away from Maggie. The trouble was that in spite of everything he knew about her, he didn't want to stay away from Maggie.

So he sat back in his seat, letting his mind wander, trying to keep Davis's face out of his head. And then there it was, like it had been there all along but he hadn't noticed. He suddenly knew where the diary was.

* * *

Maggie was sitting on the settee drinking. He'd found her in that pose so often he wondered how much time she spent doing it when he wasn't around. Surrounding her was the wreckage of the police search. He'd been away all day, but the place looked like they'd just left. The altar had been ripped from the wall. The statue of the Virgin Mary was face down on the floor in the opposite corner of the room, the contents of the drawer scattered around it. There were broken pieces of vase ground into the carpet and the photograph of Maggie and Charlie on their wedding day had been thrown across the room. A door of the sideboard hung open on a broken hinge. It was a mess. Somehow the Christmas lights survived, still lit as they lay on the floor. The only clear surface was the coffee table. It had nothing on it except for a bottle of whiskey, half empty. She lowered the glass from her lips when he entered.

'Jesus Ken, have you just got out?'

'Yeah, they liked my conversation so much they kept wanting more.'

'You've been locked up all this time?' There was a note of concern in her voice he hadn't heard before.

'That's right.'

'For a while there I thought you might have run off on me.'

He smiled at her. His absence seemed to have brought out something new in her. This was the first time she'd shown any interest in where they stood together. In spite of what Davis had told him, he was still drawn to her. The strength of the pull frightened him. When he was with her he couldn't believe she was guilty of anything.

'No, Maggie. I'm still here for you.'

'Then come and sit down.'

He sat on the other end of the settee, keeping a little distance between them. For all the fresh warmth she was showing him, he knew he had to get some answers from her. He took a breath.

'Maggie, what happened with Charlie?'

She turned and looked at him. 'What?'

'The police – they said they found something.'

'Something?' She looked away and took another swig of her whiskey. 'Is it the rat poison you're talking about?'

He nodded.

She didn't say anything. He looked at her. Her face held a faraway expression.

'They think I killed him with it, then?'

'Maggie, that stuff – they're doin' tests.'

She gave an irritable sigh. 'Let them.' She got up off the settee and began walking round the room as if bored by the conversation. She seemed suddenly high. He had never known her to smoke so much as a single cigarette, never mind a reefer. Maybe she was drunk, but walking amongst the chaos of her flat, her broken belongings, she seemed in a strange, serene state.

He was confused. It was as if he'd brought her good news. 'But what are they going to find?'

'Find?' She turned to him. He could have sworn he saw the wisp of a smile. 'Nothing, Ken. They're not going to find anything.'

'So what was that poison for?'

'Rats – what did you think? We had a great big thing in here one time. They say they climb up the waste chute.'

He watched her, baffled by the performance she was putting on. She came and sat by him, slipped her arm through his and fixed him with her blue eyes.

'What else did they say?'

There was an interrogating edge to her voice that reminded him of Davis. He suddenly felt defensive. He'd arrived back at the flat wanting to tell her everything that happened. Now he wasn't so sure. But her eyes were on him and he had to say something.

'They'd been pretty nosy about me an' you. They knew that I lived here – all that.' He could see it wasn't what she was after. 'So they'd started thinkin' that I'd helped you kill Charlie.'

Her smile disappeared, replaced by a look of amused disbelief. 'You?' she said, and gave a short laugh as if the idea was too foolish for words.

'That's what they think.'

'Jesus,' she said, 'what in God's name gave them that idea?'

He had to tread carefully. He couldn't mention his fingerprints on the packet of rat poison. 'I don't know,' he said. 'I got a feelin' they were probably just fishing. Cops're always itching to find someone like me guilty of somethin'.' He was playing her game, sliding away from telling her everything.

His answer seemed to satisfy her.

'So are they going to arrest me?' she said.

'They still got to get the report on the poison.'

She nodded thoughtfully. 'Well, we'll cross that bridge when we come to it, won't we?'

She stood up again, the conversation over, and looked around the room. Now she seemed full of pent up energy. 'God, this place is a mess. Give me a hand to get it cleared up, will you?'

He watched her, standing with her hands on her hips in the middle of the room. She looked like she'd won some kind of victory. She didn't act like somebody about to face a murder charge. She had an answer for everything and didn't seem bothered by anything. But she didn't act like a widow of two weeks either. Was she putting on a brave face? For a minute he mulled over the idea that she might just be crazy – some kind of psycho. Was he going to believe anything she told him? He should hold back, not get too involved. She would take him down with her. But right now he had to hang on to something if he wasn't to go crazy himself. He got off the settee and started tidying.

* * *

The clear-up took them the rest of the day. In the evening Maggie went out to phone Ernie, leaving Ken cooking them a meal of potatoes and a cut of brisket she'd bought at the market. She seemed to sober up quickly and, with her new energy, wanted to reconvene the meeting that Davis had interrupted and get down to the business of the shebeen.

After his conversation with Maggie, Ken put his thoughts on hold. He'd arrived back at the flat convinced she'd killed Charlie with the rat poison. Now he didn't know. Davis could be just tricking him into finding the diary. Or maybe not. Trusting the police wasn't easy. Trusting Davis was harder.

He wasn't sure what to do with the brisket, so he stuck it in the oven to roast. He realised he'd hardly eaten all day, and the smell of the cooking meat rising from the oven made his stomach rumble. Something like this was going to need a bit of gravy with it. He searched the cupboards for some *Bisto* but there was nothing. He hadn't sampled much of Maggie's cooking, but he'd worked out it wasn't her favourite pastime. If he wanted gravy he'd have to go out and get some. Most of the shops were shut now, but the off licence a couple of streets away kept a few groceries as well. After all they'd been through recently they deserved a decent meal.

* * *

Walking through the dark streets, he found himself thinking about Maggie's performance earlier on. If she was feeling any grief for Charlie, she wasn't showing it, except maybe in all drinking she was doing. And he'd got himself so bound up with her he'd lost sight of Charlie. Charlie's death had cut him adrift. He'd hardly realised what was happening to him – he been so numb, but in the effort to protect himself from that unwanted freedom, he'd been desperate to grab onto the first person to hold out their hand – Maggie. He let her take him over and become his new shelter from the storm. But she was turning out to be a bit of a mystery; wanting him, not wanting him; giving him no straight answers about how Charlie died. She wasn't going to be a replacement for Charlie. Nobody could be. That hole in Ken's life could never be filled. If Davis wasn't lying, and she had killed Charlie, he had to find out why. She had taken away the only person that ever really mattered to him. But he felt half blinded by her right now, his head clogged up with thoughts and feelings he couldn't resolve. Maybe he really was part of some plan of hers, or maybe he was just something she thought she owned now, along with the shebeen. Did she know about the diary? He'd made a sudden decision back there to say nothing about it when she was questioning him. He'd try and get hold of it tomorrow. For now it wasn't something he was about to drop into the conversation. But he knew that in spite of everything he was going to do whatever he could to get her off the hook with Davis, even if he couldn't justify it to himself. How can you love a woman who'd killed your best friend? He was riding the storm, waiting to see where it would take him, hoping for a soft landing.

* * *

As he re-entered the flat he heard an unfamiliar man's voice – loud, harsh – which stopped suddenly as he shut the front door. The silence that followed felt loaded. Pushing open the living room door he saw Maggie sitting unnaturally upright and rigid on the edge of the settee. Her lip was swollen. She looked at him and shook her head, as if warning him. Beyond her, Ernie was here, leaning against the balcony door – or pretending to. He looked awkward and uncomfortable, as if his legs wouldn't support him but the door he was leaning on was full of nails.

'You must be Ken,' said the East End voice off to his left. 'Come in and let's have a look at you.'

Cautiously, Ken entered the room. A big, thickset white man in a black Crombie overcoat stood in the kitchen doorway glaring at him.

'Hello,' said Ken.

The man walked over and punched him hard in the stomach, catching him as he doubled up in pain, and lowering him carefully to the floor.

'Now the greetings are out of the way, we can finish our conversation,' said the man. 'I was just explaining to Ernie and Maggie here about the importance of letting a bit of meat like that cook for a decent time.' Ken was suddenly aware of the smell of the joint still in the oven. 'Brisket's a cheap cut, ain't it? So it needs a good long while. You want to get yourself a pressure cooker like my old mum. Comes out a treat when she does it. You a good cook, Ken?'

Ken, still recovering from the punch, looked up from his position on the floor and shook his head.

'Nah, you black bastards know fuck all, don't you. Probably know how to boil up a missionary, that's about it.'

The man strode around the room, pausing to examine the dark spot on the wall where the altar had been, briefly turning his back on them. He was so sure of himself – that no-one would jump him from behind, or if they did, that he could handle it anyway. For all the lightweight chat about the brisket, he had a menace about him that put him in a different league from Meatball. He stopped by Ernie. Ernie's face too had received the attentions of this strange, dangerous man. Blood was trickling from his nose and he was trembling.

'Anyway, I've got off the point, haven't I? What I want to talk about's something even more important than brisket and that's –,' he jabbed Ernie with a finger to emphasise the words, 'settling your debts good and prompt. Ain't that right Ernie?'

Ernie gave a half nod, as if too much of a response might attract more of the man's wrath.

'I've come along to clear up any lingering doubts you might have on the subject.'

He grabbed Ernie by the scruff of the neck and hauled him cringing into the middle of the room. 'Ernie, old son, don't think the twins don't respect you.' He casually kicked Ernie's legs from under him, forcing him to drop to his knees. 'You and them go back a long way. We all know that.' With sudden violence he lashed out with his thick brogue, sending the toe of it into Ernie's ribs. 'But friendship don't put bread on the table, does it?' Another kick, harder than the first. Ernie let out a wail and rolled over on his side. 'So I'm here to give you a taste of how things go if they start to get unfriendly.' Another kick. 'You might not think it, but I can keep this up all night if I want to.' Another kick. 'So if I were you, I'd make sure there's a down payment over at the office by Friday. Friday is payday, see?' He walked round Ernie's curled body until he was behind him and sent another kick into his spine. The scream from Ernie made Ken clench his eyes shut and curl up where he lay on the floor. 'And the rest of it better be there by the Friday after. Got that?' He took a step back, pulled a handkerchief from his top pocket, and bent down to rub the toe of his shoe with it. 'That's the best I can do for an old friend of the family.'

He turned to face Maggie. 'Lucky for him he's an old man. If I hit him too hard he'd croak. You two - ,' he waved his arm to take in Ken as well, 'you're young and fit. I can do you a lot of damage before either of you snuff it. In fact,' he walked over to Maggie and took her jaw in his hand, jerking her face up to inspect it, 'you're not bad looking, are you? We could have a decent night with you, me and the lads.' He glanced over his shoulder to where Ken lay on the floor holding his stomach, terrified of the man's attention. 'And your boyfriend'd do for the queers. We could have a right old orgy with you two – before we fucking pulverise you.' He let go of Maggie's jaw. 'Well, I'll be off now. You'll be wanting your dinner I expect, so I won't keep you.' He turned at the door and smiled grimly at Maggie. 'With a bit of luck, you won't pay.'

* * *

The Northern Line tube wound its way up through Hampstead, Golders Green and Brent before Ken got out at Hendon Central. Another bit of London outside of his world. He had on his most sober attire; a brown suit, purple shirt and an old pair of brown Italian loafers. He had a feeling Hendon was going to be a sober kind of place and he didn't want to stand out. As he walked away from the station he could see it was a land of suburban streets where quiet, worthy lives were lived and nobody beat or threatened you. People went about their business in a calm and orderly way. Maybe he could like it, living up here, where you can be anonymous and invisible. Except he couldn't be invisible here. With the only face that wasn't white, he stood out like a smudge on a clean shirt.

The street the Dolmans lived in had trees along it. It looked good in the autumn sunshine. The houses were semi-detached but not as big as Ken expected. It was such a neat place. Even the bushes in the gardens looked like they'd been combed into place.

He aimed to get there around eleven. At that time of day husbands were usually out working and the women were thinking about that little break they like to give themselves – 'elevenses'. Hazel Dolman might be out shopping but she wouldn't be at work. Women in Hendon didn't work. It wasn't that kind of place.

He rang the doorbell and it made a gentle two-tone chime. There was silence for a long time and Ken thought his luck was out but then the door opened. Hazel Dolman took one look at him and shut the door in his face. He realised from her expression that she hadn't recognised him. She'd just seen the colour of his skin. He'd had that reaction plenty of times before. His colour made him conspicuous and invisible at the same time. He rang again. Nothing. They didn't get a lot of coloured visitors in these parts. He leaned down and put his mouth to the letterbox.

'Mrs Dolman,' he shouted. 'Hazel Dolman. I'm a friend of Charlie's.'

The door opened again. This time it had a chain on it.

'What do you want?' She was aggressive, as if she was angry about something.

'I knew Charlie.'

'So what? He knew all sorts of layabouts and ruffians.'

He was struck by 'ruffians'. A Hendon kind of word.

'I knew him from the home. Me and him were real close. I saw you at the funeral.' He smiled.

She looked him over, then nodded. 'I remember. What are you doing here?' she said.

'I wanted to talk to you about Charlie.'

'Well I don't want to talk to any of your like about him.'

'Then just tell me why you think Maggie killed him.'

For a second Hazel Dolman was completely fazed. 'I've

never even suggested Maggie had anything to do with it.'

'Then why do the police think she has?'

The door closed then opened again, this time without the chain.

'Come in,' she said. As she spoke Ken could see her looking up and down the street. He knew what that was about. She was afraid her neighbours might see her taking a coloured man into her house.

He followed her into a flowery room. The wallpaper was flowery, the chairs were flowery, the carpet was flowery. There were real flowers on a little table in the window.

'Won't you sit down, Mr – er?'

'Just call me Ken.' He sat in one of the armchairs and felt himself sink deep into it. She perched herself on the edge of the other one across from him. She was dressed in that same conservative but expensive way he had noticed the day of the funeral, except today she was wearing a yellow dress – it had flowers too – with short sleeves that were pleated in some tricky way that was probably the fashion up here in Hendon. He could see something of Charlie about her that he hadn't noticed last time, something a little square about the face. She had a lot of freckles like he did too. But she looked younger than Charlie; it must have been a couple of years or so. And for all her air of the classy Hendon wife there was still a bit of the little girl in her she hadn't left behind yet.

'I take it you don't often get up to Hendon.' She had traded up her accent from East End to middle class north London.

She was checking out his clothes. Ken wasn't about to be disturbed by that.

'I'm more a West London kind of guy. You go there much?'

'Occasionally. When I want something a little more exotic.'

'Yeah, that's generally what I'm doing there too.'

'So you were in the home with him, were you?' she said.

'That's right.'

'I remember he mentioned you in one of his letters.'

'But he never mentioned you.'

'I was his secret.' She looked shyly at him. The little girl coming out.

'Charlie liked his secrets.' said Ken.

Her hand played with the tassels that hung from the arm of the chair. 'Perhaps he had his reasons.'

'What kind of reasons?'

She looked away from him, out of the window. 'I would have thought you knew better than me. You were there, in the same home as him.'

'Well I didn't know. I heard all the stories but I never knew nothing – not really knew.'

'Charlie knew.' She said it suddenly. She was looking at him now. The light from the window caught the big lashes around her brown eyes. 'That's why they killed him.'

For a few seconds Ken watched tiny bits of dust rise up through the sunlight.

'Who're they?' he said.

'The people from the home. The people who used to visit it.'

'The ones the police are looking into right now?'

'Are they? I didn't know.'

'It's been in the papers.'

'Not here,' she said.

No, he thought, it wouldn't be. It was only some children's home in the East End of London. A different world. Why would anyone in Hendon care about it?

'It must be the same people.' she said. Ken only half heard her. He was struggling with a confusing sensation. This news about people having killed Charlie had made his heart leap. He suddenly felt good.

'But would they do that – kill somebody?' He was playing for time, trying to untangle his thoughts. If these people, whoever they were, had done this to Charlie, then that meant – .

Hazel leaned forward, her hands clasped together over her knee. 'They might do anything to protect themselves. They might still be important people.' she said. Ken was silent for a moment, collecting his thoughts.

'You must have known something.' She was still on the edge of her seat, her voice earnest. Ken shifted in his chair. She was asking him about things he had put behind him and tried not to think about.

'Charlie never told me anything. He protected me. But I knew something was happening. Every week we'd get a bunch of people showing up for an inspection – we got a lot of inspections. Then at night they'd stay on and some other people would turn up. There'd be a party. Charlie would be there, other kids too. I knew some of them – Sheila and another kid called Cliff. The rest of us didn't know what went on, but we weren't stupid. We knew Charlie and the other kids were the entertainment, getting passed around among those important people. Sometimes Charlie and the others looked like they'd – .' Ken had to stop. Something caught in his throat. He couldn't go on talking. For a second his mind went blank. He couldn't reach into the dark place where his memories lay. Not right now. Besides, there were other things going on inside him. He didn't want to think about the home. He didn't even want to talk about Charlie. He wanted to think about Maggie. He'd been wrong – hadn't he?

It was all starting to make sense now. They were the ones who did it. It had to be. They wanted Charlie shut up for good and they had done it. Now he wasn't around to talk to any police investigation. No statement from Charlie, the man who knew the names, the dates, the filthy things done – to him, to others, but not to Ken. Charlie had been his guardian angel. And Maggie was innocent. The only problem was the police didn't think so.

'Are you all right?' Hazel Dolman's words broke into his thoughts.

'Yeh - er - I'm fine. Cool.'

'They must be painful memories.'

'They're kinda mixed, to tell you the truth.'

After a minute Ken realised he was still wrapped up in his thoughts and Hazel was still looking at him. He made an effort to snap back to this room in North London.

'So what's your story?' he said. 'You seem to have come out ok for someone from the homes.' His question caught her off guard. She blushed, gave him that shy look again. Then she got herself back under control.

'Perhaps it looks that way now, but believe me I've had my share of painful experiences.'

'You had the same thing at your home?'

'No, not that. The home was all right. Apart from the occasional beating we probably had a better time than most. But I was fostered out a few times.'

'Yeah, that happened to me once. It didn't last two weeks. I was too black for them.'

Hazel Dolman lowered her eyes and blushed a little more. 'Well, with girls of course it's the sex thing. If it's not the older boys in the family it's the father. It could be bloody awful. You can't go to the mother – she'll take against you. You're trapped. And of course they expect you to be grateful anyway.'

As he listened, Ken started to get an uneasy feeling, that somehow he hadn't suffered enough. That he'd had it too easy. And Charlie and his sister, and others too had taken his share of the suffering instead. They had all been through it for him. It was all about luck; his good luck and their bad luck. They had been in the wrong place at the wrong time. They were too handsome or pretty. They had appealed. His luck was to get to know Charlie before he had started to appeal as well. He should feel bad about that. But he couldn't. He couldn't let out the things he should feel – that he wanted to feel. They were locked away.

'Then I was adopted.' Hazel was still telling her story, a distant look in her eyes.

'A good family?'

There was a long moment before she answered.

'Actually it was John and his first wife.'

Ken realised they were talking about her husband.

'You mean – you were adopted by the Dolmans?' he said. She was gazing back out of the window now.

'Yes. But John and I – well we simply fell in love. They say it can't happen like that – I was only fifteen, he was thirty one – but it did. We couldn't help ourselves.' He noticed how her voice was different when she talked about John. Those feelings were still pretty strong. Now she was looking at the flowery carpet and her voice changed again.

'Of course there was a scandal. Patsy divorced him and he was lucky the whole thing didn't come to court. He could have been struck off. Fortunately he's a Freemason.' Here, he could see the Hendon housewife again – proud of her man's position in their upstanding little community. 'We had to move away. Patsy kept the house.'

He sensed the bitterness. But the way people here handled their messy problems was something he couldn't relate to. They shared out some money, some property, and acted like it never happened. Like nobody got hurt. They pretended everything was all right and pain didn't come into it.

He suddenly realised why she was being so frank with him. There was no-one else she could tell this story to, no-one else who could understand. Despite the gap between them now, their backgrounds bound the two of them together in a way only they could recognise. It was a good moment to get to his purpose for coming.

'Charlie told me he kept a diary,' he said.

She shifted uneasily on the edge of her chair. 'Did he?

'I got a feeling people are looking for it.'

'The people that killed Charlie?'

'Maybe.'

She was silent.

'Have you seen it?' said Ken.

She nodded. 'I've got it upstairs.'

'You ever read it?'

'Of course,' she said, surprised.

Ken was surprised too, after the questions she'd been asking. 'Then you know more than me what went on.'

'Perhaps I do.'

'Are there names in it?'

She pressed her lips together, her eyebrows coming together in disapproval. 'Oh, yes, there are names alright. Names – some of them – frankly – Charlie knew exactly what he was doing when he wrote that diary.'

'Have the police been asking about it?'

'When Charlie gave it to me, he told me to give it to the police if anything ever happened to him.'

So that was Charlie's insurance – hidden away with the secret sister in the dull suburbs of north London. Hidden so well, he could treat Trevor the way he did and get away with it.

'But you didn't – give it to them.'

She looked away. 'I was going to, but no, I didn't.'

'Why not?'

She looked back, her brown eyes on him. 'The one I spoke to, Detective Inspector Davis, he said he knew the home. The minute he said it, I just – .'

'What?'

'I – er – I,' she struggled to find words. 'I just had a feeling it was best not mentioned.'

'How come?'

'There's a policeman in the diary, you see. It can't be him, he would have been too young, but if he knew the home, he must know that policeman too.'

It seemed a reasonable guess. She might live like a suburban housewife, but she had a survivor's instinct.

'So what did you tell him?'

'That Charlie had told me stories and mentioned names. I gave him the names of two of the people in the diary but I simply said I remembered them from Charlie's stories.'

'But you never mentioned there was anything in writing?

She shook her head.

'Looks like Davis found out about the diary anyway,' he said. He let her think, aware the silence would let her apprehension grow.

'Am I in some danger?' she said finally.

'If I could work out you've got it, he can too,' he said, leaving a pause before adding, 'I'm surprised he hasn't already.'

'I see. And is this why you came – to warn me?'

This was going better than he expected. He hadn't come with the intention of frightening her, but now she was afraid it would be easier for him.

'Kind of. I was thinkin' of asking you to give it to me.'

She looked at him, a hint of suspicion coming to her eyes. 'Why?'

'They think Maggie killed Charlie,' said Ken, going into his rehearsed story. 'I thought maybe I could trade the diary and get them to forget about that.'

'But you can't go to that policeman. He's one of them isn't he? He would destroy it – make sure they never got caught. Surely he's made up the accusation against Maggie just to get hold of it.'

She could be right about that. He wanted her to be. But Davis had a nearly empty packet of rat poison with Ken's fingerprints on it and was waiting for a toxicology report that he alone would decide what to do with. That was evidence as far as Davis was concerned – against Maggie, against himself, or both. Without the diary, Ken had nothing to bargain with.

'Maybe,' he said. 'But he can still make it stick. The police can prove anything if they want to.'

She looked at him, absorbing his words.

'Then what? You just hand it over and hope they'll stop

pursuing Charlie's wife?'

Now she said it, it didn't seem much of plan after all. But it was all he had.

'What is she to you, anyway?' she asked suddenly.

Ken met her eye. 'I'm doin' this for Charlie. He loved Maggie.'

She looked away. 'I'm sorry.'

'At least you wouldn't be holding it if anyone comes looking for it,' he said. He knew he was back to trying to frighten it out of her.

She was silent for a long time. 'What is the right thing to do?' she said.

He watched her struggle – her north London morality pitched against her fear of a visit from dangerous people.

'Whatever I do, I'll be doin' it for the best,' said Ken.

'So long as some good comes of it.'

'I promise it will.'

She looked at him again with her brown eyes, her long lashes catching the sunlight. Then getting up, she left the room.

When she handed it to him, she looked relieved. The small package was wrapped in creased brown paper and tied with a dirty piece of string, as if it had been wrapped and unwrapped many times. He weighed it in his hand. It felt light. This might have been what Charlie had died for. He had a sudden sense that in taking the diary from Hazel Dolman he was accepting a curse.

CHAPTER 7

Emerging from Whitechapel tube station with the parcel in his pocket, he realised that now he had the diary, finding out what was in it suddenly mattered more than anything else. He felt dirty, the way he'd got it out of Hazel Dolman, but he had to know what she knew. If he took it back to the flat he would have to share it with Maggie and he didn't want that. It was something for him alone. He thought for a moment until a solution came to him. He turned and walked briskly along the Mile End Road towards the library.

Reaching for the gleaming brass handle, he pulled open the polished wooden door. Immediately the silence and the smell of old books took him back to when he was a boy. He hadn't been in a library since then. Every Saturday morning at the home he joined a little group in the hall that one of the staff would form into a crocodile and lead down to the local library. There they spent an hour looking at books and deciding which to take out on their library cards. It was a break from the routine of the home, and a small moment when they could decide something for themselves. Ken always liked picture book stories of westerns, with their lone heroes standing against hordes of baddies or Apaches, and he'd worked his way through their entire collection a couple of times. Then

Trevor arrived and the trips to the library stopped.

The only occupants of the dusty space were three old men reading newspapers. He found an empty seat as far away from them as possible and sat down. Taking the diary from his pocket, he untied the string and carefully unwrapped it. Even so, it made a rustling sound and one of the old men turned and glared at him.

The diary itself was a small leather-bound notebook which he recognised straight away. Before Trevor, the home had been run by Mr Fry, an old man who had once been a school headmaster. The children in the home seldom saw him. He spent most of his time in a room he called his 'study' writing in notebooks exactly like this one.

He licked his fingers and turned to the first page. Charlie's scrawl, or a younger version of it, was spread across it. The first date was 13th March 1946 – not long after Trevor came to the home. Charlie would have been eleven.

'I am writing this diary to tell what happens here. If I die I hope someone will find it and tell everyone about this place and about Trevor. He pretends to be nice when grownups are around but he is a bad man and he knows lots of other bad men. They came last night and me and Cliff had to go downstairs and stand in front of them all so they could look at us. There was six men all sitting round and drinking. One of them I've saw before. He is Mr Harshaw from the Council and he comes to inspect. They called him Wally. There was a policeman there as well. He had a uniform on with pips on the shoulders like a general in the army. He showed us a big metal box with wheels on top and said we was going to watch a film, like at the pictures. Trevor started the film and we had to sit with them and watch it. It was naked men doing things with boys. They stuck their nobs right in the boys bumholes. The man I was sat next to said we were going to do the same thing when the film stopped. I was afraid and he laughed. Then the film stopped and Trevor made Cliff stand up and said to the men how much will you bid for him. The men all said how much they bid and the winner was Mr Harshaw because he said five pounds. He gave the money to Trevor like it was nothing then him and Trevor took Cliff next door. Then Trevor came back and told me to stand up and said how much will you bid for him. They bid higher this time. The winner was the policeman. He said ten pounds. He gave Trevor the money and then he said he didn't want to go to another room he wanted to stay here and do a show but he wanted five pounds from everyone to watch it all. The men cheered and gave him their money. I thought he meant we would sing a song or something but he didn't mean that. Him and Trevor twisted my arm and bent me over the settee and stuck my head in the cushion so I could hardly breathe. Then they pulled my trousers down and did everything in the film.'

Ken closed his eyes and rubbed a hand slowly across his face, trying to wipe away the image of what he had just read. This was what Charlie had protected him from. To see it written here in blue biro was like being there, back in that terrible place. He opened his eyes. His hands trembled as they held the notebook. The voice of the younger Charlie sounded so much like himself. But the anger that made him write it all down was there in the words too, in the details. He'd been trapped in that home, weak and overpowered, but he'd found a way to tell his story.

There was page after page of it. He could see where Charlie had started making his writing smaller to save space. After that there was less and less description, instead just dates and a list of initials. He flicked back to before the initials started and read another page at random. It was dated 18th June 1947.

'A new man was there tonight. WH brought him in and said he was Lord Percy. The man said he was just Percy. He had a moustache. He had a gold watch and a gold tiepin and a gold cigarette case. Trevor got very creepy round him laughing at everything he said and giving him the armchair. Me and Cliff and Sheila stood up for him to look at. He pointed at Sheila and said she is too old have you anything younger. Trevor went out and got the new girl who came last week. I think she is Sally. He pointed at me and said he is a big lad is he any good. Trevor said he had no complaints. Percy said he wanted to take me and Sally away for the night. Trevor didn't look happy but Percy took his wallet out and counted out thirty pounds. I've never seen so much money. He took us up West in his car. It looked like a Jag but he said it was a Daimler. Sally didn't know what was going on she is only about seven. We went in a big house and there was men in uniforms like guard the Queen. Lord Percy said I've brought you a present and pushed me into the room with them. I was afraid because there was lots of them and I knew what was coming. Sally wasn't afraid because she didn't know and she went with Lord Percy.'

Ken stopped. Poor Sally. He didn't know. She never said – and he was her friend. She was seven years old when they'd started on her. He'd thought about her so often, ever since she'd run away when she was – what – ten? Now he knew why. He felt tears well up and quickly wiped them away. This place was too quiet for tears. He couldn't read on. It turned his stomach. But he also realised why the diary was so important – and so dangerous. Some of the men Charlie talked about were big fish; Lord Percy; the cop. This was sixteen years ago. If they were still around they'd still be big fish – maybe even bigger. They were never going to let any of this get out.

He flicked forward to the last entry. The date was 25th July 1951. After the lists of initials, here was a final description. Charlie was nearly sixteen then, just before he left.

'Trevor said he can have me killed whenever he wants. He is a lying bastard but I keep a knife on me now just in case until I get out of here. I will stab him in the eye. I will stab myself if I have to and say it was them. Then there will be an even bigger mess than before. Harshaw said to me if he had his way anyone could come in this home and do what they wanted with us because we are nobody and nothing. They feed us and put a roof over our heads and the least we can do is be useful in any way we can to show our thanks to them. He is right. We are nobody and nothing. Our lives do not matter. Nobody's life matters in this place. Trevor knows that too now.'

Ken closed the diary and carefully re-wrapped it, ignoring the glares from the old man. So this is what happened to Charlie. When had they met? He'd been nine, so Charlie must have been about thirteen or fourteen. All the time Ken had known him, he was going through this. That was why Charlie kept Hazel a secret. He didn't want her caught up in it.

He needed to think carefully about what to do with the diary. What did Davis really want with it? If he was just interested in covering up what happened it would be better if it was never found. But Davis was going to charge him with Charlie's murder just to get hold of it. And he could make it stick, he knew he could. That feeling in his stomach again – 'butterflies' they'd called it as kids. But it wasn't a butterfly – more like a rat, gnawing away at his innards, eating him from the inside.

He turned his thoughts back to the times he'd seen Davis at the home. As far as he could remember, Davis was just a door-opener for his boss. Charlie didn't mention him in the diary so far. So he wasn't trying to protect himself. Most likely he was still looking after his boss. Why else would he be interested in it? Was this diary the reason Charlie died? Something didn't make sense. If Davis's boss, or someone else whose name was in these pages, arranged Charlie's murder to stop him telling his story, why would Davis be so keen to find the diary?

He could try and puzzle it out, but he had to think about himself, about Maggie. Even if Davis's job was to make the diary disappear – made this whole story disappear forever – did it matter, so long as they were off the hook? He'd made a promise to Hazel Dolman. But they were looking at being hanged or doing life for a murder they hadn't committed. The thing had to go to Davis, no question. But it was a risk. Once he handed it over, it was gone. Davis could do whatever he wanted. He could take it and still stick the murder charge on him, on Maggie, on them both.

He massaged his temples, trying to make his brain work better. He looked around the library. All those books full of knowledge. If only he could open one that would tell him what to do next. But he had to decide for himself. He was alone now.

One thing he knew for certain was he couldn't keep the diary on him or at the flat. It had to be hidden in a place where no-one would think of looking.

* * *

Ken stood in the darkness of the quiet cobbled street watching the shebeen. Not much business on a Monday, it was a night for playing cards or staying in with your wife, things you needed to be sober for. But a few of the weekend leftovers laughed and chatted, the sound of their fun carrying into the clear night sky.

The bouncer on the door was different tonight. Mr Elegant was gone. Instead a skinny kid in a pork pie hat and dark glasses leaned against the wall and picked his teeth. It would be a while yet before the club closed for the night. It was cold. He took a walk to kill a bit of time, warm up, wondering if this would work, and if it did, whether they would raise enough cash to satisfy the hard man and his bosses. He passed the shop doorway where he and Maggie had hidden only a few nights ago. Further on, on the waste ground beyond the boarded-up shops a group of Mods were playing with their scooters again, trying a few stunts. One of them spotted him and rode over.

'Hey man. How you doin.' He was just a kid, seventeen maybe, trying to talk the jive.

'Fine, man. Doin' fine.'

'Neat shirt.'

Ken had on a new black Fred Perry, a present from Cheryl, another of his clients.

'The Perry is *it* right now,' continued the kid.

'Is that so?' Ken heard the other scooters approaching. The hairs on his neck began to rise. They started to gather round him. Surround him.

'What d'you reckon to the trilby then?' said the kid.

'The trilby?'

'Yeh. Is it still cool d'you think?'

'Depends on the weather I suppose.'

The kid laughed and the others followed, like Ken had made a sharp remark. 'That's a good one man. You dig the Ska sound, man?' He said it like it was something new.

'Sure. I dig it.'

'Rocksteady – that's where it's at now, man.'

'That right?'

'You from that club down there?' The kid nodded towards the arches.

'I been there once or twice.'

'We wanted to get in but they wouldn't let us. Not black enough.'

'Is that what they said?'

'The coon on the door says to me 'You in favour of the colour bar?' and I says 'No', so he says 'Well I am, so fuck off out of it'.' The kids' mates laughed again and Ken had to smile.

'That's too bad.'

'All right if you're a bird though. The colour bar don't apply to them.'

'Women get special treatment. It's the way of the world.'

'You coloureds like the white chicks don't you? I wouldn't touch any bird'd been with a nigger. No disrespect like.' The kid was watching him. Ken didn't like the turn the conversation was taking and he couldn't see an escape route.

'You ain't exactly one yourself, are you?' The kid seemed to think he could get that personal.

'I'm half and half.'

'So which way round was it? Was your dad black, or your mum?'

'I never knew either of them.'

That seemed to take the edge off things for a second. The

conversation was getting too serious. The kid didn't have a comeback.

'Typical,' he said finally. 'So can you get us into that club?'

Ken let out a little laugh. 'Man, right now I couldn't get myself into that place. If I was you I wouldn't waste my time. Place is about to close up for the night.' Ken could sense the disappointment in the air. That's what it was about – just a bunch of white kids looking to join in the cool black scene.

'Ok man,' said the kid. 'We got to be going. Take it easy.' He revved his scooter, and the others did the same. Then they roared away, leaving Ken in a cloud of oily exhaust.

He walked on, making a circle around the streets and coming back to the shebeen. Nothing had changed in the half hour he'd been away, except the youth was leaning in a different place and had stopped picking his teeth. He looked at his watch. Nearly half past two. He was going to have to walk a bit more.

* * *

Maggie and Ernie were standing under a street lamp next to the truck, their breath rising on the cold night air. The truck was huge, some kind of furniture lorry.

Ken walked over to them and nodded at the big vehicle. 'How many shebeens are we blaggin' tonight?' he said. Ernie looked offended.

'It's a decent size, all right. It'll get the job done.'

'You can drive this thing?'

'I'm a quick learner,' said Ernie.

'Anyway,' said Maggie, 'we're not robbing anybody. I'm taking what's mine. That's what they said I should do isn't it? Are they out yet?'

Ken had watched the barman – Scarface – come out of the club and fit two padlocks to the door a few minutes ago. It was just after four.

'Yep,' said Ken. 'Place is a graveyard.'

'Then let's get going,' she said.

Ernie pulled a pair of bolt cutters out of the lorry and handed them to Ken. He and Maggie walked the few yards into the next street where the shebeen stood. With its doors shut it looked no different from the garages and spray-shops housed in the other arches. Behind them, the sound of Ernie trying to start the lorry broke the silence, the engine turning slowly with an uncooperative wheeze. Arriving at the door, Ken glanced around and got to work. Charlie's old lock was gone. There were two big hasps held shut by two heavy duty padlocks. He lifted the bolt cutters. His hands started shaking and he gripped them tighter to stop himself. He realised he was afraid. He'd never done anything like this before, and he'd spent more time worrying about the diary and Davis the cop than what they were going to do tonight. He worked the bolt cutters onto the first padlock and heaved on the long arms. The cutters snapped shut and the lock dropped clattering onto the cobbles, the noise echoing like a gunshot along the arches.

'Christ,' he said. Maggie picked up the padlock. They both

stood and listened. There was nothing to hear except the lorry's engine turning over and then shuddering into life. Ken lifted the cutters again and tried to get the jaws around the second padlock.

'They won't fit,' said Ken.

Maggie looked around. 'What?'

'They won't fit. It's a bigger lock. It won't take them.'

Maggie was silent for a second. 'Let me see.' They both inspected the lock and Ken tried again. He couldn't manoeuvre the jaws of the bolt cutters onto the lock.

'I need to work this out,' he said.

'I'll fucking work it out,' she said through her teeth. She grabbed the cutters from him and took a swing at the lock.

'Hey, woah there!' He caught them in mid-swing. She tried to jerk them from him. 'Take it easy' he said. 'We don't want to wake the whole East End.'

'We're getting in.'

'Ok, ok. I'll find a way.' They stood for a moment with the bolt cutters between them, neither willing to let go. Even in the darkness he could feel the heat of her eyes on him. Then she relaxed her grip.

'Go on, then,' she said with a goading edge. 'Find a way.'

He took them and turned back to the door. He was irked by her manner, as if she constantly found him inadequate and this was just more evidence. He felt around the lock and realised that the part of the hasp the padlock passed through was thinner than the lock itself. He put the cutters up to it and managed to squeeze them in behind the lock. Again he heaved. They snapped through. He did it again on the other side of the hasp. This time Maggie caught the lock before it fell and the only sound was the piece of hasp that held the lock tinkling to the ground. Ken rubbed his hand across his forehead and was surprised to find it covered in cold sweat. He lifted the latch and pushed the door. It swung open.

Behind them they could hear Ernie manoeuvring the lorry into the lane. He was taking his time. Maggie reached for the light switch and flicked it on.

The one low-watt bulb threw a pale, inadequate light over the bar and the dance floor. The rest was in deep shadow. The silent, dim place had an eerie feel to it. Ken closed the door and they walked through the tables to the bar.

He wasn't feeling good. The break-in he'd been through in his head. This part – being inside – he hadn't thought about at all, and he was uneasy. The last time he had been here when it was this quiet was with Charlie.

And he still burned with the heat of the tussle he'd had with Maggie outside. The way she'd snatched the bolt cutters from him. 'You don't think much of me, do you?' he said.

Maggie was already behind the bar pulling a case of Bacardi up onto the counter.

'What are you talking about?'

'You thought I wouldn't get that door open.'

'No I didn't. I just wanted to be sure.'

'Because you weren't sure about me.'

She gave an exasperated sigh. 'About the lock, Kenny boy. Give me a hand here.'

'Maggie I'm with you, every step of the way.'

'That's great to hear – so give me a hand then.'

'You ain't listening Maggie,' he hissed, trying to cut through her indifference. She stopped and looked at him.

'Look, I know you're with me, Ken. But when I take something on, I do it, and to hell with the consequences. It's the way I am.'

'Just trust me, Maggie.'

She came down the bar to where he stood and took his hand in hers.

'Of course I trust you, Ken.' She leaned over the bar and kissed him.

'Hey lovers, you got the wrong place for kissy-kissy.'

They looked round. Ken didn't know what surprised him most. The fact that Mr Elegant was here, that he was wearing a pair of striped pyjamas done up to his neck, or that he had a gun pointing at them.

* * *

The big Jamaican smiled at them as he walked over, his massive bare feet slapping the stone floor. Ken could just make out a camp bed in the shadows behind him.

'We didn't mean to wake you,' said Ken as calmly as he could. He tried to concentrate on the gun and not the tremor running through him.

'Well I'm glad you did.' Mr Elegant pushed Ken back against the bar and stared at him. 'Well, well. If it ain't the half nigger.' He patted Ken's pockets for weapons. Then he walked round the bar and did the same to Maggie, stopping to feel her breasts as well.

'You're nicely built,' he said to her. 'I wouldn't mind some of that.'

Ken felt the heat rise up his face. Elegant noticed.

'Take it easy, man. I ain't goin' to fuck your woman.' He turned a grin on Maggie. 'Not yet, anyway.' He snorted out a quick laugh. Then he cocked his head as he caught the sound of the lorry.

'That'll be our friends,' said Ken.

'That's right,' said Maggie. 'We've a few here to help load the goods. You didn't think we were alone, did you?'

Elegant weighed up their words for a second, went back around the bar, and backed towards the door, keeping the gun on them all the time. There was a noisy crunching of gears and they could hear the lorry reversing up the narrow lane, the whine of the engine getting louder. Elegant, his back to the door, reached a hand behind him for the latch. With an ear-splitting crash the lorry hit the door and it flew open, cracking Elegant hard on the shoulder and throwing him forward. Ken judged the gap between him and Elegant at about fifteen feet and he had a split second to decide to go for him. He took a step and stopped. He'd never make it. It was too big a distance. Already, he could sense Maggie's disapproval.

But it wasn't over. Elegant was spinning round towards the door, thinking he was being attacked from behind. It was enough. Ken sprang across the floor, his legs turning to jelly as he ran the few paces. But Elegant was recovering – realising there was nobody behind him. He turned back, saw Ken coming and raised the gun. The black hole at the end of the muzzle stared at Ken. He dived at Elegant as the gun fired, the explosion so close to him it filled his head, the flash blinding him, heat scorching his face. He piled into Elegant, sending him stumbling backwards as he reached for the man's thick neck. Elegant managed to stay on his feet and they began to struggle. Ken knew he had to stay close in to stop Elegant getting another shot or using his strength. He could smell his rancid breath. They wrestled, Ken trying to get him off balance, the man's powerful hand pushing him away while he sought to aim the gun with the other. Ken knew his hold on the man's throat wasn't strong enough to put him down quickly. His mind raced, looking for another move as they staggered and lurched. Then the butt of the gun suddenly smashed down on his head. The blow stunned him but he clung on, thinking faster. He took his hand off Elegant's throat and jammed his fingers as hard as he could up the man's nose. Elegant squealed in pain and surprise and dropped the gun. He grabbed Ken's head in both hands, pressing the sides of his face, then bringing his thumbs down on Ken's eyes. The power of the hands sent a sickening shudder through Ken. The strong thumbs pressed into his eyes – the pain stabbing through his head. He cried out – from fear as well as pain. His eyes were being squeezed into his head, the hard thumbs pressing without mercy. Elegant was going to blind him. In a growing panic, he grabbed at Elegant's wrists but they were so thick, so strong, it was like gripping two steel bars. He couldn't stop him, and he gave a sudden sob of terror. Then a sound – 'thunk' and the pressure on his eyes seemed to ease. Another 'thunk' and Ken found himself looking into Elegant's own eyes. The angry glow in them seemed to fade and he suddenly slumped forward, his grip on Ken vanishing. Ken dropped to his knees, his strength drained. The big man stood in front of him, arms hanging by his sides, his eyes dull, like a boxer out on his feet. Maggie stepped from behind him. She swung the bolt cutters. They hit Elegant hard on the side of the head – 'thunk' – and he collapsed onto the floor.

Ken pulled himself to his feet, blinked several times, and put his fingers to his face. Bright, fresh blood trickled down his hand. He was glad to see the vivid redness of it, glad to be dazzled even by the dim light that hung above him.

'Is he dead?' said Maggie.

He bent to Elegant's unconscious form on the floor and put his fingers to his neck.

'He's alive.'

The door opened and Ernie stepped in.

'Friend of yours?' he said.

'We've been gettin' to know each other,' said Ken, still blinking and rubbing his eyes.

Ernie rolled Elegant over, pulled out the pyjamas cord, then rolled him onto his face again and tied his hands behind his back.

'That should keep him out of mischief,' he said. Then he looked at Ken's face.

'Bullet took a piece out of your ear. Lucky.'

'That's me,' said Ken, 'all the luck.'

'Needs a bandage, though,' said Ernie. 'It's bleeding like a bastard.' He went over to Elegant again and began to pull off his pyjamas bottoms. Elegant was starting to come round.

'Wha' da fuck?' he grunted.

Maggie was standing by him, and jabbed him with the bolt cutters.

'Don't worry sweetheart, I'm not going to cut your prick off – yet.'

Ernie tore the pyjamas bottoms in half and threw one piece to Maggie, then tied a gag round Elegant's mouth with the other. Maggie walked over to Ken. He saw the look in her eyes and was surprised. They sparkled with fun. She was enjoying all this. She smiled at him.

'How's my Kenny boy?' She stroked his face. 'You did well.' Putting the pyjama bandage under his chin, she drew it up over his bleeding ear and tied it in a knot on top of his head.

'There,' she said, 'that'll do you.' There was laughter in her eyes.

Catching himself in the mirror behind the bar, Ken realised he looked like a cartoon character with toothache, but said nothing.

'Come on. Let's get to work,' said Ernie. He opened up the big double doors and let down the tailgate of the lorry. The three of them went behind the old brown curtain and looked at all the cases.

'Wow,' said Ken. There were a lot, far more than Charlie ever had, and more even than they had seen on their previous visit. There was enough to supply the shebeen for months. 'Must be a hundred cases. Maybe it's a store they use for other places as well.'

'Lorry hi-jacks,' said Ernie, 'big business these days.'

'God,' said Maggie. 'It could take all night to shift this lot.'

'It'll fetch a good price though,' said Ernie. He brought up a two-wheel sack barrow and parked it in front of them. 'You two load,' he said. 'Ken, you wheel it over and throw the cases up to me. I'll stack.' It sounded like Ernie was an old hand at this.

They got busy. The loading and wheeling weren't too bad but Ken soon realised he'd drawn the short straw when it came to throwing the cases up onto the truck. The first three or four were fine. After that they got heavy.

* * *

By the time they got back to the flat Ken was ready to lie down and die. It had taken them nearly three hours to load the truck, so when Ernie finally got behind the wheel and drove off, a cold dawn was already breaking and they could hear the moan of ships horns as they reached the docks on the morning tide.

Ken bathed his ear and Maggie stung it with iodine before re-bandaging it. He lay down on the settee intending to spend a few minutes basking in the heroics of the night. He got as far as remembering Maggie telling him he'd done well before he fell asleep.

An instant later he was woken by someone banging on the door. He looked at his watch – half past ten already. He crawled off the settee and answered it. Ernie stood there, looking spry and dapper in fresh clothes, apparently untroubled by the night's labour or the lack of sleep.

'Wakey, wakey,' he said. 'Time to see what Uncle Ernie's got for you.'

He stood in the lounge looking pleased with himself while Ken roused Maggie. She came out in her dressing gown.

'God almighty, Ernie. You're bright-eyed and bushy-tailed.'

'You don't piss about with a lorry-load of nicked booze. You get rid.'

'You've flogged it?' said Ken.

'And got a good price,' said Ernie, rubbing his hands.

'Who from?' said Maggie.

Ernie tapped the side of his nose and winked. 'Friends,' he said, 'south of the river. Come on, let's sit down and take a look.'

Ken, still dazed, was quietly impressed with the old man. He'd managed to convert the lorry-load of alcohol into cash in a matter of hours via his 'friends south of the river.' Ernie, in spite of the risks it seemed to involve, was very well connected.

Ernie gathered them to the kitchen table, then held up a hand, his leathery features assuming a more serious look.

'First,' he said, 'you've got to get out of this place. Those Jamaicans are going to be very pissed off soon and they're going to come looking for you.'

Ken looked at Maggie. He could see she hadn't realised the danger either. But now that Ernie said it, it was obvious.

Maggie sighed and looked around the kitchen. It was clean and bright. The little window over the sink looked south to Greenwich and Blackheath. Giving up the place wasn't part of the plan. 'It's worth it to get back at them bastards,' she said quietly.

Ken wasn't so sure. He was going to miss this place where Charlie lived and he and Maggie had been through so much. But Ernie was right. The next knock on the door could be anybody, and not just the Rudies.

'You need to do it soon – today or tomorrow,' said Ernie. 'And look for somewhere with a back way out. If anyone's at your front door in this place, you're fucked.'

It was practical advice from a man of experience. It had to be done.

Maggie sighed. 'Fine,' she said.

'OK. Let's get down to business,' said Ernie.

They watched him pull a battered brown envelope from his inside pocket and take a thick wad of cash from it. He spread it out in front of them.

'Five hundred quid,' he said.

Ken whistled and glanced at Maggie. It was more money than he had ever seen in his life. He could buy a brand new car with that – if he knew how to drive.

Maggie's eyes were wide in surprise too. 'Is that all?' she said. 'There must have been more than a thousand quids-worth there.'

Ernie bristled. 'When you sell on the black market, five pence in the shilling is pretty good,' he said defensively.

Maggie sighed. 'Maybe so. But where does that leave us with what we owe?'

'Well,' said Ernie, 'It gives us a decent down payment for Friday.'

'But what about the next Friday – the final payday?' said Maggie.

'We'll still owe a big slice, but this'll take the sting out of it. It's not small beer we've got for them. With a bit of luck and my sunny smile we'll get a deal out of them.'

'What kind of deal?'

'Who knows,' said Ernie, 'more time at least. But let's not get ahead of ourselves. We've got five hundred in front of us, and the first thing we need to decide is how much we let them have.'

Ken's eyes widened. It hadn't occurred to him not to hand it all over.

Ernie took in his expression and smiled. 'They don't know how much we've got, do they? And if it's not going to clear the debt, what difference does it make if we keep some for ourselves?' He scooped up the bundle of notes and began counting them out. Fifty pounds in front of Maggie, fifty in front of Ken, and fifty for himself. He smiled round at them again. 'There, what do you say to that?'

Ken looked at the money. He was being given an equal share. Up to now he'd just worked with the idea he was helping Maggie out – earning his keep. He glanced at her, then at Ernie.

'Fair's fair,' said Ernie. 'You did your bit – nearly got your head blown off. The people I work with wouldn't piss on a coloured if he was on fire, but I speak as I find.'

Ken took a second to marvel at the sentiment from this old white East Ender, but he knew Ernie was anything but typical. He took the cash. It was hard to say no. He hadn't made any Friday trips up West recently and was skint. He knew it was the first cash Maggie had seen in a while as well. The weekly rent on the flat hadn't been paid for a month.

Ernie was still talking. 'We'll bung 'em this lot Friday – that should shut them up – then we'll worry about next week.'

'How much more do they want?' said Maggie.

Ernie tilted his head thoughtfully, as if unsure whether to answer her. 'Eight hundred all told, so that leaves four fifty. And don't be surprised if there's some extra this or that to keep us on the hook. That's how they are.'

Ken reeled back in his chair. Maggie looked shocked as well.

'Then let's put this back in,' said Ken, throwing his money back on the table.

'Forget it. If we're short, we're short. It don't matter by how much.'

'So how do we get rid of them?' said Ken.

Ernie shrugged. 'We don't. We just do some other deal with them.'

'Like what?'

Ernie gave another shrug. 'Something.'

* * *

The front door of the rooming house had seen better days, the ancient brown paint weathered and peeling. It opened to reveal a dark hall lit by an underpowered bulb with no lampshade. The landlady, a sharp-nosed little woman in a wrap-around apron and a hairnet looked them up and down suspiciously.

'You've got a room,' said Maggie.

'That's right – for the right sort of people.'

'May we see it?' Ken spoke with his best refined accent – the one he had picked up from his West London life. He'd always been quick to absorb how people spoke and the power it gave them.

'Are you black?' said the woman.

'I'm from Spain,' said Ken, his well-rehearsed alter-ego kicking in.

Maggie raised her eyebrows at him.

'I've got Italians here,' said the woman relaxing a little. 'They're alright – pays their rent on time.' She opened the door wider to admit them. They followed her down the narrow corridor and up the bare stairs to the first floor. The place smelt of cats and fried onions. She opened the door of the room and switched on the light. It was as weak as the one in the hall.

'Bathroom and toilet's down the corridor. You only share with the Algerians and they're at sea mostly.'

They made a show of inspecting the room. The lino floor was worn through in places, and the small sink by the window was overlaid with many generations of stain. The bed sagged in the middle and there was a brown patch on the ceiling above it.

'It looks grand,' said Maggie.

'Are you two married, then?' said the woman.

Maggie smiled and held up her hand to display her wedding ring.

The woman nodded.

'How much is the rent?' said Ken, now giving his new voice a Spanish inflection.

'Fifteen shillings all in. I'd want two weeks in advance.'

Ken pulled out his wallet and extracted two notes, a pound and a ten bob. The woman took them, examined them closely as if she suspected they might be fake, before shoving them into the pocket of her apron.

'I'll get you the key then,' she said and disappeared through the door.

He turned to Maggie. 'I've seen worse,' he said.

'Have you?' She walked around the sagging bed.

He looked at it then at her. 'Should be snug.'

She didn't answer.

* * *

Ken and Maggie, wrapped up against the cold breeze, walked arm in arm through the bustle of Roman Road market. He loved the heave and churn of the mid-week crowd – people buying, selling, looking, or just there to be seen. The fruit and vegetable stall-holders called out their wares, their sing-song voices carrying over the heads of the throng. The clothes stalls that he so often visited were crowded with browsers. Here, and in the little shops behind the stalls, was where you came for fashion if you couldn't afford Carnaby Street and the other expensive boutiques up West. So when he needed something his women hadn't supplied, this was where he came. And here was every kind of cool kid from the East End who wanted to make the cut on a Saturday night. Teenage girls in black and white miniskirts rifled through the racks seeking out the bright new colours and even shorter styles that were filling the pages of the magazines. Mods were there, in and out of the little tailors for their made-to-measure tight suits and thin ties, checking the record stalls for the new music. Those stalls were where he came too, but not for the bland white crooners of the Hit Parade. It was Ska from Jamaica – Derrick and Patsy, Prince Buster – and blues from America – Jackie Wilson, Martha Reeves – that everyone came here for.

After all that had happened, Maggie seemed more relaxed, her prickly edge less evident. Taking the stock from the shebeen had calmed her anger. And away from the prying eyes of the tower block, they'd settled into their new room with an ease that had surprised Ken.

A bright November sun did little to warm them as they strolled. Maggie was dressed in a new coat, bought at a stall further up the market, her old one carefully folded into the shopping bag she carried by her side. Ken too was wearing a new overcoat – something he had never owned, even through the long bitter winter of last year. It was a dark blue French-style trench coat she had picked out for him. When he'd stood in front of the stallholder's mirror he'd thought it a little conservative for his tastes, but Maggie had bought it for him. Like all his women, she wanted him to look the way she wanted him to look – to make him hers. He was always careful to make sure he wore the right image for each one. But he wanted to please Maggie more than he had ever wanted to please anyone. So this coat was special; it was the first thing she's ever bought him. He'd live with the conservative look.

At a shoe stall Ken, after an extended consultation with Maggie, bought himself a new pair of loafers, and tried unsuccessfully to get her to buy a pair of thigh-length patent leather boots.

They came away from the stall laughing, and a man with a cockatoo on his shoulder and a camera around his neck approached, one of the street photographers always on the prowl wherever there was a crowd. Catching their laughter, he raised the camera.

'Smile!' he called.

They held their smiles, even after the flash had popped. He handed them his card and Ken took it.

'Ready in an hour,' he said with a cheery grin. 'That'll be a good one. I know, ten years I've been doing this – and cheap too. I do the best price in the East End.' He moved on.

For a while they lost themselves in the day to day pleasures of spending a few pounds and feeling good in each other's company. For Ken it was a moment of pure bliss. They were together, like a real couple. He could never be like Charlie, but he'd managed to show a bit of courage the other night. It had been by accident, but that didn't matter. What mattered was it seemed to work on Maggie. She felt closer to him, like she was letting her guard down a little – thinking better of him. He knew it wouldn't be like this for long. In a couple of days there would be a reckoning with Ernie's so-called associates. But Friday felt a long way off right now, and anything could happen before that. The Jamaicans or the cops could catch up with them by Friday, and they could be dead or in prison. So many possibilities – why worry about just one of them? He pushed away the thoughts.

Maggie's own brightness was subdued now, and he guessed her own thoughts wouldn't be much different from his own. So the afternoon began to take on a sombre air, the glow of their feelings fading with the sun.

As they reached the end of the market Maggie suddenly grabbed his hand and pulled him into a pub.

'Let's cheer ourselves up with a drink,' she said.

The Young Prince was crowded with market stall holders and shoppers, winding down after the work of the day. The atmosphere was ripe with loud voices, cockney accents, and the coarse laughter of early evening drinking. Ken edged his way to the counter, pulled out a pound note and tried to attract the attention of the barmaid. A fat woman in a tight dress, she was perched at the far end of the counter, talking to a punter. She looked round and noticed Ken.

'I'm not serving you!' she called.

'What?'

'Didn't you see the sign?' she said, walking down the bar towards him. 'No blacks allowed in here.' She pointed to the handwritten sign above the bar.

NO GYPSIES

NO BLACKS.

Ken felt the heat of the insult rise through him.

But then she smiled. 'Still, you're a good-looking boy, aren't you,' she said, checking him out. 'Not even proper black neither.'

'My money's as good as anyone's,' said Ken, still reacting to her first sharp words.

'Better than most, I'd say. This your lucky lady, then?' she said, eyeing Maggie. Maggie smiled demurely. 'I ain't prejudiced meself,' she continued, leaning over and lowering her voice, 'I just got to keep me customers happy, that's all. What can I get you?'

Ken ordered the drinks, the angry thought welling up inside him that winning permission to be served here was the kind of victory he could do without. He'd had stuff like this so many times before. Half-caste and good-looking, his nearly-status landed him halfway across some line between outcast and pet poodle. She'd be asking how big his cock was next, as if that was all he was good for – him and all the other darkies from the jungle. And when he thought about how he made his living, maybe she was right.

They stood at a tall table and drank, but the incident deflated him and he could feel the eyes of other drinkers on him. Maggie, sensing his withdrawal, put down her half-finished drink and slipping her arm through his. 'Come on, I'll get you a nice cup of tea.' She began leading him through the crowd to the door. 'We've got enough to worry about without this little thing.'

He let himself be walked out of the pub by her. Outside in the street, he began to feel restored. He'd been protected by his looks. The story of his life. But that first public insult twisted inside him. He hated always having to negotiate his way, justify his place. To be half-caste was always to be half of something. Only ever half.

Maggie was saying something about photographs, and steering him back towards the market. The stallholders were packing up, the Council men pulling carts of trestle tables away for the night. It slowly filtered through to him that she was talking about the photo they'd had taken earlier. She wanted to collect it. It seemed odd that she, of all people, was walking him away from a scene that might have got angry. It could only be a good sign. His mood improved.

They found the shop, its lights blazing out into the gathering gloom of the evening. The assistant put the photo on the counter for them to inspect. There they were in their new coats, Maggie, eyes looking straight into the camera, he giving it a sideways glance that made him look shy. They both had ridiculously wide smiles, the laughter of the previous moment still in their eyes. It was a picture of perfect happiness and he felt a lump in his throat as he looked at it.

She paid. 'My treat,' she said, and they left the shop. He was a little calmer now. Maggie had done the trick with the photo, replacing an awkward moment with sweet one. If only it was always that easy.

But Maggie's hand suddenly gripped his arm. 'Listen,' she said.

His attention was grabbed by the call of the newspaper seller in front of them.

'Bartlett House – Police find a body!'

The paper he was selling wasn't the local one, it was the Evening Standard. The news had made the main London paper. Ken bought a copy and they looked around for somewhere to sit and read it. He was wary of going into another pub. They kept walking in silence, a sense of dread beginning to grow inside him as his mind raced over the possibilities of the headline. They found a cafe, went in and ordered two teas. They were the only customers. At a wobbly table, Ken pulled the paper from his pocket and spread it out so they could both see it.

'BARTLETT HOUSE – POLICE DISCOVER BODY.

Following recent investigations into historical activities at an orphanage in Forest Gate, East London, police today disclosed that they have discovered a body in the grounds of the house. A spokesman described the body as that of an adult male, probably aged between twenty and thirty, and said it was badly decomposed. It had probably lain there for a number of years. It was removed to the central mortuary later this afternoon where forensic tests are being undertaken to establish the identity of the deceased and the cause of death. Police are treating the death as suspicious.

'It has been revealed that an investigation has been under way for some time into the activities of staff and visitors to the home. There have been two appeals for former residents to come forward. No arrests have been made to date. This latest development changes the nature of the investigation and the home and surrounding grounds are being treated as a potential murder scene. Large numbers of police and their support staff were seen arriving during the course of the day and the area around the home has been cordoned off. House to house enquiries are under way. The spokesman renewed the appeal to former residents to come forward, and said a further statement would be made when new information became available.'

'That home,' said Maggie grimly, 'it was an evil place. How come you didn't know what was going on there?'

Ken shook his head slowly. He'd asked himself that a lot lately. He offered the only explanation he had. 'Charlie,' he said, 'he saved me.'

Neither of them had touched their tea. Ken felt a queasy sense of relief. His first thought was that it would be one of the kids – someone he knew. But it was an adult. This whole thing was getting big. Nobody really cared what went on in a kid's home, but a dead body was something different. That mattered more. And it meant the diary mattered more too.

CHAPTER 8

The telephone box smelled of stale piss. Ken flattened out the scrap of paper with the number of Stepney police station on it and dialled. Inserting his two pennies, he asked for Detective Inspector Davis. There was a long pause and he had to put more money in while listening to the sounds of men talking in the distance. The story in the newspaper had given him the kick he needed. He had been stalling ever since he'd read the diary in the library, fretting about Davis's motives. This phone call might be a mistake, but he had to do something. It was his one bargaining chip and he had to use it. The distant talking on the other end of the line ended in a burst of laughter. Finally he heard footsteps approaching the phone.

'DI Davis.'

'It's me, Ken. I got the diary.'

There was silence.

'Where is it?'

'I got it safe. I want to do a deal.'

'No fucking deals. You know what'll happen if you don't hand it over.'

'I saw the paper. You got a body now.'

'So?'

'More important case, ain't it? Everyone interested in it.

You gonna be the big man in charge. You don't want to go wrong on it.'

'What the fuck do you want?'

'This thing with Charlie. Me and Maggie both – we got to come out of it clean.'

'You've got to be joking haven't you? That's a murder case too.'

'Only if you say so. You're the one who decides. Ain't that what you said?'

'It depends what's in the toxicology report.'

'The report comes to you though, don't it?'

'It's not that simple.'

'The diary, there's plenty in it – names, dates – everything. Some big names.'

'What do you mean 'big'?'

'Names you see in the paper sometimes.'

'Like who?'

Ken didn't answer. The pips sounded, indicating more coins were needed. He quickly put in another tuppence.

'Ok,' said Davis. 'You want a deal? Then bring me the diary – but don't bring it here. I'll tell you where.'

Ken scribbled down the place Davis mentioned on the edge of the piece of paper.

'Tonight, eight o'clock,' Davis was saying. 'Make sure you've got it with you – all of it. No missing pages or any shit like that.'

Ken put down the phone. He'd just agreed to meet Davis in a dark place on his own with the diary.

* * *

He didn't share the Eastenders' taste for Chinese food, so it was rare for him to venture down this stretch of the Commercial Road at night. Limehouse was the East End's Chinatown, and most nights of the week crowds converged on the cheap restaurants scattered along the road. Now it was just before eight and the evening crush was building. He always felt nervous being out in the East End at this time of night; a lot of people about, several drunk, all of them white. It was a good time of day for a coloured man to find trouble. But in this light his golden skin protected him a little and he mostly passed unnoticed – which was how he liked it. He dipped his head and kept walking. A little further on, he found the turning Davis told him about. He walked down a narrow passage between buildings, barely wide enough for a single car, which opened out into a cobbled lane. It seemed to be completely deserted. On one side were more railway arches just like the street the shebeen stood in, on the other, a school playground surrounded by a high wire fence.

He'd thought hard about this meeting with Davis, wondering whether he really should bring the diary or not. But he had no choice. Davis was going to get the diary or he would come after them both for Charlie's murder. That bit was simple. But what happened after Davis had the thing was out of his control. What went on at Bartlett House was out in the open now, and the diary was important evidence. But if Hazel Dolman was right, and Davis was part of a cover-up that had got Charlie killed in the first place, they were fucked. And if the toxicology report showed rat poison had killed Charlie, how could he and Maggie run from that? Davis had the power. He had nothing except the diary. So any chance was worth taking. Still, he felt exposed and nervous standing there holding on to the package. It was like carrying explosives. He wanted to be as careful as possible. What if he just got jumped by some drunk who made off with it? It would be the end of the faint hope he had of getting Maggie and himself out of the mess they were in.

It was a clear night, none of the freezing fog they'd had recently. He'd expected Davis to be in a car, but there was none parked along the lane.

He reached the appointed spot – opposite the school entrance, and checked his watch. It was gone eight. In the distance he could hear a clock chiming and the sounds of people talking and shouting. He looked up and down but the lane was silent.

Minutes passed. He watched his breath rise into the night. He could easily let his mind wander over all the subjects that fought for his attention, but he focussed on keeping it blank. That was the skill he'd acquired long ago – blanking things out. He was good at it. It took almost no effort, and he knew that if he wanted to, he would be able to forget all this too in time. It wasn't a bad thing. What was wrong with forgetting the things you don't want to remember? When all this was over he would go back to living in the here and now and keep himself happy that way.

He started to get cold, so began walking up and down flapping his arms across his chest, blowing on his hands. By eight thirty he'd seen nobody at all, the only activity a rat scurrying across the playground. Davis wasn't coming. But why not? He'd made it plain to Ken that he'd do whatever he had to to get his hands on the diary. He started to feel nervous again, remembering the thought he'd had after the phone call. He had been careful to deny any knowledge of what went on in the home, but maybe that wasn't enough. Perhaps he shouldn't have told Davis about the names in the diary. It meant Ken knew something now, something he shouldn't. That was enough for him to decide he wasn't going to wait any longer, so he made his way out of the lane and back into the lights and the noise of the Commercial Road.

* * *

The tiny room was different when he returned. As he opened the door he was hit by a delicious smell of lamb cooking. A big saucepan of stew bubbled on the gas ring. The place looked brighter. On the bed was the coloured counterpane from the flat and he recognised the saucepan on the gas ring and the kettle as well. But what really changed the room was the presence of the altar, reassembled on top of the ancient chest of drawers, the plastic Madonna once more surrounded by her Christmas lights.

'You been to the flat.' said Ken, stating the obvious.

'Yep. What do you think?'

'Better,' said Ken. 'Bit risky though.'

She laughed, flicked a hand at him, dismissing his concerns.

He took the hint. 'Looks good, though,' he said, wandering around and nodding his approval, 'makes the place a little cosier.' He hadn't seen this side of Maggie before – the home-maker. He wondered what it would be like to live like that, in a real home, shared with a loving woman, shared with Maggie.

'You have to make the best of things,' she said. She was at the sink filling the kettle.

He went over to the altar. The last time he had been this close to it was when he'd secretly looked through the contents of the little drawer under the figure's feet, searching for the diary and finding the rat poison instead. A guilty twinge ran through him at the memory.

'Your lady goin' to be keepin' an eye on us, then,' he said, staring at the luminous figure.

'She's not 'your lady', she's Our Lady. And it's mostly you she'll be keeping an eye on.'

'Why me?'

'I won't be here. I've got a job.'

Ken turned to her, eyebrows raised. 'Doin' what?'

'Same thing as before I met Charlie – stitching. The rag trade's always looking for fast workers, and I'm fast.'

'That's for sure, Maggie. You been busy.'

'That's me, no half measures.'

Ken had to agree with that. After all the sitting around

drinking, suddenly she was different. The brittleness she often had in her manner with him was gone too, and she looked good this evening. She wore a pair of dark slacks and a light, tight blouse he hadn't seen before. If it wasn't for the weight of the problems they were carrying, he'd have said she was happy.

'Something smells good.'

'Irish stew. And I'll bet you thought I couldn't cook.'

Another guilty twinge. 'You got plenty of talents, Maggie. I ain't never doubted it.'

When it was time to eat, Maggie sat on the upright chair and Ken sat on the bed, plates on their laps. In spite of these awkward arrangements a quiet intimacy fell over them. After they ate, they shared the washing up. The confined space by the sink reminded him of when he was small, playing house in the garden of the children's home with Sally.

It was still only half nine when they'd finished these mundane chores. Ken wondered how they would get along, squeezed together in this small space every day. He realised Maggie must have been wondering that too, which must be why she'd gone and got herself a job. Apart from the money, she needed an excuse to be out of the claustrophobic little room. He never needed excuses. He lived out there, in the world of the streets and the crowds. Being indoors – at home – was something he only did after he'd done with everything else. But maybe one day, if he really felt he belonged somewhere, that might change.

There was no particular reason why they both turned towards one another after Ken hung up the tea-towel. It seemed to happen without either of them thinking about it. But they faced each other, and without a word between them, he simply began to undo the buttons of her blouse.

They fell into the ancient bed, their hands finding their way through their clothes to each other's bodies. But the bedsprings seemed to have been specially designed to discourage such activity, squeaking in protest at every movement, so they dragged the blankets onto the floor in front of the little two-bar electric fire and began to make love in its warm orange glow. When he kissed her breasts he felt a hunger for her that was different from everything he'd ever known before. With her he was no longer just a performer satisfying a client – a hard cock and a bit of skill. This was no transaction. With Maggie he wanted not to satisfy her but to inflame her, to make her want him more and more, so she would bind herself to him, body and soul, and never let him go. And tonight, in this little room, she too seemed to want more from him. They moved slowly, leisurely, taking their time. The long evening's love-making built towards one climax after another. In between, they rested, held, touched, whispered, and laughed, before starting all over again. When they finally tired and she turned from him to sleep, she snuggled against him and he held her, enjoying the heat of her, the smoothness of her skin, the salty taste of her sweat, until he too fell into a deep sleep.

When he stirred at his usual time of around ten the next morning, it was with a strong sense that something new and good had happened between them, that the fears he'd harboured about the closeness they'd imposed on themselves – the potential for Maggie's temper to reach flashpoint; for his own weaknesses to become more obvious to her – all those demons faded with the coming of the morning light. Instead, there was something he tried not to let himself think about – hope. Was it really possible they could make it work – be happy together? He closed off that thought. It skirted too close to a cliff edge he had to stay away from. He'd be happy just to carry on where they'd left off in the early hours. But she wasn't there. She'd gone to work.

He got out of bed, grabbed a towel and walked down the corridor to the freezing bathroom. The house was silent, the low thrub of London in the background. There were dripping nylon stockings and knickers that probably didn't belong to the Algerian sailors hanging from a line over the chipped bath. Condensation ran down the dark green walls into mould-edged pools on the lino floor. As he shaved, the light above the sink blinked and went out. He turned it off and on with no results, so he began shaving by the poor light of the window, its cracked glass yellowed by years of London smog.

He knew the way the evening had gone was Maggie's doing. She'd created it all. He'd just been the willing dupe. Life with Maggie was like the shaving light, turning light and dark in ways he couldn't influence. She had him on a leash, he knew that. He wasn't complaining. He'd be happy if things went on like this forever.

CHAPTER 9

Ken and Ernie walked down a small street in Bethnal Green, past little shops full of curtain and dress materials, cottons, ribbons, coats and dresses, and towards a narrow doorway beneath a faded green sign announcing the 'Regal Snooker Club – members only'. A big man wearing a sheepskin coat and check cap stood outside reading the 'Sporting Life'. The coat hung open to accommodate his massive beer gut.

'What the fuck do you want?' he asked brusquely.

'It's Friday ain't it?' said Ernie. 'We owe a bit.'

The man looked them over then jerked his head towards the door. As they climbed the stairs, the sound of clacking snooker balls grew louder, until they found themselves in a big hall with about a dozen baize-covered tables. Only two were occupied. The walls were painted the same green as the sign outside, except for the several places where it peeled away to reveal an ancient, dirty cream. Ernie led them straight ahead, past the tables and towards an office partitioned off from the snooker hall by frosted glass panels. As they passed, Ken felt the eyes of all the four men playing follow them across the room.

Ernie had wanted to go alone. In spite of the beating, he seemed to think he had some kind of privileged access to this world and he was reluctant to share it with anyone else.

Maggie couldn't face handing the cash over to the ape who'd paid them a visit the other night, and Ken knew by now that if she was here things would not go well. Besides, she had her job. But neither of them wanted the old man walking around alone with all that money in his pocket. What if it got stolen before he handed it over? The thought was enough to make Ken sweat. And he wanted to see where this transaction took place, how it went. Ernie had been grudging at first, but, as Ken expected, couldn't in the end resist the temptation to show off his credentials as wheeler and dealer amongst the hard men. So he got to come along.

Inside the office there was no-one at home. For a moment Ernie seemed unsure of himself as he placed the brown envelope with the cash on the empty desk in front of him.

'What now?' said Ken.

'We wait.'

Outside in the snooker hall the silence was broken by the occasional smack of balls and a muttered oath. Ernie sat down in a battered leather armchair. Ken wandered back into the hall. The two men at the nearest table cast him aggressive stares. He was in the lion's den, but he didn't feel afraid – not yet. They were just the goon squad. They didn't know who he was and they needed the boss's permission to make any moves. At the other table, one of the men, middle-aged but muscular, gave him a cooler look. Ken knew that look well but wasn't expecting to find it here. He held the man's gaze, checking he wasn't misinterpreting what he saw.

The man came over. As he got closer, and away from the others, his face broke into a smile. 'Got a minute?' he said.

'Depends,' said Ken.

'On what?'

Ken rubbed his thumb and forefinger together in front of the man's face. The man nodded in acknowledgement.

'How much?'

'Got to be a quickie,' said Ken, 'I got business.' He jerked his head at the office where Ernie sat patiently waiting. 'Call it two.'

The man nodded again. 'Let's go outside,' he said.

* * *

When Ken reappeared, Ernie was still waiting. 'Where have you been?' he said tersely.

'Bloke needed a hand with something,' said Ken.

As he spoke, the thug who'd beaten up Ernie the other night came through the door. Ernie flinched at the sight of him. The man flung himself into the chair behind the desk.

'I was beginning to think you weren't going to make it,' he said.

'Well I'm here, aren't I, Tommy?' said Ernie grimly. Ken's eyes widened as he realised Ernie knew the man. 'The twins about?'

'Nah – don't see much of them these days. They're always off with their fancy friends up West.'

'Getting their names in the papers, I see,' said Ernie. 'They want to watch that. They still got that place – Esmerelda's something?'

'Esmerelda's Barn – yeh, but I hear they're getting shot of it. Just as well, the things that go on in that place,' Tommy rolled his eyes. 'Their old man'd have a fit.'

'That's the rich and famous for you – pretty queer sorts.'

'Yeh, bloodsuckers the lot of 'em. So it's down to the likes of me to do the hard graft and keep the business going. What you got, then?'

Ernie opened the envelope and emptied the cash onto the desk. 'The down payment.'

Tommy looked at the money, then smiled up at Ernie. 'You've been a busy boy, haven't you? What'd you do – rob a bank?' He laughed at his own joke then drew the money towards him and began counting it. It took him barely a couple of minutes. He tapped the wad of notes on the desk with a satisfied air.

'Nice work, Ernie, old son. Just another five and a half to cough up.'

'Four and a half,' said Ernie sharply.

Tommy's lips tightened in a mirthless smile. 'Late payment penalty.'

They glared at each other.

'One more payday to go,' said Tommy.

'I might need longer.'

Tommy's expression changed immediately. 'Don't come that one with me, you old fucker. I meant what I said the other night, so don't push your luck. The deadline's next Friday, and not a minute later.' He stood up and gathered the money together. Raising his eyes to them again he said 'You still here? You can piss off now.'

* * *

Waiting for the woman in the phone box to finish her call, Ken nervously turned over the coins in his pocket. It was cold and the arrival of thick cloud had brought the darkness early. He should have worn his new overcoat. He had to talk to Davis again after his no-show the other night. But any contact with the cop made him edgy, even at a distance. He'd managed to squeeze a deal out of him last time but something had gone wrong. Was he going to have to go through all that again? There was one thing he had decided, though, their next meeting place would be more public than a dark side street.

The woman finally came out of the box and Ken entered, the heavy door closing with a bump behind him. He inserted the coins and dialled the number. It rang for a long time before anyone answered.

'Stepney CID,' said a voice.

'I want to talk to Davis,' said Ken.

'DI Davis?'

'That's right.'

'What d'you want him for?'

Ken hesitated. 'I got something for him.'

'Yeah? What?'

'He'll know,' said Ken.

'What's your name then?'

'Ken.'

'That it – just Ken?'

'Yeah.'

'Well, he's about somewhere Ken, but I can't see him right this minute. He's probably in the crapper. So tell you what, give me your number and I'll get him to call you back.'

'I'm in a phone box.'

'That's ok, he'll call you in a couple of minutes.'

Ken read out the number.

'Got it,' said the cop. 'Sit tight and he'll be with you in a tick.'

Ken replaced the handset and waited. After a few minutes there was a rap on the glass behind him. An elderly man stood there. Ken opened the door a crack.

'You done in there?' said the man.

'Just waitin' for a call back. Won't be long.' He closed the door again. More time passed as he pondered how it would go when Davis finally called. He was taking his time. Then another rap on the glass. He opened the door again.

'Come on, Mr Sambo, its bloody freezing out here. I could have made my bleedin' call by now.'

Ken wasn't listening. He was watching the speeding police car, its bell ringing and blue light flashing, as it jumped a set of red traffic lights and raced directly towards him. No-one was calling him back – they were coming for him.

He ran.

* * *

The police car followed, overtook and skidded to a halt in front of him, blocking his path. The doors flew open and three plain clothes cops jumped out, sprinting at him. He turned, ran across the road dodging the traffic and hurdled the barrier onto the opposite pavement. As he landed he saw an alley in front of him and darted into it. It was unlit and he had no idea where it led. His leg connected with something hard and he leapt clear of it, his shin stinging from the contact. He ran on. Behind him a curse as one of the cops collided with the same thing. There was a high wall on his left and shadowy buildings to his right but no end to the alley in sight. In front of him a light shone from a door in one of the buildings. He reached it, grabbed the handle and turned. It opened and he flung himself through it. A steamy kitchen full of Chinese men. They all turned to stare at him. At the other end of the kitchen was another door, out to the restaurant. As he made for it someone grabbed his shoulder, spinning him round. He found himself facing a huge Chinese man in a chef's hat and a dirty apron. The man rammed him against the wall, his thick arm pressed across Ken's throat. The meat cleaver in his raised hand glinted along its razor edge. When the cops burst through the door and grabbed him to handcuff him, Ken was almost grateful.

* * *

The car hurtled through the evening traffic, forcing other vehicles aside with its light and bell. They weren't heading for Stepney police station. Instead they were driving through the City, its pavements thronged with office workers on their way home.

Ken sat between two cops in the back seat. They were big men, and there was barely room for his slim frame between them. His arms, held behind him by the handcuffs, ached from being squeezed by the shoulders of the men, and his scorched arm throbbed. No-one said anything. The lights of the West End sped past until Big Ben loomed up in front of them. The car made a sharp right and pulled up at the entrance to a tall Victorian building, its walls blackened by the soot of ages.

His minders hauled him out. They each shoved a thick hand under his armpit and frogmarched him up the steps into the building. The sign by the entrance read 'New Scotland Yard'. Inside, it was alive with uniformed police, cleaners, men in overalls, and others who wore no uniform or mark of their trade. A tea lady pushed a rattling trolley past them containing a huge silver urn. They quickly climbed a wide, ancient staircase, then another and another, the two big cops lifting him bodily off the ground when he began to flag. Now they walked down a long corridor where secretaries in seamed stockings and sensible shoes carried files back and forth between offices that echoed to the sound of radio operators talking to squad cars. No-one took any notice of the three of them. At the end of the corridor a door opened onto a large, dimly lit office.

The men shoved him through the door and brought him to a halt on front of a very big desk with nothing on it except a reading light, an ashtray and a thick file lying open. Behind the desk, sitting reading the file was a man, his face in shadow beyond the reading light, the badges on the shoulders of his uniform indicating a senior rank.

'Thank you gentlemen. That will be all,' he said in a nasal South London accent. Ken's ear caught the way he'd modified it to a more clipped, superior version, as people did when they went up in the world. The two cops withdrew and the man in front of him looked up. He was middle-aged, with deep crow's feet spreading from either side of his dark eyes, and thinning grey hair combed back and slicked down with Brylcreem – an old fashioned style. He was a man who spent time on his appearance, but not to good effect. He reached into his pocket and drew out a packet of Senior Service.

'Smoke?'

Ken shook his head. The man took one and lit it, the smoke curling up to the light and out into the darkness of the office.

'I understand you want to get in touch with Detective Inspector Davis of Stepney CID.'

Ken didn't respond.

'What business do you have with him?'

'Why am I here? I ain't done nothin''

'What business do you have with him?' repeated the man.

'Who are you anyway?'

The man leaned back in his chair and surveyed Ken for a moment.

'Commander Baldwin. I'm in charge of all CID operations

across the Metropolitan Police area,' he said. 'That means every CID officer in London answers to me.' He leaned forward and tapped a finger on the file in front of him. 'This file was one of DI Davis's cases. It concerns a children's home in Forest Gate. Your name is in it.'

Ken realised it was the same file Davis had been looking through when he interviewed him. 'So where is he, then?' he said.

'DI Davis has been assigned to other duties.'

'Why's that?'

Baldwin studied him for a moment, deciding how to play it. Ken could almost see the wheels whirring.

'Since the discovery of a body, the case has taken on greater significance. It's been passed to me to oversee.' He reached a hand out and gestured at the empty chair on Ken's side of the desk. 'Won't you sit down Mr – ,' he glanced down at the file, 'Smith.'

It was a long time since he'd heard his surname – if it was his real one. He'd never really known for sure. Was it his mother's or his father's? The small, grubby birth certificate didn't give him anything to go on. He settled into the chair.

'I still don't know why I'm here. You arrestin' me?'

'Not unless you've committed a crime. You're helping us with our enquiries.'

'I don't know nothin',' said Ken.

'But yet you had – have – something of interest for DI Davis. What is it?' Baldwin's gaze rested on him. So Davis hadn't told

Baldwin about the diary. He had to think fast. His own wheels needed to whirr. He had a glimmer of an idea.

'Information. I had some information for him.'

'And what is it?'

'It's about a diary.'

A moment's silence.

'The one mentioned in this file?'

Ken shrugged. 'I suppose.'

Baldwin's interest was so intense he stared at Ken as if he was hypnotised. 'That could be a highly important piece of evidence.'

'Yeah, Davis thought so too.' Ken took the plunge. 'That's why me and him made a deal.'

Baldwin raised a sceptical eyebrow. 'Really? And what, may I enquire, is the precise nature of this 'deal'?' The flowery way with words didn't seem to go with the accent.

'If I let him know where the diary was he'd close the file on Charlie.'

Baldwin's hypnotic stare stayed on him – the same way Davis's did. Maybe they learned it at cop school. As the silence lengthened, he started to wonder if Baldwin even knew about Charlie and Maggie, then Baldwin put his cigarette in the ashtray, pulled open a drawer and took out another file.

'That would be this file, would it?' He placed it on the desk in front of him and opened it to the first page. 'Concerning your girlfriend Mrs Margaret Ward and her newly deceased husband?'

Baldwin had done his homework.

'Yeah,' said Ken.

'You're still living with Mrs Ward at –,' he ran a finger down the page, 'Stifford House, I presume?'

The tower block. So he still had one advantage. 'That's right.'

'I wonder what the neighbours think.' Baldwin eyed him then began to flick through the file. 'DI Davis doesn't have the authority to make a deal like that,' he said without looking up. He continued to study the file in silence, letting his words sink in. Ken mulled them over. Baldwin could be telling the truth – probably was. Davis had committed to a deal he couldn't deliver. Finally Baldwin leant back in his chair, the leather creaking, and sighed, as if he'd made a decision.

'There's something you need to know about DI Davis, something of a delicate nature. Can I trust you to keep it to yourself?'

Suddenly they were going to be pals. 'Sure,' said Ken.

Baldwin seemed to ponder further before finally speaking. 'We have reason to believe that DI Davis was undertaking the investigation into Bartlett House in order to protect himself and others known to him.' He sounded like he was reading a statement. But it made sense. Ever since he'd recognised Davis from the home, he'd wondered about his motives. 'So you will perhaps see why he was so keen to get hold of this diary – and why it's vital that we get hold of it ourselves.'

Ken nodded along to these comments. He had been right to be suspicious of Davis, but his deal with him was gone. He was back where he started.

'Unlike DI Davis, I do have the authority to make mutually beneficial accommodations,' said Baldwin, as he continued to look through the file.

'Make what?'

Baldwin looked up at him and began speaking slowly, as if to a child. 'I have the authority to make that deal.' He leaned forward and put his hands on the big desk, reducing the distance between them but not by much. 'So do you have the diary?'

They looked at each other for a second. Ken had no plans to turn over the diary to this stranger without some time to think it through. He'd just learned that Davis had probably lied to him about doing a deal. It was all getting complicated and, although what Baldwin said made sense to him, his instinct told him to buy some time. The man was very sure of himself, and, like a lot of white people, imagined Ken was stupid. People like that were easy to play.

'You got the authority – that's cool. But are you really goin' to make the deal, this time?'

Baldwin's face softened. He looked ready to smile but decided against it. 'It's a big decision of course, but yes – if you actually have the diary.'

'And you reckon what's in it could be a help?'

Baldwin gave him a look of grave sincerity. 'Absolutely. It could prove vital in the case against these awful people.'

'I don't want to get involved, though. I just want to live a quiet life.'

'I give you my word that just by handing it over you will have played your part.'

'And me and Maggie? No more stuff about how Charlie died?'

Baldwin leant forward. 'Don't underestimate what I'm doing for you. Your girlfriend is guilty of poisoning her husband. This toxicology report confirms it.' He tapped the file he had taken from the drawer. 'The only reason she's still walking free is because I wanted to have this conversation with you first.'

So, it was true. After all the suspicions, the doubts, the hope he'd been mistaken, here it was in a few cold words. If Baldwin had punched him in the gut, he'd feel less beaten, less winded. But right now he had to hold it in. He let a little silence pass as he seemed to consider Baldwin's words while he pulled himself together. The deal was on again – if he wanted it. He'd got to play it right, and any thoughts about what Baldwin just told him had to be put on ice.

'I'm doin' this on trust,' he said finally.

Baldwin smiled again, this time with sly satisfaction. 'I've built my entire career on trust.'

Ken smiled back – the smile he would give a man in a park to let him know it was ok. 'I ain't got it – not anymore, but I know where it is.'

Baldwin stubbed out his cigarette and produced a notepad and pencil from the desk. 'Let's have it,' he said.

'There's a man called Meatball,' said Ken. 'He does some work for a rich guy with a load of properties called Blake.'

'And how do we find this man?'

'He'll be in your records. He's done a stretch. Spends a lot of time around Notting Hill.'

'How did he come to be in possession of the diary?'

'He stole it from me when he evicted me.'

Baldwin put down his pencil and again gave Ken the hard stare again.

'Why did he do that?'

Ken's imagination was in full flow now. 'He took a lot of my stuff. The diary was with it. He didn't know what it was.'

'And how did you come by it in the first place?'

He answered quickly. He had to protect Hazel Dolman. 'I've always had it. Charlie gave it to me years ago after he left the home.'

Baldwin watched him, his eyes dark. 'Have you read its contents?'

Again Ken made sure there was no pause before he answered. 'No. I can't read.'

The heat went out of Baldwin's stare.

'So why didn't you just tell DI Davis this information when you made your deal with him?'

Ken hesitated. He could afford to this time. 'I wasn't sure I could trust him. I wanted time to think about it.'

'And today you decided you could trust him?'

'That I had to.'

The sly smile again. 'It's lucky for you that you're talking to me instead.'

'Yeah, I guess it is.'

'OK Mr Smith,' said Baldwin getting out of his chair, 'you've been a great help in a very important investigation. That diary could be the breakthrough we need.'

Ken got up too. Baldwin came round the desk. For a moment he thought he was going to shake hands, but instead he handed him a neat white business card. 'In case you think of anything else that might be useful.' He went to the door and pulled it open to reveal one of the cops who had brought Ken there.

'Geoff, see our friend out will you.' He turned back to his desk as if Ken was already gone.

* * *

Outside Scotland Yard, Ken turned up his collar against the rain that drifted fitfully over the streets, driven by a blustering, icy wind. He made for the tube station. This new turn of events sucked him further into the quicksand. Maggie really did kill Charlie. The report was right there in that file on Baldwin's desk. He had seen the signs but he'd brushed them aside. Now he knew – and he hated knowing. If Baldwin hadn't slapped him in the face with it he could have gone on pretending. He wouldn't have to sort out his feelings for Maggie. Now he'd have to make some kind of choice. Charlie had been everything to him for so long – even after Maggie came on the scene and Charlie put the distance between the two of them. He'd protected Ken – fought for him even – while he suffered at the hands of those men in the diary. And he never let on – never tried to inflict any burden on Ken, call in any favour, ask any price. In this entire world of people Charlie had been his one true friend. So what was he doing, lying with Charlie's woman, trying to get her off a charge of murdering him? How could that be right?

If he could at least understand why she'd done it, maybe that would help. He stopped walking as he re-examined those words. Help him how? Only by finding a way to forgive her. He didn't like where that idea lead him. Every little step down that path would take him away from Charlie and towards Maggie. And that was wrong, wrong, wrong. Charlie had to come first. Charlie was in his blood. Everything felt twisted up inside him. But she had to have a reason for doing it, didn't she? Maggie never did anything without a reason. But she'd made no effort at all to explain anything. Instead she'd got under his skin like no woman ever had. The image of her looking at him over her glass that night after Charlie died came back to him again. He'd let himself be drawn in by her. Up to now he's always kept women at a distance, never got too involved. But this one, the one who should be safe because she was Charlie's widow, she'd worked her spell on him. Last night in the room together – everything seemed so perfect. She'd got him feeling he had a heart to give – had already given it. What was the benefit to anyone of putting her on trial, finding her guilty and maybe even hanging her? Those people who sat in their cosy armchairs reading about it all in the newspapers would feel good, people who lived inside their safe lives and didn't care anything about the likes of him and Maggie, who would never give them a second glance if they passed them in the street, except to look down on them. They'd be happy, but no-one else. Now he thought of it, he might be the only thing standing between Maggie and the gallows. That brought him to a halt as well. All he had to do was deliver the diary to Baldwin. If he didn't, Maggie would be gone too, and he'd be alone.

He stood looking up at the lights of the tall buildings and the dark sky beyond, the rain running down his face. Could he trust the man in his big office? He had no idea. Davis was off the case, and that had to be good news. But it meant the only deal around was with Baldwin. Why had he hesitated? If Charlie was still alive he'd have had someone to talk to, to help him work it out. But he had nothing but instinct to guide him so all he could do was go with it. Things were getting clearer in his mind. In the meantime he needed to call Betty and warn her that Meatball and her husband were about to get questioned by the police. Thick Rick was going to have another reason to be angry with him.

* * *

All through the night, Ken's thoughts churned as he stared up through the dark of the room and into the blackness of the stain on the ceiling. So much had happened during the day his head could barely hold it: Standing in the phone box dialling Davis's number, then Baldwin's office. And now he was lying next to the woman who had killed his best friend.

Why did she do it? He just couldn't understand that one at all.

When he finally dozed off he found himself lying awake in his dormitory bed in the home, while the door slowly creaked open. Then a whisper in his ear, so close and clear; 'I'm here,' said Charlie. He jerked awake. It was daylight and he had the bed to himself. He lay recovering from the unsettled night, his head still spinning with it all. Charlie wasn't here. He never would be again. He was on his own – except for Maggie. She was still here, and he knew he wanted her to stay. Part of him hated himself for admitting it. But what could he do? If that was the truth of it then he had to admit it. He'd spun all the way back to where he'd been with Davis. He was going to have to hand the diary over to Baldwin.

CHAPTER 10

Leaving the rooming house behind, he made for the comfort of the busy streets. It was cold again after the rain, but at times like this walking London's pavements was his release. He could lose himself in the crowds without thinking or doing anything – blank it all again. Out here it could all stop for a while. And besides, now he'd made up his mind, he was already feeling lighter. Once the diary was gone he wouldn't have to worry about it anymore, and Maggie would be free. He'd have kept his promise to Hazel Dolman, and if Baldwin was as good as his word, everyone in it would be rounded up and put behind bars. Only Ernie's friends to worry about then. Friday was getting closer, and the deadline was starting to prey on his mind. Was there some way he could raise the cash? How long would he need to spend in Regents Park to make five hundred and fifty quid? He started on the mental arithmetic and quickly realised it was a waste of time. Regents Park was the best spot he'd managed to find in London. But he went there on a Friday because that's when the pickings were richest. Any other day was a lot quieter. It was hopeless. He couldn't earn his way to that kind of money in a couple of days – or even a couple of weeks. And anyway, Baldwin would soon have every copper in London looking for him. If he was going to sit around on a bench looking for pickups in one of the busiest parts of London he might as well paint 'come and get me' on his forehead. Time to blank that out too.

The thing to do was ask Baldwin to pay for the diary. If it was as important as he said, then forking out for it shouldn't be a problem. Cops paid for information, didn't they? It would be like a reward. Maybe he'd get his name mentioned in the papers as well. The man who'd brought them all to justice. He'd like that. Yes, that would be the way to honour Charlie. He started looking for a phone box.

Ahead of him, the headline board of the 'East London Advertiser' had only one story on it: 'BARTLETT HOUSE – MORE BODIES FOUND'. He was already sick of seeing the stories about the home, but he had to know what they were finding, even when he was afraid of it. He bought a copy from the street vendor and stepped into a doorway to read.

'The continuing investigation at Bartlett House Children's home took a macabre turn yesterday when police using heavy digging equipment uncovered what are believed to be two more bodies. The statement from the police gave no further details, but sources close to the investigation say they understand the bodies are those of children. This latest revelation has brought national attention to an operation that began as little more than an enquiry into allegations of misbehaviour by some members of staff. Scotland Yard has assumed direct control of the investigation. It will be led by the highly experienced Commander Jack Baldwin. In addition to a large team of officers carrying out house to house enquires in

the Forest Gate area, it is also understood that Missing Persons files, dental records, and records from the Children's home itself are being examined in an effort to identify the victims. The first victim, an adult male discovered last week, has yet to be identified. Full details on pages 2 and 3.'

Ken turned the page. A big photograph of the home filled half of page 2. He read through the detail, but quickly realised it was just filler and there was nothing new to add to what he'd already read.

These new bodies were children. The chill of the word ran through him. When they finally identified them he was going to know who they were. It was a near certainty. It all happened while Trevor was in charge, that was obvious, and he had been there for seven years of Trevor's reign. The men in Charlie's diary were a sick, perverted hard core that Trevor must have brought together over years. The kids were nothing to them, a handy bunch of available victims invisible to the world. They'd snuffed out some lives that didn't matter – just part of the entertainment. How did Charlie survive it? By being bigger and tougher than the rest? It made his own survival seem even more miraculous. He owed Charlie a bigger debt than he'd ever realised.

He turned back to the front page and read it again. Beneath the main story was a final line he hadn't noticed before. *'Police Officer suspended – see page 5.'*

The story at the bottom of page 5 was short. *'Detective Inspector Malcolm Davis of Stepney CID, who initiated the original enquiry into Bartlett House, has been suspended from duty while investigations are carried out concerning possible impropriety in public office. No further details have been made available.'*

Davis was out of the picture altogether – maybe even a suspect.

Ken lowered the newspaper and looked out across the street, his thoughts taking him back to the years in the home again. Until Charlie died he'd all but forgotten his time there – had deliberately put it out of his mind. Now that all this was resurfacing in the papers, his own memories were being dragged back up with it. That skinny kid Dan, coming out of Trevor's office after a beating with the Strop, trembling, his face white, and dropping down on the floor like he was dead. Two of the staff filled a bath with cold water, stripped him and flung him in. They held him under until he came round, lashing out and struggling. Ken and the other kids were gathered at the bathroom door watching while they pulled him out and sent him running to his room, naked, wet and shivering, while they laughed and shouted after him: 'Skinny little bastard!' And he was skinny, and he was little, and he probably was a bastard too. That's how it was there – everything calculated to grind you down, make you into a zero. It was all he knew, so he'd come to believe that's how kids everywhere got treated, even those with parents. Maybe it wasn't supposed to be like that. Maybe some kids somewhere were happy. But for all the routine misery of the place, he'd been the lucky one. His one encounter had been with Anne, and that felt more like a rite of passage. It hadn't led on to anything else, so that must have been her own bit of private enterprise.

As his eyes came back into focus from these unwanted memories he found himself looking at a man standing on the other side of the street. The man was staring back at him. For a second he thought it was someone looking for a pick-up. But it wasn't. It was Davis.

* * *

As Davis crossed the road towards him, he thought about running. But Davis wasn't a cop now. He was suspended. Did that make him less dangerous, or more?

'Hello Ken.'

Ken didn't answer. Davis was unshaven and looked like he'd slept in his clothes. Close up he smelled of booze.

'Read the paper then, I see,' said Davis nodding at the newspaper in his hands.

'You're suspended,' said Ken.

'That's right. Some bollocks to get me out of the way.'

'Meaning what?'

'I was getting too close.'

'Yeah? Maybe you was always too close.'

Davis gave him half a smile. 'You've met Baldwin, haven't you? After the diary, is he?'

'Maybe.'

'Don't give him it.'

'Why not?'

'He's in it.'

A shred of memory came to Ken; what Charlie had written about the cop in uniform.

'Listen, its cold out on this street and I don't have a nice warm police station to invite you to any more. Let's get a drink. There's a place just here.' Davis pointed at a pub called the White Hart on the corner along from where they stood.

It was a public place, and Davis wasn't officially a cop anymore, so he couldn't be arrested or charged. He might learn something from listening to him. At the very least he wanted to know what Davis had to say about Baldwin.

The pub was big and old, with faded gilt on winding pillars rising from the bar, and screens of polished wood and stained glass separating the bar from the snug. The floorboards were bare and unvarnished. It wasn't long after opening time and still almost empty, just a few early drinkers occupying some of the tables, chatting or reading the paper. Two men stopped talking and stared at Davis. He stared back. They both knocked back their pints and left in a hurry. Behind the bar was a huge mirror advertising Truman's Stout. Ken looked at their reflections in it. He thin and well dressed, Davis rough, overweight, middle-aged and ill.

Davis ordered a pint of bitter and a whiskey chaser for himself and a Guinness for Ken. The barman scanned Ken then pursed his lips and primly pointed to the familiar sign stuck to one of the wooden screens: 'NO GYPSIES, NO BLACKS.'

'Fuck off and get our drinks,' said Davis, eyeballing the

barman, his cop's authority at full throttle. The barman did as he was told.

Davis chose a quiet corner and they sat at a table. He took a long sup of his pint, placed it on the table then knocked back the whiskey. 'That's better,' he said.

'So what is this, coincidence?' said Ken.

'I followed you.'

Ken was stunned. 'What for? You're not even on the case now.'

'There's a reason I've been shoved out of the way and it's nothing to do with any 'impropriety' shit. That was just an excuse.'

'Didn't do a good enough job at hushing it all up?' said Ken.

Davis glared at him for a second. 'Don't be thick. I'm the one who started all this.'

After his visit to Hazel Dolman, Ken had more or less worked that out for himself. The stories in the newspapers about the home started after Hazel Dolman spoke to Davis about Charlie's death.

'How come?' said Ken, wanting to hear Davis's version of the story.

'That sister of Charlie's – Hazel – she told me what home Charlie was in and I said I knew it. She told me a couple stories about the place she said she'd got from Charlie and it all fell into place for me.'

Davis didn't realise how close he'd come to getting the diary handed to him. But his admission that he knew the home had thrown her, brought out an instinct for self-preservation just strong enough for her to keep quiet about it to him.

'But you were there. I remember you,' said Ken.

'That's right, I was. But I'll bet there's nothing much about me in that diary is there?'

He'd already been thinking back over the passages he'd read; the initials on the pages. There was no MD, no mention of Davis. He shook his head. 'What were you doin' there then?'

'I was playing Baldwin's fucking chauffeur, wasn't I?'

Ken looked closely at Davis. The man had been a copper too long to ever completely lose the sneer, but there was something different about him since they'd sat opposite each other in the interview room. It would be a stretch to call it honesty, but maybe it was as close as he'd ever get.

'I was young then,' continued Davis, 'did as I was told and didn't think much about it.'

'So what makes you think Baldwin's in the diary?

Davis shrugged. 'Isn't he?'

'There's some cop – no name though.'

Davis looked disappointed.

It was Ken's turn to shrug. 'So why're you tellin' me all this?'

'You've still got the diary, haven't you?'

He felt a sudden unease. Was this whole thing a set-up? Would Baldwin's men come bursting into the pub to beat the location of the diary out of him? No. If that was going to happen it would have been yesterday when they first picked him up. Davis already knew he'd got the diary, so any little scheme between him and Baldwin would have worked its way out before now.

'You know I have. Why didn't you show up for the meet?' he said.

'That's the day I got chucked off the case. I spent six hours waiting around at Scotland Yard for Baldwin's side-kick to tell me what he could've told me over the phone. Baldwin wanted to show me who was boss now – rub my nose in it.'

It made sense of Davis's no-show.

'You started all this because you thought they'd killed Charlie.'

Davis gave him a thoughtful look. 'Yeah, for a while.'

'A while?'

'That was Hazel Dolman's theory. And your Charlie made himself invisible after he left that home – working cash-in-hand on the building; running that shebeen – yeah,' he said, catching Ken's expression, "course I know about that place. Even the Council flat's not in his name. It's like he was covering his tracks. It didn't take long to work out they hadn't got to him. He was the Invisible Man.'

Ken mulled that over. Another side of Charlie he'd never guessed at. And maybe another one he'd benefitted from as well.

'Why Maggie?'

'Who else? She was the only one there when he died. Most murders are done by the nearest and dearest.' There was something straightforward, open about Davis now. Maybe he wasn't as bent as the rest.

'So if Maggie was in your sights for Charlie, why'd you start on the home?'

'I always had my suspicions about what Baldwin and the rest used to do there, but no evidence – and no idea there was murder involved. Hazel Dolman gave me an excuse to turn over the stones. I convinced my Super there was a connection between the home and Charlie's death.'

Ken raised his eyebrows. 'Big risk.'

Davis gave him a lop-sided smile. 'No shit. What're you going to do with the diary?'

Ken shrugged. 'Baldwin's offering me the same deal – me and Maggie off the hook if I hand it over.'

Davis flared his nostrils in contempt. 'Yeah, I thought he might.'

'So? Why shouldn't I take it?'

Davis took a sip from his pint. 'Because you're not on any hook.'

Ken shook his head in bafflement. Davis leaned in until his face was inches from his, about to speak. It was too much like their last interview at the police station, just before Davis grabbed him. Ken instinctively drew back.

'What I mean is,' said Davis with exaggerated emphasis, 'Baldwin's lying. The toxicology report didn't show anything up. Your mate Charlie died of natural causes after all.'

* * *

Davis was still talking to him, but the words flowed past

unheeded. All he could think about was that Maggie was innocent. Baldwin had lied. There was no poison. There was no murder. And he'd been stupid and wrong to fall for it – stupid and wrong to doubt Maggie. A tension he didn't even know he'd been feeling flooded out of him, and with it went the fear that she had been using him all this time. He could float away, he felt so light. He itched to jump up, shake Davis's hand and rush off to tell Maggie. He had to get away. They should be celebrating. Suddenly all the suspicions and uncertainties, all the barriers to his feelings for her, were gone. He knew now, instantly, that what he felt for her was something stronger and deeper than he'd ever felt for any other woman. She deserved only the truest, purest form of love that he could offer. This moment was historic. He would remember it forever.

'Are you listening?' said Davis.

'What?'

'I said you've got no reason to give him the fucking thing now. If you do, it'll disappear, and him and his filthy mates'll get away with it.'

He reluctantly turned his attention back to Davis's words, and to something else that was puzzling him.

'Why're you doin' this, man? You're a cop just like he is.'

Davis's face took on a look of professional seriousness. 'No – we're not the same. Believe it or not there's some of us who joined the force to catch criminals and put 'em in prison, not cover up for them.'

'And look where it's got you.'

Davis sighed. 'Yeah. I'm fucked.' He leaned in again and dropped his voice. 'But there's some good men in the Met – some that'd be glad to see Baldwin and all those other dirty bastards go down. Some of us still know what we're here for. You've got that diary. How're you going to use it?'

That was the big question. Ken had no answer now. His elation at Davis's news about Charlie's death was giving way to new doubts. Could he trust Davis? Was this, after all, some complicated plot to get the diary out of him?

As if on cue, Davis spoke. 'If you were to let me have that diary, I'd make sure it got into their hands.'

They stared at each other, Ken's mistrust so clear on his face that Davis just held up his hands in surrender.

'Ok, but what else is there? You're nothing on your own – just some nig-nog nobody'll listen to. Baldwin's a senior officer in the Metropolitan Police. He's a mason. He's got influence. And don't think he'll honour any deal you try and make. He'll want you out of the way. Prison if you're lucky, but – ,' Davis's finger tapped the newspaper headline about the bodies, 'he's got other options. If you want it to do some good, I'm all you've got. Think about it.' He reached into an inside pocket and produced a pen. Taking the newspaper, he wrote a phone number along the edge and pushed it back across the table. 'You can get me on that.' He stood and buttoned up his overcoat. 'One more thing,' he said, looking down at Ken. 'You did a runner from the tower block but I still found you and followed you. If I can so can others. Remember that if you're planning to move the diary around.'

* * *

The journey back to the room was a blur of faces, colours, sounds. Everything felt bigger, brighter; the air smelled sweeter. He was drunk on elation, floating and skimming through the crowds. All his life he'd held himself back, making sure he never got involved. There had been women – men too – who'd wanted him for themselves, but he'd resisted. Something inside him always held him in check. If he didn't let himself fall for anyone, he could never be rejected, never be pushed any further out into the cold of the world. Now it was different. He could surrender to his feelings. It felt good – it felt great.

The road to the rooming house sped by beneath his feet. He burst into their little room, out of breath from the pace he'd kept up.

'Maggie!' he gasped. 'Great news.'

The room was empty. Of course it was. It wasn't one o'clock yet and Maggie wouldn't be back from work for hours. He'd forgotten. People who spent the daytime at work hadn't featured in his life until now and he was thrown. He sat down on the bed, deflated by her absence.

The last part of his conversation with Davis had been a haze. He'd barely been listening, but now his words came back. They were off the hook – there was no hook, so he could call Baldwin and tell him what to do with that phoney deal he'd offered him.

But the cop was still desperate to get his hands on the diary, so was it possible he could instead get the cash he needed in exchange for it? If everything was like Davis said, then he'd be taking a big risk. Davis knew it was Baldwin in the diary, even if the diary didn't spell it out. Baldwin didn't know what was in it, which is why he had to have it. He was covering his tracks so that made Ken a target too. He told Baldwin he hadn't read it, but he knew it existed, and that was too much knowledge. No. Like Davis said, if Baldwin wanted it all hushed up, Ken would be sticking his hand in the fire trying to deal with him. The diary would disappear and everything Charlie and the others went through at the home would be buried and forgotten. But that wouldn't be the worst part. Baldwin could do anything he wanted to Ken and no-one would care; find some new crime to fit him up with, bury him in prison for the rest of his life – maybe just bury him. But what about Davis? His words had the ring of truth. Davis's attempts at uncovering what went on in the home had got him suspended. And he still hadn't given up. He had to be genuine. So if he wanted the diary, he'd have to pay for it. That was the way to solve all this. Then Davis's friends in the Met would use it to go after Baldwin and all the rest of them. With Baldwin out of the way and the debt paid off, he could set Maggie free – free to be with him. They could lay Charlie to rest and look ahead.

But he just couldn't keep his mind on the diary right now.

What really mattered was that Maggie was innocent. She hadn't killed Charlie and she wasn't going to prison. Nor was he. He was too excited to sit still for long. He got to his feet and paced about the room. What a day this was turning out to be. He was in love, he knew that now. He wondered if he'd ever been this happy. The diary could wait a couple of hours. There was going to have to be a celebration first. He had nothing to celebrate with, so he decided to go out and find some flowers or chocolates – maybe a bottle of something fizzy if there was such a thing in the East End. Tea and flat beer were the only things he could ever remember drinking in this part of London.

Searching the small shops in the Mile End Road he managed to turn up a bouquet of a dozen different coloured roses. They were expensive, and were more thorn than rose, like they were the leftovers from a wreath or something. Still, it was the best he could do. He'd never given Maggie flowers before.

Looking at his watch, he still had too long to wait. He was restless but she didn't finish until four. She must get a break. If he could remember where she worked he could go round and surprise her with the news. He knew it was a place that made dresses on Brick Lane, close to Petticoat Lane with its market and endless cheap clothes shops.

He dropped off the flowers at the room – she wouldn't be able to do anything with them at work – then headed for the lane while he searched his memory for the name of the place. He had to be on the move. He had to see her. If he went down there he was sure he'd recognise it when he saw it.

* * *

He must have been the only man in the street without a sack barrow to push. Stacked bundles of clothes, long rolls of coloured materials, and strange metal pots of liquid all rushed past him as he picked his way through the sweating men trundling their goods to and fro along the cobbled lane. Further on, lorries loaded with beer barrels roared out of Truman's brewery and sped down the street, the drivers blind to those in their path. He had to jump quickly back onto the pavement to avoid being hit.

He was more of an outsider here than he'd ever felt in his life. It looked like all the races of the earth were here. He could have been in India or Africa or somewhere. He felt foreign. Maybe those white East-End lorry drivers were making some point by the way they drove.

He was right; as soon as he saw the name 'Jacobson and Sons' he recognised it as Maggie's place. But now he was here he wasn't sure how he'd get to talk to her. The place was big, several floors of dirty windows and a loading yard to the side. There was a front door where people in suits went through, but he couldn't see another way in. But then at the far end of the yard he saw a group of women sitting around smoking on the stone steps leading up to another entrance. He went over to them.

'Hi ladies,' he said, giving them his sunniest smile.

Their tired gazes, incurious at first, took in his chisel-toed shoes, tight, grey check hipsters, narrow-lapelled jacket and finally his smiling face. One of the women, younger than the others, smiled back.

'You're a sight for sore eyes. Those trousers don't look big enough for you, mate.'

The other women laughed, raucous and loud.

'Got plenty on him, I'd say,' said another.

'More'n your old man,' said the first.

'How'd you know that?' replied the other. More laughter.

The first one looked at him again. 'I still got ten minutes on me break. Fancy a trip round the back?' She grinned and tipped her head towards the back of the building.

He carried on smiling. On a Saturday night she might look good, but today her face was haggard and weary. 'If I wasn't already spoken for I'd definitely take you up on that.'

'I knew it. All the best ones are taken,' she said. 'Who's the lucky girl?'

'Maggie – she's new.'

'Not that stuck-up Irish cow?'

'Er – could be.'

She got up, sighing. 'I'll get her. I don't reckon she deserves you though.'

He waited while the women continued to eye him. But they were quiet, even shy, without their mouthpiece present and settled back to puff on their cigarettes.

Maggie appeared in the doorway. She gave him a nervous smile. 'What are you doing here?' she said, stepping down through the other women. They turned and walked through the yard towards the street. 'I'll have to go back in a minute.'

'I've got some news that can't wait.'

She gave him an anxious look. 'What? What is it?'

'I saw that cop – Davis. Maggie, he told me there wasn't no poison. Charlie died natural.'

She stopped walking, staring straight ahead. He waited for her to speak, but nothing came. She continued to stand in the yard as if she was frozen.

He put an arm around her. 'It's over Maggie. You got nothin' to worry about any more.'

She yielded slowly to his embrace. 'No poison?' she said. Her voice was far away, like waking from a dream.

'Yeah. He said the report didn't show anythin' up. They was wasting their time.'

She slipped out of his arm and started walking again until she was out in the busy lane. It wasn't the reaction he was expecting, but he knew by now she never reacted as he expected. He caught up with her. 'It's great news, Maggie.' He wanted her to feel as happy as he did. He put an arm around her again. 'All that crap from the cops – it's over and done with. We can put Charlie to rest now.'

All of a sudden her weight was against him and he was supporting her, her legs no longer carrying her. He held her tight. She turned, her face sliding into his shoulder. He heard a muffled sob, reminding him of their first night together. Apart from that one time she'd kept her tears away from him – kept so much of herself away from him. He was oddly happy that here, in the street, the news he'd brought her finally made her give way.

They stood for a while, him doing nothing more than holding her, stroking her hair, and whispering to her as the teeming bustle of the lane flowed past them. The celebrations would have to come later. The burden he'd taken off her shoulders – the lightness that came with it – was too much to bear.

She looked up at him. 'Why did he tell you?' she said.

He stood back, confused by the question. He realised there was a lot he hadn't told her. 'I met him. He's been suspended from his job. But he's seen the report – what it said.'

'Has he?'

Again her question made him doubt himself. Had Davis some motive to lie to him? Did he need the diary to justify his actions to his bosses – to get his job back? Surely the bodies coming out of the ground at the home gave him that. But Maggie was making him question everything.

'He was tryin' to help.'

Maggie's head went back, suspicion in her eyes. 'Davis was trying to help? Why would he do that?'

He saw his mistake. Davis's actions only made sense if he told her about the diary – something he still didn't want to do. If she didn't know about it she couldn't tell anyone. It would protect her as well as him. Besides, it was private, a connection to Charlie he had and she didn't. And that still mattered, even with his love for her.

'Davis is an honest cop,' he heard himself saying. 'He wanted me to help with what was goin' on at the home.'

She continued to watch him. 'What help?'

Ken thought. 'He wanted a statement out of me.' Why was he doing this? He was getting lost in these lies. But he just wasn't ready to share the diary with her yet.

'What can he do with it if he's suspended?'

'He wants me to give it to some other cop. Maggie, relax. This is good news.'

She watched him for a few more seconds, and then her face broke into a smile he hadn't seen for a long time. 'You're right,' she said, 'it is.' She put a hand to his head and stroked his hair. 'You never doubted me, did you?' She was watching him again, looking for his reaction.

'No Maggie, never for a second.'

'Doesn't solve our problems, though, does it?' She was moving on, the conversation about her not being a murder suspect any more already over. 'I've got to get back. I'll see you later.' She turned and was gone.

For a minute he barely moved. He didn't know what to think. She was right. If you believed in her innocence all along the news from Davis couldn't have been anything else. There was no poison to find. It was something that only existed in his head – and Davis's. And it was true – they still had plenty of other worries. So the sooner he put them to bed the sooner he could claim her undivided attention.

CHAPTER 11

Under the heavy November sky Ken walked back to the Mile End Road and turned in the direction of the library. Maggie had sewn new doubts in his mind about Davis. He wanted to see the diary again. When he'd scanned through it before, he thought he'd got a pretty good picture of what had been happening in the home. But it had been too hard to take it all in on that first reading, and he'd given up. Now he'd seen those headlines about the bodies he was past shying away from the truth – of being sensitive to his own feelings. He would learn from Maggie and toughen up – deal with what went through his head when he opened the black covers again. The bodies weren't the only things rising from the past.

The library was even quieter than last time, with only one of the old men poring over the newspapers. He took the set of wooden steps and moved them over to the section where thick, ancient reference books lined the high shelves. Climbing to the top, where 'Tolley's Tax Guide 1956/57' and 'The London Gazette 1950-1955' had enough dust on them to tell him that no-one had handled them in years, he glanced around to see who was watching. Nobody. He wasn't even sure the old man was awake, and in any case up here he was out of sight. He reached over the top of the huge wooden book case until his fingers found the package containing the diary.

Once unwrapped, the little book looked less sinister than the first time he'd handled it. He began to browse through it, this time skimming over Charlie's description of events and concentrating on the names. He particularly wanted the passages that featured the cop. Did Charlie ever put a name to him?

He flicked past the early entries he'd read the first time and began at the new passages. It was more of the same. Week in week out, the men kept up their Wednesday visits. But over time there were changes. New names were added and then became initials. They meant nothing to him. Maybe they were the men in the photos Davis had shown him. But all the way through the diary, the cop was a regular visitor. But he played a clever game – appearing in uniform to intimidate the kids while at the same time knowing the risks he was taking and making sure he never identified himself in front of them. He became known as 'Uncle' to the others who joined him for the weekly parties. But there wasn't much description of what he looked like, and if Baldwin denied it was him, there was nothing here that would pin it on him. It would take Davis to point the finger for anyone to be sure.

Ken continued to browse through the diary. In the last half there was almost no description, just dates and initials, page after page of them. He picked through them, stopping randomly, but finding nothing new. He closed it and stared at the black cover. Charlie must have given this to his sister some time in his last year there – before that time they tore the place apart searching for it. They knew about it already by then. He must have threatened them with it. 'Tell them to remember Charlie's diary,' he's said in his letter. They knew.

His thoughts turned to his friend Sally. She was in here too. She had disappeared when she was ten – another runaway, according to Trevor. But was that really what happened? A sudden shudder ran through him. Who were those bodies in the garden? If they were the victims of this bunch of perverts then it would be written here, in the diary. Did he want to know? He had to face the sick, dirty truth.

He opened the diary again and turned to the section dated 18th June 1947, when Lord Percy first appeared. Sally had been chosen that night. Until he'd read it in the diary, Ken knew nothing about it. When he and Sally were together she never spoke about what had happened to her. She was a quiet kid anyway, so maybe it wasn't that surprising, but then nobody ever really said much. He'd known Cliff and Sheila too, the others that Charlie wrote about. Sheila was the same age as him. But again, they never told anyone what happened. It was like knowing half a secret. Everyone knew things were going on. They saw the men come and go, they saw the kids disappear at night, they even heard the muffled cries and – worst of all – the low repetitive moans that went on and on, travelling through the walls, drilling into your brain until you pulled the pillow over your head and pressed it against your ears to shut it out. But the kids never said anything.

Ken turned the pages. She cropped up regularly after that first night, a favourite with Lord Percy, who came to collect her several times, and with Wally, the Councillor, who took her into the back room at the home, paying Trevor five pounds a time. The cop never touched her, or any other girl. He only went for boys – especially Charlie. He turned back to look again at the entries before she disappeared and tracked them slowly forward. By now she was just 'S'.

It was a simple weekly routine. 'W' or 'P' or 'C' would take her to the back room. Now and then the lord 'LP' would turn up and take her away. It was hard work wading through all these pages of initials. Turning another page, he found himself looking at words instead – two precious pages full of them. The first for a long time. The date at the top of the page was 15th November 1950.

'I told them what would happen and now it has.' Charlie's writing was bigger and more jagged than usual, like he'd written in haste or anger. 'I said I wasn't doing it any more. They sent that twat Ian for me. They thought he would be better than Trevor. I told him the same. He pulled out a quid and shoved it in my top pocket like I was a tart. I went mad then. I smashed one into his face and he went down like a ton of bricks. I was on him, kicking and kicking. Trevor pulled me off. I had blood all over me. The cunt just lay on the floor with his tongue hanging out. Trevor nearly shat himself. I felt great, like when I'm pissed only better. I didn't know he was dead. Everyone went mental. The cop sorted it out. He yelled at everyone to shut up and ordered them around. He punched and kicked if they didn't move fast enough. They took it in turns to dig a hole and carried him out in a blanket. The cop told me to have a bath and he took my clothes and put them in the hole too. He told me to keep my mouth shut or I'd hang for murder. After, they all told him what a great bloke he was for taking charge. They kept calling him Jack. I never knew his name before. Trevor told me to go to bed, like I was a naughty boy. I laughed when I saw how they all looked at me. They're scared shitless of me, even the cop. They're all in on it. They won't touch me again. Not now.'

Ken's hand was squeezing his jaw so hard it hurt. Ian – the nervous little bearded guy who didn't stay long. He was the adult body the newspaper talked about. That explained why Charlie could get away with the things he did in his last year there. If they'd let the police get involved, if there was any kind of investigation, the lid would have blown off the place. The kids and staff would be interviewed, the men's presence would have to be explained. It couldn't be allowed to happen. And the cop took charge to make sure it didn't. Ken took out the business card that Baldwin had given him last night: 'Commander Jack Baldwin, Metropolitan Police'. And he was doing the same again now.

Hazel Dolman couldn't have seen this. If she had, she would never have given the diary to him or anyone else. He'd missed it himself – twice. It was easy to do among so many pages of initials and dates.

All this time, thirteen years, the secret had stayed locked away. Charlie quietly invisible, the diary carefully hidden away in an anonymous north London suburb where no-one would think of looking. That was the unspoken deal – the standoff. Baldwin and his cronies left Charlie alone and he left them alone. It was like one of those unexploded bombs left over from the war, just lying there underground until someone dug it up by accident. It wasn't his fists or even the knife he carried that protected Charlie, it was the diary.

He looked at the date of the diary entry again: 15th November 1950. He'd been friends with Charlie a long time by then. What did he remember? He couldn't recall anything in particular from that night. The fight must have happened in the bedroom right next to his. But so much went on any night there – shoutings and beatings, laughter from the parties, people coming and going from the bedrooms. It was all normal – so normal that Charlie could kill someone a few feet away and he probably slept through it. The guilt of his privilege came to him again. All this stuff was going on around him, but he hadn't been chosen. He wasn't the only one. There were others; those who were too ugly, too fat, too skinny to catch the eye of the men who came. But he was different. He alone had caught their eye and been protected. So he'd become one of the grateful invisible – those who knew but turned away, who turned their faces to the wall when the bedroom light came on and Trevor's shadow passed across them and stopped by someone else's bed.

But Charlie told him nothing about what happened. He must have seen him the next day or the day after. They spent a lot of time together then, but he hadn't noticed any change in Charlie. Though thinking about it, he did remember a change in Trevor. Was it that time? He was the same to everyone else but he avoided Charlie like he'd got leprosy or something. Everyone noticed. The word was Charlie and Trevor had a fight. But that was just the story that filled the space. No-one really knew except the two of them. Ian wasn't around to say anything. And people like him came and went. The children might ask about them for a week or two, but then they were forgotten. The home was a place where a little group of Trevor's friends was always there, and everybody else just passed through. It was no surprise to anyone that Ian was part of Trevor's circle one minute and gone the next. Trevor was fickle with his favours.

But it was Sally's story he'd been looking for, and he hadn't finished his search yet. He took a breath, licked his thumb and turned more pages.

The last time she appeared was 16th May 1951. 'LP took S out' at the end of the entry. Ken kept going, looking for her initial again. Nothing – her name no longer mentioned, no remark passed about her. He flicked back and forth to be sure. It was so easy to miss; Lord Percy picks her up, just like he had many other times, and then she was gone – vanishing like a ghost. And afterwards nothing, the diary stayed silent.

What did that silence tell him? Maybe she really did run

away. It was just part of the every day. Kids disappeared almost as often as the House Parents did. They got reported, but unless they were unlucky enough to get caught by the police, that was the end of it. A week later some new kid would be sleeping in their bed. He was relieved though. He'd been afraid of finding something about her, something terrible – even more terrible than what he'd just read about Charlie. But amongst all these pages of initials there was nothing to solve the mystery of what happened to the little girl who used to be his friend.

He closed the diary again. Baldwin was the cop in it. Had his apes rounded up Meatball and Blake yet and found out they knew nothing about it? If they had, they would be looking for him again. He must get the diary to Davis. He would call him. But first he needed to get back to the room. He still had something to celebrate with Maggie.

* * *

She would be home soon. Killing the time waiting for her by trying to rehearse some lines didn't do any good. The more he thought about what to say, the more tangled his thoughts got. Every conversation he'd had with her stopped before he got to where he wanted. He didn't want that to happen again. This new thing in the diary about Charlie and Ian didn't help. It weighed him down, blocked his thoughts. It made Charlie different from how he remembered. That was always the problem with Charlie when he started fighting. No-one could stop him. He became a wild man, a devil that just kept going. It was terrifying to watch. And now it turns out that's the kind of man he was even after he'd kicked someone to death. But Charlie was still dead. However much it changed things in the past, the present counted for more. Since he'd had the news from Davis, the flame that burned inside him for Maggie had become a house fire. He had to make sure she understood his feelings for her. The endless doubts he'd had about her were created by suspicions that were false. That was all in the past too now.

When she finally came into the room he got up, eager to start, and handed her the roses he'd bought earlier.

'Maggie – ,'

'Don't Ken. Let me in the door and get my coat off,' she said testily.

He stood back, flowers in hand, watching her. Even in the drab dress she wore for work, she was more beautiful than ever. He wanted to take her in his arms. She went to the sink and filled the kettle, set it on the ring, then struck a match and lit the gas. He couldn't tell what kind of mood she was in. Finally she turned to him and looked at the simple bouquet.

'They're nice.'

He handed them to her. 'Best I could find.'

'I need something to put them in.' She went to the altar, reached up for the new vase that sat in front of the Virgin Mary and began to arrange the flowers in it. 'Is this in honour of my freedom?' Her tone was light, playful.

'Yeah, I thought it needed celebratin'.'

'And why not? It's a great bit of news, isn't it?' She seemed a lot happier than when he'd met her at the factory. It was finally sinking in.

'The best,' he said, coming up behind her. He slid his arms around her waist. 'Maggie –.'

'There's hope for us yet. Maybe she's answering my prayers after all.' She broke free from his grasp and put the vase of roses up in front of the plastic Mary figure, the Christmas lights brightening the colours of the petals. She turned to him, a sparkle in her eyes. 'Kiss me.'

He kissed her, holding her body tight. The heat of her aroused him. But he'd been caught out and confused by her so many times now. He had to get through to her, to know that he was dealing with the real Maggie, to know the real terms they were on.

'Maggie, you can stay as cool as you like, but I got to get this off my chest.' She gazed up at him. 'Maggie, I'm in love with you. I know you think that's a line I give out to every woman, but it ain't. The women I know, they don't need to hear it because they're not interested in love – not mine anyway. In fact, to tell you the honest truth, I only ever said it once before in my whole life. But I'm sayin' it to you, Maggie.'

She put a hand to his cheek. 'Oh Ken, you're such a sweet lad, aren't you.' She was smiling at him now, but he sensed she was working out her response. 'Look, its grand having you around, we might make a great pair when things get settled. But give me time, Ken. Charlie's not even buried yet. Let's just see if we can get through all this in one piece and then see where we are.' She kissed him. 'Don't worry. It'll be fine.'

It was meant to be a peck, but he pulled her to him again and kissed her fully. They fell backwards onto the bed, his body sliding on top of hers. His head was spinning. What did he have to do to hear the word 'love' from her; to be heart to heart with her as well as body to body? He ached with hunger for her. The taste of her lips, the smell of her skin and her hair burned him with their sweetness. Yet still she held back.

She broke her mouth away from his. 'Not now, Ken,' she said, a laugh in her voice.

He kissed her again, his hands on her breasts, his thigh between hers.

* * *

Afterwards, he wanted to get out and on the move again. It hadn't been the great consummation of their love that he'd hoped for. It wasn't like the other night. There was more duty than passion in her this time and he regretted it. It had gone wrong again. Maybe she was still getting over the news of her freedom. She needed time to adjust. He'd underestimated the strain she'd been under. Perhaps she wasn't as tough as she made out – how could she be? Or maybe he was just making excuses for her.

Walking away from Maggie and the rooming house, he let out a long sigh. In his head he'd pictured a big scene, with the pair of them declaring their undying love for each other and she falling into his arms. But nothing seemed to move her. 'It'll be fine,' she said, but it wasn't fine – not for him.

There was a whirlwind blowing through his head, so he did what he always did at times like this. He blanked his mind – no thoughts, no feelings. His feet were taking him to the tube station, and all the way there he saw and heard only what was in front of him – people, cars, buses, trucks, noise, smoke; the ebb and flow of traffic as the lights changed. And when he got to the ticket office, he asked for a ticket to a place he wasn't thinking about either – West Kensington.

CHAPTER 12

Betty rolled over and reached for her packet of Sobranies. She drew out a pink, gold-tipped cigarette and lit it from her small Dunhill lighter.

'God, I needed that,' she said. 'I haven't had a decent shag in weeks. Where have you been, anyway?'

They were in her favourite hotel in Bayswater – anonymous and discrete – the sort of place where Mr and Mrs Smith checked in several times a day.

'A few things on my plate,' said Ken.

'Yeah, well you're not the only one. Rick can't shit for coppers crawling up his arsehole.'

'Oh?' said Ken, 'how come?' His heart leapt in panic as he remembered his conversation with Baldwin. He looked her over. She didn't seem to have taken any punches lately.

'He's been having a bit of bother.'

'What kind of bother?'

'Some boys from the East End been trying to muscle in on him – want to take over some of his properties. There was a bit of Cowboys and Indians. Someone got shot, so the law's been all over him.'

'East Enders?' said Ken. He was trying not to look too interested. 'Bit outside their – er – manor?'

'Oo, get you. Proper cockney.' She reached for the ashtray. 'There's a couple of right ones called the Kray twins who've made it big down there and they've been moving up West.'

'They own a place called 'Esmerelda's Barn' don't they?'

'S'right. Know 'em, do you?'

'Heard of them.'

'Everybody's heard of them, Ken. They're not like most villains. They don't mind courting the limelight.'

'I thought Rick and his rent men could handle stuff like that.'

'They can – usually, but this time Meatball ended up in hospital.'

'Not Meatball – my favourite bastard?' Ken held up his still bandaged arm. 'I hope he's the one who got shot.'

'Oh ha ha. As it happens, he wasn't. But it's got Rick in a right strop – getting it from all sides like that. He pays those coppers good money to stop this kind of thing happening.'

'What's he goin' to do?'

'He's done a runner.'

'You're kidding. Where to?'

'Spain. The law can't touch him there so he's got his golf clubs and holed up in a hotel to plan his next move.'

'I thought Rick was the man who could handle anything. He met his match?'

'Dunno,' she said thoughtfully, 'I got a feeling they're better connected than he is. Those coppers taking his money aren't going to see any more of it now. Something bigger's happening.' She turned to him and stroked his cheek. 'So anyway, while he's away, we can have as much fun as we like.'

He smiled. 'Great.' He wondered where Baldwin fitted into all this. 'So did the coppers catch up with Rick and Meatball then?'

'Flying Squad lifted Meatball. They missed Rick. Second lot were well pissed off when they found out they'd been beaten to it.'

'Second lot?'

'You're nosy aren't you? What's it to you?'

He rolled over and stroked her breast. 'Just taking an interest.'

'I dunno who they were. Local plod I think.'

It sounded like his luck was in. Rick was gone. Baldwin's men had missed him. Meatball wouldn't say anything to anyone without the boss's permission – least of all about a diary he didn't even know existed.

Betty stubbed out her cigarette and snuggled up to him. He felt her hand close around his cock. 'So what have you been up to all this time, anyway?'

He browsed through recent events wondering where to start. 'I think I'm in love,' he said.

She let out a laugh. 'Who with?'

'A very special lady.'

'Blimey, that sounds serious. She in love with you?'

'I don't know.'

'Well if you don't know, she probably ain't. Not stringing you along, is she?'

He considered the question. He'd considered it several times on his way across London.

'I don't know that either.'

'Well its dead simple, Ken. Who did the chasing?'

'She did.'

'And what's she getting out of you – apart from the obvious?' She gave his cock a playful squeeze.

'I sort of got her off a murder charge.'

'Wow. Then you're her knight in shining armour. She'll be swooning at your feet, I expect.'

'Well, no, not exactly.'

Betty raised herself on an elbow and looked at him. 'But she was before you got her off?' Ken didn't answer. She gave him a pitying look. 'Oh Ken. You're a lovely boy, but you ain't the sharpest knife in the box, are you?'

* * *

She wanted to spend the next morning taking him around her favourite shops to buy him some new clothes. It would be like old times, she said. But he didn't want to take the things back to the room with Maggie. So instead they went down to Soho and had coffee in some place Betty knew. According to her it was 'full of groovy people from the music business.' All he could see were some middle-age men sitting around the grubby Formica tables pretending to be Mods while a bit of mainstream Ska played in the background.

As they finished their coffees, Betty had some final advice for him.

'I don't want to lose you, Ken, but I've never known you

find anyone you thought was special. So if you really think you have, then you've got to find out for sure. Whatever's standing between you, you got to break it down.' She smiled and put a hand to his cheek. 'Faint heart never won fair maid.'

After they parted he felt in no hurry to step back out of this bubble of West End life and he wandered down Shaftsbury Avenue to Piccadilly Circus. The flashy arcades were crowded with punters who never tired of pouring their money into the one armed bandits. In among them he saw the boys moving about – the runaways and the homeless – strays like himself, wandering and watching the fruit machines, hanging around until some man came up and took them away for half an hour. Some were very young; ten maybe, but then he'd been that age himself when Charlie first took him down here and showed him a whole new world.

He must have known Charlie a year or so by then. They'd started skipping out on Saturday afternoons when Trevor wasn't around. In the beginning it was down to the sweetshop for some thieving, but when they got bored with that they'd slip under the barriers at the tube station and go down to the markets at Roman Road and Petticoat Lane to see what they could pick-pocket. Charlie was brazen. He'd walk right up to someone, barge into them and start an argument. Ken's job was to slip a purse or a wallet out of their pocket while they were distracted. Then they'd spend the money on crisps and bottles of Tizer before heading for the cinema. The Lone Ranger was always Ken's favourite, but he liked the old war films too. Best of all was 'Ben Hur' – a real man; strong and brave, who overcame every hardship, never gave up and won the chariot race against his mortal enemy.

How long had Charlie been slipping under the sheets with him at night by then? In his head it felt like it had always been that way – the two of them nuzzled together in the narrow bed, Charlie's heart beating against his back, his big hands holding him, touching him.

Just the memory was enough to send a shiver pleasure down his spine. It had been love – for him at least, but for Charlie too he felt sure. They were inseparable then. He followed Charlie around like a faithful dog. Whatever Charlie did, he wanted to do it too, because Charlie was big and strong and right about everything, and he belonged to him. So when Charlie said he was going up to Piccadilly to 'make some easy money', he wanted to go too. Charlie was his hero, his soul mate, his love, his blood brother. He knew the world and how to handle it, and if people got in his way, he'd kick them out of it. When Ken was with Charlie, he was safe, loved, protected.

Even down the Dilly. That first time he'd come here, he'd been dizzy with excitement. He'd never been to the West End before and the crowds and the traffic and the busyness amazed him. He was dazzled by the big neon-lit adverts that danced and flickered high above him. But as they pushed their way into the beeping, buzzing arcade he was suddenly fearful. Charlie took his hand and led him through the crowded, noisy place, the smell of sweat and the body odour thick in his nostrils. Charlie had some money and he started playing one of the machines. Then a man was standing by them, watching him play. He was tall and thin and unshaven, with a big beak of a nose.

'Hello Charlie,' he said.

Charlie had looked up at him and smiled.

The man stroked the back of Charlie's head. 'Shall we?' he said.

'My mate wants to come too,' said Charlie

The man looked at Ken and scowled in irritation. 'I don't think so.'

'Got to be,' said Charlie. 'He wants to learn.' He turned to Ken, 'Don't you?'

He didn't know what else to do except nod.

The man considered. 'OK.' He turned away and headed out of the arcade, Charlie and Ken following behind.

Out in the alley, Ken watched as the man gave Charlie a pound note and then Charlie knelt in front of him and sucked him off. It seemed strange to look at something that he and Charlie had only ever done in private before. But he wasn't afraid or shocked or anything like that. It was just people doing things with each other, like talking or dancing, or like when he and Charlie wrestled. It wasn't like real fighting, or like being beaten with the Strop. No-one was getting hurt. It was over in a few minutes. And afterwards Charlie held up the pound note in front of his face and grinned.

'See? Nothing to it.'

So it had been easy for him. Charlie made it easy. Down here, the men were never a problem. Mostly they were just sad ghosts drifting around the arcades looking for escape from what looked, even to Ken's young eyes, like grey and miserable lives. And they were grateful. Payment up front for doing simple things – the kind of things Charlie'd taught him, things he loved doing with Charlie. So he took his place on the meat rack with the other pretty boys and learnt how to make money from other people's needs.

They'd come up here whenever they could. Charlie still liked to go thieving or pick-pocketing sometimes, but Ken couldn't see the point. Life here was how it should be lived – easy, friendly. Once the punters got to know him, they'd buy him a meal or get him to run errands – delivering pills to teenagers who hovered nervously in side streets. It was better than anything he'd ever known, and when he felt Charlie's arm around his shoulder on their way home, he glowed with the pleasure of being wanted, being included, being part of something good.

The only aggravation came from the other kids. For him and Charlie, the money they made was extra. Most of the others lived on the streets and relied on what they made to feed themselves, find shelter, and buy the uppers they needed to keep doing it. So the street kids resented them and sometimes there was trouble. But whenever Ken was cornered, Charlie was there. Up here it was a little rough, a little wild, but Charlie was still king.

He wondered now about the stuff in Charlie's diary. How different it was – the things that went on in the home. There, kids got hurt – a lot. That was the attraction for the men who came. They could do whatever they liked and no-one cared – force themselves on kids who couldn't say no and had no-one to complain to. That was how they got their real fun, not from the sex, but inflicting pain and watching it with a cold sadistic eye. It's what Charlie knew all about, and had protected him from. By comparison, being a Dilly Boy was freedom – it was paradise.

Why didn't Charlie just run away? He had plenty of reasons to – and he knew how to survive. He could have disappeared amongst the other street kids. Ken never allowed himself the luxury of thinking it was because of him.

What would Charlie have been like if those things never happened at the home? Would he have been different? Maybe he would never have been interested in Ken, or any other boy. And if that happened, what would he, Ken, be like? He had loved Charlie. But would he have loved another boy if Charlie hadn't been around? He wasn't sure about that. He'd always got on better with girls than boys. Women always seemed to like him. His only other experience of sex in the home had been with Ann – someone who was supposed to be in charge of him. He hadn't minded that. He just accepted what came his way. And it was the same with Charlie. Things just happened and it felt good. Did Charlie make him the way he was now? Did Ann? All those men he met in Saint James's park – they didn't grow up in children's homes, so what made them different? Who really knows what makes us what we are? It was hard stuff and he couldn't think about it. But some things were easy to see. For him, life under Charlie's wing had been good. For Charlie it had been different. He'd started out as a victim. But over time his anger and his strength made him safe – until he got too angry and killed someone.

The journey back to the East End was gone already – passing without him noticing. He'd realised on the way that Betty was right. He had to find out if Maggie had any real feelings for him. She might just have been using him. After all, if she hadn't seduced him and turned his head, how would he have felt when the police started questioning her about Charlie's death? There wouldn't have been any doubt he'd be on Charlie's side. So it had served her purpose – except for one new and important fact: there was no murder. Charlie died of natural causes. So the more he thought about it, the more he was certain she did want him. They'd both been cast adrift by Charlie's death. And now they could start again, on a better footing. Trust was what it was about. If she could trust him enough to tell him what was in her head – in her heart – then he was ready to do something he'd never done with any other woman; commit himself.

* * *

As he walked towards the rooming house, a familiar figure approached from the opposite direction. Ernie looked sprightly, greeting him with a broad smile. He wore a wide-brimmed hat and was smoking one of his cigars, the thick, sharp smell hitting Ken before they were close enough to shake hands. He knew by now that Ernie always seemed at his most chipper when trouble was in the air.

'Watcha Ken,' he said. 'Maggie in?'

'Don't know. Just back myself.'

Ernie raised an eyebrow, waved his cigar. 'Where you back from?' He wasn't usually inquisitive.

'Just out and about.'

Ernie grinned. 'You don't have to tell me nothing.' He winked, and gestured for Ken to go ahead of him up the path.

This wasn't the return he wanted. He'd hoped for time alone with Maggie. She would be back from work by now and at the very least, he wanted to explain his absence. He'd left her too quickly yesterday, irritated by the wall she'd put up against him.

As he entered the room, Maggie was standing at the sink, washing some clothes. They looked at each other silently as Ernie entered, cigar smoke lingering in his wake. The landlady would have something to say about that.

'Hello Maggie,' said Ernie, 'Fancy a stroll in the park?'

She looked at Ken again, a reproachful look, he thought. 'Why not?' She dried her hands. 'I'll get my coat.'

The three of them walked towards the little Bethnal Green Garden a couple of streets away.

'Not a lot of park round here, is there?' was Ernie's only

comment. His usual chatty manner was gone and he showed no inclination to talk while people were passing them in the street, so they remained silent.

By the time they reached the small park the early evening darkness was setting in. There was no-one around. The gates would close in an hour or so.

'This looks like a good spot,' said Ernie, indicating an empty bench. They sat down with Ernie in the middle.

'That place you're in,' said Ernie, 'the walls are so thin you could hear a mouse fart in the next room.' He glanced at each of them, looking for a reaction, and when he got none, he looked a little closer until he got a sense of the atmosphere between them. 'So, it's Friday tomorrow. We need to talk about it,' he said.

'And we've got nothing,' said Maggie, matter-of-fact as always. 'What'll happen when we don't pay?'

Ernie took in Maggie's glum expression. 'Don't despair, girl,' he said. 'We might be down to the bones of our arse, but there's always a way.'

'What way?' said Maggie.

'Well they've had a good hit out of us, remember that. But we've still got a card or two we can play, I'd say.'

Ken's interest sharpened, but without allowing himself to hope.

Ernie looked at each in turn, checking they were paying attention.

'We're all ears, Ernie,' said Maggie impatiently.

'Well, we might be able to throw them the shebeen,' he said smiling at them.

'The shebeen?' said Ken. He had to suppress a flare of anger.

Maggie looked at Ernie, her eyes shining. 'No,' she said. 'It belongs to me.'

'Anyway,' said Ken, 'what would be the point? Even if they flung the Jamaicans out, it's not worth anything to them.'

'Well,' said Ernie slowly, 'if you want a new deal out of them you've got to put everything on the table – shows them you've got fuck all else to offer.'

Maggie was silent for a moment. Ken could see why. It meant handing over the only thing she had left.

'And when they say 'no'?' she said sceptically.

'They might say yes. Remember they're villains. They want to bleed people dry. We're none of us any use to them dead, are we? In fact, we'd be a nuisance – three bodies to get rid of.' Ernie's attempt to lighten the tone wasn't helping. He tried again. 'Look, one thing I've learnt in life is that it's not what you've got to sell that matters it's how you sell it. If I dress it up a bit, they'll bite. Those lads are good at throwing their weight around but they ain't that bright. They don't say 'thick as thieves' for nothing.'

In Ken's head, the image of Tommy beating and kicking Ernie as he lay on the floor of the flat played out again. The ultimatum he'd given them was all too clear to him. 'Tell you the truth, Ernie' he said, 'that sounds like nothin' to me. A key to a rented lockup? A club for people they hate? How're you goin' to get anyone interested in that?'

Ernie wagged his finger at him. 'You don't know those boys. They'd sell their own mother if they thought they could make a few quid. Darkies, Four-be-twos, shirt-lifters – it's all the same to them if they're making money. Ronnie's queer as a nine bob note himself. You should see what goes on in that place they've got up West. You wouldn't want your granny going there.' He eyed Ken, and finding him unconvinced, a note of impatience entered his voice. 'Look, the shebeen's illegal – that's not going to bother them, in fact it's a plus. If they control it they could use it to support other parts of their business operations. We saw what the Jamaicans were doing with it – shifting lorry-loads of nicked booze. The boys could do that and more besides – probably launder a bit of cash from wages snatches through it as well. It's perfect. And if they don't go for it, then at least we're negotiating. There'll be a deal to be had.'

Maggie sat upright and faced him. 'Ernie, the key to that place is the only thing I've got left. I'm not giving it up.'

'But what's it worth to you, Maggie?' said Ernie, 'Screw Face is still using the place. All you've got is a key. Tommy and the twins, they've got the muscle to do something about it.'

Ernie had a point, Ken could see that. The Jamaicans would have replaced the stolen stock and be back in business by now. The place was useless to Maggie.

She was silent and he could sense her anger. This was her contrary side coming out. He knew she wouldn't give in.

'*If* there's any deal to be done, I want to be part of it,' she said finally.

Ernie turned a puzzled eye on her. 'What do you mean?'

'If they get the shebeen, they get me too. I'll run it.'

Ken traded shocked looks with Ernie. 'Maggie,' he blurted, 'you'd be putting yourself on the hook with them.'

'Took the words out of my mouth,' said Ernie.

'That's the deal,' said Maggie.

'You'll pay hell of a price,' said Ernie.

'I'm already paying hell of a price.'

Ernie shook his head in disbelief. 'You'd do that, just to get back at the Jamaicans?'

Maggie said nothing. But her face had taken on that look Ken was starting to recognise. Her decision was made. There was no more room for argument.

Ernie gave a sigh and looked at Ken. 'Talk some sense into her, if you can.'

Ken shrugged.

'Anyway,' said Ernie, 'all this could be a waste of time. They might just decide to drop me in the river instead.'

'You?' said Maggie, 'What about me?'

'I've been trying to keep you out of it,' he said, suddenly angry, 'but if you want in, you can be in.' This was another Ernie, the hard man he kept concealed from them. There was silence. The park was completely dark except for the light of a nearby streetlight. 'Let me meet them alone to start with – see the whites of their eyes. They'll probably give me a good pasting anyway. But then we'll know where we stand.'

Maggie's eyes were on Ernie. 'You can't go alone,' she said.

'It's the best way.'

'Why?'

Ernie picked up her hand and placed it against his cheek.

'Feel that? Like leather ain't it?' He put her hand gently back down on the bench. 'People've been beating my hide since the day I was born. That's the world I live in. It's like water off a duck's back to me.'

'I can't let you do it, Ernie,' said Maggie.

'Don't worry about it. It's happened before and it'll happen again.' He dropped the remains of the cigar and ground it out with his heel. Then he got to his feet, suddenly keen to be on his way. They rose too, and he shook hands with each of them, stiffly, formally.

'I've known these lads since they were kids in short trousers. It'll be alright. I'll call for you at noon tomorrow; let you know what's what. Then we'll go down, sort it all out, and do a deal with them. High noon.' He winked at them, then turned and walked away. They watched him in silence until he reached the gate and disappeared into the early evening rush.

* * *

They walked slowly back to the flat. He could think of nothing to say. He wanted to talk about Davis and Baldwin, but the urge to keep that stuff away from Maggie was stronger than ever. She had so much to deal with. The news that she couldn't be accused of murder already seemed old. The shadow of tomorrow hung over them. He felt weak and useless in the face of the looming deadline. Ernie's plan sounded hopeless to him but he had no better ideas. And Maggie – digging a hole for herself like that. What was she doing? And when Ernie had walked away from them the picture that came to mind was his frightened face the first time he'd told them about the debt.

The last of the streetlights to come on glowed pink amongst the orange of the others. Maggie surprised him by slipping her arm through his, and then again by resting her head on his shoulder. He moved his arm up around her.

'Did you enjoy your day off from me?' said Maggie.

His heart jumped. This way she had – closing off one thing and moving straight on to another – it unsettled him every time. He tried to refocus.

'I needed some time,' he said. It sounded lame, so he added, 'My mind was all mixed up.'

'Did running away help?' Her tone was light, with no edge that he could detect.

He turned and looked at her. 'Yeah, as a matter of fact it did.'

'Well,' she said, as they turned up the path to the house, 'you'll have to tell me all about it.' Now it was soft Maggie, understanding Maggie. What was going on?

They walked up the stairs and let themselves back into the room. His chest was still thumping, his head still full of Ernie, the showdown tomorrow; Davis; Baldwin. So much pressing in on him. But this was the moment – the one that mattered to him most of all. Maggie was making it the moment. He had to get it right.

Without taking her coat off, she sat down on the bed facing him. 'So?'

'I want – ,' he tried to find the words, but the way she looked at him – her eyes beguiling, disarming – he was suddenly a confused kid again. She could switch it on whenever she wanted to. He struggled to control his feelings. 'Maggie, I've got to get this straight with you. I've never felt like this about a woman before, but when I try and tell you, you just give me the brush off.'

She shook her head, amused, surprised. 'No I don't Ken.'

'You blow so hot and cold.' He was speaking louder than he intended. 'I don't know where I stand with you.' He strode over and stood in front of her. 'I want to know how you really feel about me.' It wasn't going right.

She looked down and sighed. 'Ken, I like having you around, I like having you in my bed.' Lifting her head again, her gaze was on him once more. 'Isn't that enough?'

'It's not enough, Maggie. You're more to me than that. Can't you see that?'

'For pity's sake, Ken.' Her voice was steady, 'after everything's that happened since Charlie died. I've had to work it all out for myself. I can barely breathe with all I've had to cope with.' She was going to push him away again, he could see it. But she was right. What was the matter with him? His anger began to fade. Almost every moment since

Charlie died had brought some new twist. Charlie not even in the ground yet. And yet he'd somehow come to believe this thing he had with Maggie would replace everything he'd once had with him – everything Maggie'd had with him. He sat down on the bed beside her.

'I'm sorry – .' He didn't even know what he was sorry for. His selfishness? His blindness? His stupid belief that he meant as much to her as she did to him? 'I just wanted to find out if you – ,' he broke off again.

'Find out what?' she said. 'If I'm leading you on – is that it?'

'Yeah, somethin' like that.'

She put a hand on his shoulder. 'Ken, you're a lovely boy. But I don't want to be your mother.'

He jerked his shoulder away in surprise. 'What?'

'It's who you're really looking for, isn't it – that face in the photo you keep in your wallet?'

He stared at her. In this half-light the resemblance was strong; her hair, her face, the shape of her lips. Where had this come from? She'd homed in on the darkest place in his night-time thoughts, and she was prodding it. Was she playing with him – manipulating him, using it as a way to throw him off? Maybe she was right. He'd been alone all his life, didn't even know what having a mother felt like. When he looked at the photo in his wallet he was looking at the only history he had, where he came from. And it hurt him to look, to stare at that face. But he could never see behind the photo, never know what went before. He knew nothing about his mother, what kind of person she was, or why she'd left him. He never had, and he never would. So now, facing up to the question she was asking, here, in the dim light of the fading day, he knew it wasn't true. The Maggie he wanted was the Maggie in front of him, not the ghost in the picture. He shook his head, more determined to get through to her. 'No Maggie. It's not about her, it's about you. You're the one I love. I know what love feels like.'

'Do you?' She gazed back at him, her face softening, her blue eyes catching the light.

He found himself sliding off the bed and onto his knees in front of her. He took her hands in his. 'I'm on fire for you.'

'You're so sweet Ken. But you shouldn't burn so bright.'

It was that lilting, inviting voice. Her words pushed him away while the voice drew him on. He gazed up at her. She was doing it again – casting her spell.

'With you, I can't help it.'

'It'll fade away, Ken. Nothing lasts.'

'You have my soul – can't you see, Maggie?'

She lifted her hands to his face, caressing it, holding it. She smiled at him. 'You're lost aren't you?'

'Lost in you.'

'You shouldn't.'

'I want to.' He searched her face for signs of the love he sought. Her smile was soft, gentle. But her eyes. In them was the look, the one he'd seen that night – Charlie's body laid out in the bedroom and her watching him over her glass. She was drawing him in again, bewitching him. Drawing him so close that the Maggie he was in love with could melt away and vanish before his eyes, like mist, leaving some other unknowable version of her. And he was going to be left dangling once more – if he let her. But he wouldn't let it happen. Not this time. Because what was in those eyes he couldn't put into words, but it sparked a strange unsettling feeling. It was running down his spine right now, almost making him shiver. It stopped him in his tracks, his train of thought lost. And then he understood. What was in those eyes was a secret; one he had to know if he was ever to really know her at all.

'What really happened the night Charlie died?'

She drew back from him, her face closing down, the mask she wore so often sliding back into place. But her eyes stayed on him. In the darkening room he felt them pierce him.

'Do you really want to know?'

He hesitated before nodding.

* * *

She sighed as she got up and took her coat off, then bent to plug in the little electric fire. Walking round the bed, she lay down on the other side, not looking at him, but instead staring at the stain on the ceiling. She was silent for a while, arm across her forehead, weighing her thoughts. Then she began to talk, her voice flat, neutral, as if she didn't want her feelings to show.

'I went for the job at the shebeen. The minute I saw him I could see he was handy with his fists. He was big and strong, alright, but the way he carried himself, there was no mistaking it. He'd lay about him if you so much as looked at him the wrong way.

'It was easy. He hadn't a clue. I told him about my imaginary experience of bar work and he hired me on the spot.

'I wasn't wrong about him. You know what he was like. Any trouble in the shebeen he'd be there in a flash and he'd beat the bejesus out of the lot of them – black, white, blue or green, he didn't care, they'd be out on their backsides before they knew what hit them.

'He was a drinker, and that was something I knew about from home. I had five older brothers and an old man that all drank like fish. It was a bad place to be on a Saturday night after the pubs shut. Daddy and Mammy'd be at it hammer and tongs, the boys would take sides; there'd be fist fights. I couldn't tell you how many fights I saw in that kitchen when I was growing up.

'I was the skivvy – the only girl in the family. So for me it was cooking, cleaning and clearing up after the men while they were out on the farm or away at the pub, and Mammy feeding her chickens or praying on her rosary. It was no life at all, so the minute I could, I got out. Packed a bag the night before market day and hid it under the bed. Then as soon as the men all drove off I jumped on Mammy's old bike and rode it twelve miles to the station to catch the only train of the week up to Dublin. When I saw Dun Laoghaire disappearing into the distance behind the ferry the only thought in my head was 'good riddance'.

'They always said they'd come after me. It was no secret I wanted to get out. I'd throw it in their faces when I got mad. 'I'll be gone. You'll have to clear up your own mess.' In Ireland women are there to serve the men. It's the Catholic way. The priest'll tell a man to chastise his wife if she doesn't obey him, and women who escape'll be dragged back by force if they're caught. So when I got to England I made sure I steered clear of the Irish. If word got back they'd be over for me. But I was always on the lookout for protection. It was my good luck that I met Charlie a few months after I got off the boat. Or it seemed like good luck at the time.

'He took me to Brighton for a night. We stayed in a big hotel. It was going to put the seal on our affair. I wasn't a virgin. I'd lost that to a lad called Eamonn who came to the next farm to bring the hay in when I was seventeen. He was great – knew what he was doing. We were at it nearly every day out in that field. God knows what happened to the hay. We weren't very careful the first few times, so it's a wonder I didn't fall pregnant. I'd be skivvying for him now if I had.

'It didn't go well in Brighton. I thought we'd just go to bed but Charlie wanted to see the sea and get something to eat and then have a drink. When we finally lay down together he wasn't ready. We did it in the end but it felt more like work than fun.

'Anyway, it was enough for me. Life was great compared to what I'd had at home. The club was doing well, and even with Charlie drinking so much of his takings he always had plenty of money and didn't mind spending it. When you're as poor as we were on the farm, money matters to you. I took an interest in the business and got to know Ernie. He turned out to be well in the know about business and had plenty of contacts. I wanted to learn all I could just in case I needed it in the future. Then Charlie proposed and I jumped at it. If the family ever showed up, he'd boot them straight back to the bog where they belonged.

'Things were fine at first. We got the flat. It was bigger and cleaner than anywhere I'd ever seen. We were up high, looking out across London. It's a sight I'll never get tired of, all the buildings and the cars and the people. And I had clothes – I'd never seen the like of in my life. We were going to get a phone and a television. Charlie was thinking of buying a car.

'In bed, Charlie was alright, but he was no Eamonn. It didn't seem to come naturally to him. I knew he grew up in a kid's home but he didn't tell me much about it then. It was only later on that he talked about what had happened to him there. So I put it down to the drink. But things got worse, and he'd get mad with himself sometimes if he couldn't do it, and then he'd get mad with me. The first time he hit me he knocked me unconscious. I couldn't go out for a week till the bruise went down. After that it got to be more often. I'd half expected it would happen sometime. It's how it is in Ireland. A man's not a man unless he gives everyone around him a few thumps now and then, especially his wife.'

An image of Charlie came to Ken. The fearsome way he

fought when there was trouble in the shebeen – the way men fell and didn't get up again after he'd hit them. No-one would want that Charlie coming at them. Maggie's voice brought him back. It had dropped low, as if she was getting to the part that mattered.

'But there was more to it with Charlie. It wasn't just anger or drink than made him hit out, it was something deeper. I started to wonder if he might be queer. I'd read about such things in the Sunday papers. Then one night, instead of hitting me he started to cry. That was when he told me about the goings-on in the home. It made me sick to listen to what those bastards did to him. I realised then that when Charlie married me he was doing his best to be normal, to live like a normal man, but it wasn't working. But it didn't help me. In fact it was the beginning of the worst part of all.

'The first I knew of it was the next time he was drunk. He came staggering in and I could see there was something different about him – a coldness in his eye. He put his finger to his lips. 'Keep it sweet,' he said. I didn't know what he meant.'

An unsettling ripple passed through Ken. Those words – they seemed familiar.

'He got hold of me and pushed me into the bedroom. I wasn't sure what he was going to do but I took my clothes off and stayed ready for a punch, but he threw me face down on the bed and next thing I know he starts to shove himself up my back passage. The pain of it was terrible. He was tearing me in half. I let out a scream but he pushed my face down into the pillow. He was strong as an ox. I was suffocating and he kept on shoving. I thought I was going to die that night. I'll never forget the pain of it. I passed out and thank God I did.

'That was the new Charlie. Somehow, letting out all that stuff he'd been keeping inside seemed to turn him. It was as if he'd become one of those bastards from the home. He would beat me and bend me and do that to me. The things he did, I couldn't even tell the priest. And it wasn't rage or drink any more, it was pleasure. He was never happier than after a night torturing me. He'd be up the next morning whistling and smiling and out of the door with a spring in his step. Then he'd come back later with a few flowers or something he'd picked up from the market and say sorry. As if that could make it right. I could see he meant it at the time though. It was like living with Jekyll and Hyde.

'It must have been a year ago all that started, and I spent every second thinking about how I could get out of it. When he walked out of the door I was like a bird let out of its cage. When he came back, it was like having a black mask pulled down over my face. I couldn't go back to Ireland that was for sure. I could hide in London if I could afford a place to live. But I didn't have any money of my own.

'Right from the start I thought about killing him. After one of those nights I wanted to see him lying on the floor bleeding to death. In my mind I'd bring the knife down on him a hundred times. But even in middle of the blackness, I knew he couldn't help himself. I'd have to be blind not to see he was driven by demons. It was his cross to bear. It wasn't his fault what happened to him, but there was nowhere to go for help. I begged him to go to a doctor, thinking maybe he could get some tablets to straighten him out or something. He said he would, but he never did. He didn't want people to know what he was like. The more I thought about it, the more I realised killing him was the only way. The shebeen'd be mine then, and I could work with Ernie to make a go of it. I'd need to put someone in the front to keep order, but Ernie had contacts. Putting Charlie out of his misery would be a mercy for us both.

'But I didn't want to get caught, so no knives or scissors or anything like that. It had to look like something different. I had an idea. We had a great aunt in Ireland, Aunt Bridey, whose husband had died young, not long after they were married. They said it was the drink. She wasn't exactly all there and she'd sometimes say she'd killed him. People said she was a witch, but we all thought it a great joke from the crazy old woman. Then one time, when I was fifteen, I was over at her place on my own and I asked her about it. She said it was true. She didn't like the beatings he used to give her when he was drunk so she poisoned him and nobody suspected anything. They just put it down to the drink. She's still alive now, although she must be in her eighties. So I wrote to her and asked her advice. I told her to write back to a post office so she wouldn't have my address, just in case. Back came a letter from her. If she wasn't right in the head when I'd last seen her, she seemed to have improved with age. Her letter told me exactly what to do. It was a poison from a flower called Monks Head, and if you did it right, a doctor would just think a drunk man had died on his own puke. She even put a few of the dried flowers in with letter. It was that simple.

'Charlie was drunk most nights, so I had plenty of chances. If I didn't get it right the first time I could try again. But I didn't need another go. It all went off as smooth as you like. He nearly always wanted tea when he got back. I just put some of the flowers in with it. He took bad straight away, lay down on the bed and started twisting and puking. Then his voice went and his breathing got slower. I think he knew he'd had it then, I could see it in his face. He passed out. He was dead in half an hour. I watched him the whole time and I didn't feel a thing. I just rolled him over so his face was in his sick and went out to call the ambulance.'

So there it was, spelt out for him in every last detail. She really did kill Charlie. A darkness fell on him, thick and oppressive, pressing on his chest, and a sick feeling rose in his stomach. This woman lying quietly on the bed had murdered his best friend – poisoned him after all. But the police report found nothing.

But she wasn't done with her story yet. She was still talking.

'I wanted him cremated to be on the safe side, so that meant two doctors had to take a look at him. They both said the same. Died inhaling his own vomit while under the influence of alcohol. They saw it all the time in the East End.

The death certificate was issued, and the funeral arranged. I felt light as a feather. God was smiling on me.'

She turned her head and looked at him, reached a hand in his direction. 'And then there was you, Ken – sitting there looking like a peacock in your yellow shirt. You always were a good looking lad. Everything about you said ladies' man. The way you looked me over without even thinking about it. The way you sat on the edge of the chair, like a cat ready to sidle up and rub yourself against my leg. I knew all about you, your long list of girlfriends that you lived off – Charlie told me. I suppose it must have been the relief of it all – getting away from what Charlie put me through, starting a new life, or maybe it was just never having any real – you know – when I was with Charlie, but I wanted you there and then. I've never felt it so strong as I did that night when you came over and sat on the settee next to me.'

She turned her face to the ceiling again.

'Why in God's name the Dolmans got involved I just don't know. Charlie and Hazel hardly ever wrote, never mind met. When the bloody coppers appeared at the crematorium I couldn't believe my eyes. Then they took me down to the station and started asking me if I'd killed him. I was sure they were onto me. I thought if they do any tests I'm done for. I was in a panic. So when you told me they didn't find anything I nearly passed out.

'But that wasn't the end of it. I knew nothing about his debts either. Looking back, I suppose it was too good to be true, the money he got through, as well as the drink. Now look at me. I thought I was escaping from a cage, and all I've done is climb into another one.'

Silence filled the room. All the way through her story, an aching sadness had been building inside him. This was Charlie, the one he'd loved, his guardian angel. He still couldn't square the picture she was painting of the man he'd been so close to. But it all made too much sense now. The way Charlie had cooled towards him when he married Maggie; the bruises he'd seen on her back; the anger. He felt like he'd been slapped awake from a long, deep sleep.

She swung her legs off the bed and stood up, facing the wall, as if bringing herself back from the place she had been. She walked round the bed and stood in front of him. 'There, now. There's the real Charlie for you. Did you get what you wanted?'

Her voice seemed far off. He looked up at her. He felt his mouth move, but no words came. He was shrinking, the lights grown dimmer, as if the person he used to be was fading out of the world altogether. He slowly shook his head.

'How could it be?' he asked, finally.

'You were there, Ken. You tell me.'

She was putting her coat on again, picking up her bag.

'Where are you going?'

She looked at him, a strange, weary smile on her face, before opening the door.

'Confession,' she said. 'It's time I did. God will forgive me, even if you won't.'

CHAPTER 13

A thick, misty rain drifted up the darkened street, slicking the pavement and the passing cars. The cold air felt fresh and clean after the warm fug of the room. After she'd gone he'd stayed on in the darkness for a while, thinking; not thinking. Then out of nowhere he'd started crying. He'd kept it up for a long time, an engine of tears he couldn't stop. He had lost Charlie twice over.

His instinct was to do his usual thing – wander aimlessly in the streets and let his mind drift, but it was too wet. He started walking. Whitechapel Road was quieter than usual, the rain keeping people inside and giving the street lights a hazy yellow glow.

He didn't want to be in the room and when Maggie came back. What he wanted was to lie down in a safe place and be alone. Somewhere he could curl up under a blanket and block out the world. He had to find somewhere. Maybe Betty? No, he felt defeated and didn't want to face her. There was Lucy, if she was sober enough. Maybe she could fix him up. He found a phone box. But he'd guessed right. She wasn't sober, slurring incoherently and dropping the phone before his money ran out. His old life seemed to be pushing him away.

He started working his way through his mental list. Shoving

his hands into his pockets to find some more coins, he felt something metallic and pulled it out. It was the key to Maggie's old flat in Stifford House. It would be dry and warm there. He could be alone for the night. It was exactly what he needed, and it was only around the corner.

But there was something else he had to do. There was a rage stirring in him. If Charlie had become a monster, then those fucking bastards in the home made him that way. And they were going to pay. The diary was the answer. It would bring justice for Charlie and save him and Maggie too. Now he'd met Baldwin, he knew how vital the thing was. To the scumbags in it, it was priceless. He pulled out the scrap of newspaper Davis had scribbled his number on and dialled it. It rang for a long time before someone finally answered.

'Brian's Turf Accountants,' said a woman, a buzz of voices in the background. A betting shop – and open at this time of day?

'I'm looking for Davis – the cop.'

'Who wants him?' A sharp, tinny voice cut across her; 'They're out!' The only racing after dark was the greyhounds.

'Ken.'

'I'll see if he's in.'

The racing commentary ran on, an almost continuous list of dogs and positions.

'Hello?' Davis's voice was almost a grunt. When they'd last met he'd been on the chasers at eleven in the morning. God knows how pissed he was by this time of day.

'It's me, Ken.'

'Ken?' said Davis uncertainly. Was he too drunk to remember? Then his tone changed. 'So you've come to your senses have you?' He was sobering up fast.

'I dunno if I have. I'm about to trust a cop.'

'I don't expect you'll make a habit of it.'

'There's a problem, though.'

'Here we go.' Davis's voice took on the impatient tone Ken knew from previous meetings. 'What now?'

'I need money.'

'For fuck's sake, is that all you can think about?'

'It's not for me.'

'Who then?'

It wasn't any business of Davis's, but it might help close the deal.

'Maggie. Charlie left her some debts.'

'Debts? Who with? No-one legit's going to lend to someone like him.'

Davis was sharp.

'Ever heard of the Krays?'

Davis was silent for a couple of seconds, the commentary in the background slowing as the race finished. 'Are you fucking joking?'

'I wish I was, man.'

Davis sighed, long and deep. 'Jesus fucking Christ. How much does she owe?'

'Seven hundred.' Might as well work in a little extra.

'That's a lot.' There was another pause. Davis seemed to

be thinking things through. 'OK, tell you what. Meet me and give me a few pages of the good stuff, so I've got something solid to show them. If it's as good as you say I should be able to swing it.'

Ken's heart flipped. He'd done it.

'Make sure there's something about Baldwin in the pages you bring.'

'OK. Where can we meet?'

'Remember the first place we were supposed to meet – when I couldn't make it?'

'Yep.'

'That's where.'

'When?'

'I'll need tonight to meet a couple of contacts – set them up for what's coming. I don't want to be holding that stuff a second longer than I have to. Let's say tomorrow morning at nine.'

'Have to be half past. I can't get to the diary till nine.'

'At least you're thinking straight now. Make sure it stays safe.'

'Ok.'

Ken replaced the receiver and stared at the phone for a couple of seconds. He smiled grimly to himself. Those bastards were going to suffer. Would Maggie be grateful? He wasn't even doing it for her. It was for Charlie and Hazel Dolman and all those poor lost kids he once knew.

* * *

He let himself into Maggie's old flat and wandered through to the living room, flicking on the light. Its brightness startled him after the cheap, low-watt bulbs favoured by their landlady. He stood briefly by the bedroom door and thought about Charlie, laid out there before the funeral that never happened. And he remembered the nights he and Maggie had shared the bed, until she'd sent him off again to sleep on the settee. Crossing the living room, he opened the door to the narrow balcony and stepped out into the hum of the evening. The space outside was sheltered from the worst of the rain, and the glow from the city spread out before him was comforting. He liked it up here, cut off but still part of the great, groaning beast that stretched as far as he could see.

Everything Maggie had told him was true, there was no doubt. He felt like a blind man seeing for the first time, blurred shapes coming into focus. Charlie had played the hero for him all these years, but inside he'd been ripping himself apart – trying to fight his demons and make himself normal. And Maggie got the fallout. But she was the wrong kind of woman. She wouldn't take that from anyone, not even Charlie. So she killed him. An act of mercy was how she saw it. Maybe. But it was cold and it was calculated – right down to the untraceable poison. And God would forgive her.

And yet they were two of a kind, her and Charlie. That was the attraction at the start. Maggie wanted someone tough and they didn't come any tougher than Charlie. But Charlie's strength came from the rage inside him, Ken could see that now. When it came to the thing that really mattered, the sex, Charlie had nothing for her. But Charlie never had a problem being with him. Maybe he was the one person Charlie could be real with – the one who was different to everyone else. Ken – always the exception to everything – neither black nor white, queer or straight; a darling to them all, but always on the outside. He was everybody's favourite half-hour. But no-one wanted him to stay – except Charlie. Charlie had loved him and saved him. Charlie killed Ian. Maggie killed Charlie. That chain of events didn't change anything about how Charlie had been with him. But what was Charlie's true face? The one he knew, or the one Maggie saw as Charlie pushed her into the bedroom?

And Maggie. On top of all the other things he felt for her, he now felt sorry for her. This world of real feelings had been fresh ground for him, but he was starting to find his way. He'd been out of his depth with her right from the start, behaving like a kid with a crush. Now he understood, he could forgive her for killing Charlie. But he also understood what was in her eyes last night, and it wasn't love. He didn't want to think about it anymore, needed to let his mind rest.

But there was something else floating around in his head – something still out of reach. Those words Maggie came out with, the ones Charlie used: 'Keep it sweet'. He knew them.

A noise from the corridor. At the front door a chain was rattling, or a set of keys. Someone was trying to get in. His body's reaction was faster than his brain – way faster. Before he knew it, his legs had flung him across the living room and into the darkness of the kitchen, his back pressed against the wall as whoever was out there scraped and worked at the lock. But everything around him said it wasn't enough; not dark enough; not hidden enough. The panic churning in his guts told him so. The sudden bang of the front door against the wall told him so. A surge of fear sent him climbing blindly – up onto the draining board – up again, scrabbling onto the dirty, dusty top of the big cupboard above the sink, sweat already drenching his body, his trembling fingers slippery as he heaved himself up. And then he was wriggling and squeezing, squeezing his skinny body tight against the wall, back as far he could make it go. He wanted to be small, to be invisible; to be nobody.

The kitchen light came on and someone walked in. Heavy breathing, and the sound of the cupboard door sliding back. Then steps out again to the living room. Doors opening, closing. Thumps, and then a crash from the bedroom. The balcony door flung open, glass breaking.

'What you got?'

He knew that voice. Mr Elegant.

'Nothin'.' It was Trilby.

'Wha? Don't give me nothin'. Someone turned that light on.'

The light in the living room. It had sent a beam out across London to anyone watching. And someone was.

'You find the bitch, then.'

'Maybe that half-nigger's here.'

'Not 'less he turned invisible.'

'Check that balcony again. Somethin' to hide under?'

Silence. An age of seconds crawling by. Then a sound next to Ken's ear – a single sharp, rending sound. The sound a kitchen cupboard makes when it begins to part company with the wall. Silence again. Someone came to the door, paused. He held his breath, afraid that even the movement of his breathing might bring the cupboard down.

'Nope.' The distant voice of Trilby. 'Coulda climbed around onta the next balcony. Or down.'

'Shine a light.'

'Don't have no light.'

'You got a fuckin' match dontcha?'

'In this wind? Come and look for yo'self.'

The two of them talking out on the balcony. Ken tried not to breath, almost crying with the effort. But another creak from the cupboard. It was going to give, he knew it. He thought of Maggie's God and tried praying to him.

Voices back in the living room.

'Musta climbed down. It's the only way.'

'Fuck it!'

'Let's get down there. Might catch 'em yet.'

Silence again, then Elegant. 'Forget it. If they climbed out, we've lost them. Gimme a cig.'

The scratch and flare of a match. More silence. Ken lay with his eyes shut, taking the slowest, most shallow breaths he could, concentrating on each one, each tiny act, making it as small and quiet as possible. This breathless, fearful, hiding.

It was – what was it? Deja vu. 'Keep it sweet,'– and suddenly he was there. The room downstairs at the home, the one at the back. He was sitting reading his cowboy book. So deep was he in it, he heard nothing until the door opened and they walked in, Charlie in the lead, laughing, pulling Sally behind him. And behind her came the voice of the fat man – the Councillor in the diary – Harshaw was it? The surprise on Charlie's face when he saw Ken – more than surprise, his laughter choked off – dropping Sally's hand, then he was lifting Ken by his shirt. Ken was travelling backwards, Charlie's big fist tight at his throat, holding the shirt. Charlie opening the cupboard in the corner and shoving him into it. And just before he closed the door on him, a little smile, a finger to his lips and those words: 'Keep it sweet'.

He always did what Charlie told him, so he stood there staring at the black door, its shape carved by a thin frame of light, and he made no noise. He didn't know whether to be afraid or pleased that Charlie was looking out for him. From the other side of the door came sounds. A low laugh from Harshaw, a bleat of protest from Sally, then Charlie's voice: 'Hold still.' Harshaw's deeper voice: 'Lovely.' Silence for a while, before he heard Sally again – a single word, drawn out into a frightened moan. Like she knew what was coming next – 'No'. His heart beat faster at the sound. Sally was his friend, but Charlie was his best friend. It was quiet. Then out of the silence came a grunt, followed by another and then another. The air gradually filled with them, growing louder and faster until there was nothing in Ken's ears but their continual, repeating rhythm. He was afraid now. He didn't know what was happening but he trembled at the sounds that were coming from this grown-up. He raised his fist to beat the door – let them know he was there, but he couldn't do it. Instead he put his hands over his ears and felt the piss run down his leg and into his shoe, warming his foot. But he didn't move, didn't make a noise, keeping it sweet for Charlie.

After it stopped he heard Harshaw give a big sigh and then say; 'you can run along now.' The sound of the door to the room opening and closing.

'She doesn't like it yet, does she?' Harshaw.

'Not yet.' Charlie.

'Another few weeks, she'll be great.'

'Yeah. Takes a while to break them in,' said Charlie.

'Our noble lord's going to love her,' said Harshaw. 'I hope he doesn't get carried away like the last one. Spoils it for everyone.'

The strip of light around the door went black, and Ken stayed there in the dark, listening to the silence until the piss in his shoe made him shiver with cold.

* * *

'Boss'll be mad,' said Trilby.

Ken opened his eyes and looked around for anything he could grab hold of, anything he could use that might lighten the load on the cupboard. He moved his head slowly and carefully. Nothing.

'If he finds out,' said Elegant.

'Wha?'

'You wanna deliver the news?'

'Fuck that! Why he so hot on her?'

'Hear the way she talked to him? Bitch don' respect the man, don' respect the culture. She got to be taught, man – Jamaican style.'

'I dunno,' said Trilby. 'Them Irish Paddies, they thick as shit, man. They don' learn.'

'Then she'd better fuck off back to where she came from – fast.'

'Yeah, she one o' them immigrants – needs to fuck off home. White nigger.'

They laughed long enough for Ken to catch a proper breath.

'Ok, then,' said Elegant. 'Let's get the fuck outta here. Turn the lights out, in case they come back.'

The kitchen light went out. Their voices faded as they left the flat. He listened, attuned for the smallest sound. The rumble of the lift door opening, closing. Then the slow tick, tick, tick of the lift dropping down to the ground, taking the danger away and letting his heart start beating, his lungs start breathing, and his face lift off a jagged splinter of wood he hadn't even noticed until then.

In the darkness, he began to slide over, inch by inch, trying to make himself lighter as he went. Moving his legs cautiously over the edge of the cupboard, he took a breath, ready to shift the rest of his weight, waiting for another creak.

When it came, it was a decisive rasp. Suddenly the cupboard dropped and he was hurtling towards the floor.

The explosion of glass, crockery and wood as he hit the floor made him freeze with fright, forgetting the pain of the sharp edges he'd landed on. How far did the sound travel? Who would come looking? He lay still, listening. He stayed there a long time, until eventually the broken pieces of glass and plate pressed too hard into him and he had to move.

He picked himself slowly out of the debris. His hands were wet, and he knew it was blood. But he couldn't turn a light on to look at the damage. That would be a bad idea. So he stumbled through the living room and found the door to the bathroom. In the pitch dark, he felt his way to the sink, turned on the taps and washed himself as best he could. The water stung him, and a couple of times he had to pick broken shards out of the wounds. But he was in one piece – he was still alive after his third close call with the Rudies. With Tommy and the Kray gang still to deal with, how much longer could his luck hold for?

He went out to the front door and inspected the lock. They'd picked it but otherwise hadn't damaged it, so he locked it again, this time sliding the bolt at the top of the door into place as well. Back in the living room, he pushed the broken balcony door closed against the cold and found his way to the settee. Laying down on it, he was hit by a rush of weariness, as if he'd been awake a thousand nights. But his mind still pumped with the terror of the evening. From that one little slip, they'd nearly got him. And if they had? They'd have beaten and smashed him until he gave up Maggie – and then they'd have got her too. The two of them would be dead.

* * *

A ghost of daylight was in the sky when he woke up. He hadn't meant to sleep. Even the smallest movement brought instant pain. He decided to lie still until it was bright enough to see by. No lights. The sleep had done something to him, though. He felt different – as if a switch had been thrown and the thoughts in his head were running down new tracks. It wasn't just what Maggie had told him. That memory from the home – Charlie, Sally, Harshaw – it sprung out of nowhere, and yet it had always been there. His image of Charlie had been torn to shreds, the way Trevor had ripped up the photos of his mother. Could he ever think about Charlie the same way again? The way Charlie lived his life, how he'd stormed at it; he'd wanted to live like a hero. But now the pictures of Charlie he had in his head were so different, he couldn't stick them together and see the same man. How did they fit, these two different Charlies? Jekyll and Hyde, Maggie called it. But did the bad kill all the good? Not for him. Somewhere in his heart, there was still a place for Charlie. He gritted his teeth and heaved himself off the settee.

There wasn't much he could do about the damage in the

kitchen. Clearing it up seemed a waste of time. They would probably never come back here. He looked at himself in the bathroom mirror and winced at the sight. There were cuts all over his body and dried blood smeared on his face. But when he was washed again and cleaned up, his face was the one part of him that had miraculously survived without obvious damage. He still had the sticking plaster where the bullet took out his earlobe and the bandage on his arm from the scolding, but he was still a pretty boy – from the neck up.

* * *

The cold morning air was sharp against the cuts on his hands. The damage he'd suffered felt oddly good to him. He wanted his body to feel as broken as he did inside. It was almost a pity his face wasn't smashed up too, so everyone could see his suffering. Because he knew now that he was guilty too. He'd buried the truth, blanked it. He hadn't done it deliberately, but that didn't matter. He'd done it.

He wandered down to the Whitechapel Road. The early morning rush filled the pavements. Men in donkey jackets and flat caps, flasks and sandwiches tucked under their arms, factory workers making for the eight o'clock shift, a long line of them queuing at the news kiosk outside the tube station. Instinctively he looked for the headlines but then checked himself. He wasn't sure he wanted any more news – if he wanted to burden himself with any more knowledge; any new pain. But then his eye caught the headline on the 'Daily Herald'.

'The Bodies in the Garden – Now it's Four,' it said simply. A national newspaper was carrying the story. The whole country was getting to hear about the house in Forest Gate where he grew up.

He joined the queue. It moved fast. Nearly every order was the same, twenty cigarettes and a daily paper. He paid for his paper and stepped aside to read the article.

'Police have revealed that a total of four bodies have been recovered from the garden of an East London children's home. An investigation into Bartlett House, in East London's Forest Gate, grew last night when the officer leading it announced that a further body had been disinterred from the grounds of the home. Commander Jack Baldwin revealed that the painstaking work has been under way for several days. He was unable to confirm whether the body was that of a child or if any of the other victims had yet been identified. Asked whether any arrests had been made, Commander Baldwin said enquires were currently centred on an ex-member of staff, one Ian Ferguson, whom they believe could assist them with their investigation. He appealed for Ferguson or anyone knowing his whereabouts to come forward. No further details were given.'

Ian Ferguson – the houseparent Charlie'd killed – the one Baldwin helped bury. And the first one they'd dug up. It didn't make sense. Or maybe it did. He was starting to see the picture. The cover-up was under way. Baldwin was steering the investigation away from himself and the others, and dropping the blame on someone who would turn out to be dead – or more likely just stay missing. That first body would never be identified. Baldwin held the torch now and he could decide where to shine it. He and his cronies were off the hook – and Trevor too, of course. Trevor. All these pages of reporting and so far there wasn't a single mention of his name.

He thought about the children he knew in the home again – Sally; Cliff; Sheila. Would they turn out to be the bodies? A sudden shudder of grief hit him and he stood amongst the morning crowd trembling, fighting to keep his face straight, his eyes clear. Forcing himself to move, he stuffed the paper into his pocket then found himself facing in the wrong direction. He had to get himself under control, think about what needed to be done.

He didn't have long before his meeting with Davis and he had to get the pages from the diary from its hiding place at the library. He had the advantage that he wasn't at the rooming house last night, so Davis couldn't follow him from there and jump him, if that was his intention. Taking a deep breath, he turned and headed back along the Whitechapel Road towards the library.

* * *

Commercial Road was quieter than he'd ever seen it, though he'd probably never been in it that early in the morning before. Now the rush hour was over there was no-one but a greengrocer setting out his display in front of his shop and a few old women wrapped up against the morning chill. Hardly a car passed down the normally busy road. A lone kid in short trousers and school blazer slouched across the road at the zebra crossing a few yards away. Ken turned into the narrow lane where he was to meet Davis and walked to the spot where he'd stood the other night. He stopped, breathed the morning air and looked around. On one side, under the railway arches, a car was being revved in a small workshop. Outside another, two men stood drinking tea from enamel mugs. On the other side, behind the wire of the school fence, the same kid was making his way slowly across the playground, late but still in no hurry to start his day. A diesel train trundled by on the track above him, hauling an endless line of wagons from the docks. He touched his hand to his breast pocket, where seven pages torn from the diary were tucked into his wallet, then checked his watch: A few minutes early.

The way the lane narrowed at the top near the main road gave it a closed off feel. What if he needed to run? He could get trapped here. He decided to go to the other end to see where it led. It was a dead end for vehicles, but off to the left was a narrow foot tunnel under the railway line. He walked into it, picking his way through the dog shit and pools of piss. On the far side was a silent street of terraced houses, a few still occupied, most of them empty and boarded up. More condemned slums ready for demolition. There was nobody around; not even a car parked in the road. So far, it didn't look like Davis had laid a trap for him. He wasn't going to part with anything until he was sure he'd get paid. Returning through the tunnel, he walked back up to the top of the lane where it joined Commercial Road. He found a spot where he couldn't easily be seen from the main road, but could keep an eye on the action around him. It felt a bit safer.

He ached from the bad night's sleep on the settee and the cuts and bruises of the fall from the cupboard. And that wasn't all. He was aching inside too. Maggie, Charlie, everything he'd learned. It was a deluge of pain. All this knowledge. Why did he have to know it at all? Standing there, he felt a weariness come over him, a bottomless hole opening up that he could drop into and keep falling. He wanted all this to be over, for Davis to take the diary away and make his little world well again – a world where he didn't have to keep constantly running and he could feel safe, away from everything. No more debts, no more thugs, and the past locked away again, where it couldn't reach out and grab him anymore.

In the distance, on the other side of Commercial Road, he could see the figure of a man walking fast. He watched him, knowing already it was Davis. As he looked out onto the main road from his position at the top of the lane, he noticed a green car parked opposite. Was it there before? He didn't think so. He checked it closely. The engine was running and the driver was sitting smoking a cigarette and reading a newspaper, his elbow propped at the open window. Ken was suddenly alert, looking for other signs that he was being ambushed, but the driver paid him no attention at all. If this was a trap, there would be others involved. He scanned the road. Nothing else had changed. The old women were at the shops, the road was still empty apart from a truck in the distance. Davis was nearly at the zebra crossing but still hadn't seen him in his concealed position. Davis began to cross, nodding to Ken after finally spotting him. Ken checked the car again. It was empty, but the engine was still running. The driver was on the pavement next to it. He was wearing a long gabardine overcoat and hat with the brim pulled low over his eyes, but he still wasn't looking in Ken's direction, didn't even seem to be aware of his presence. It was Davis he was looking at. He raised his folded newspaper and called out in friendly recognition.

'Malcolm! Malcolm Davis!'

Davis, halfway over the crossing, stopped and turned to see who was calling him.

When the truck ploughed into Davis, his head jerked back and exploded like an egg against the windscreen, his body flying up into the air like a sheet of newspaper on a windy day. Then he was somersaulting, bouncing onto the roof and rolling, rolling, banging down onto the flat bed of the truck before spinning off the end and landing with a soft, sickening thump in the road. The truck sped on, its window wipers working to clear a view through the thick red mess smeared across the cracked glass.

The man was already back in his car, crunching the gears and revving the engine. Then it accelerated away in the same direction as the truck.

Ken stood paralysed, his eyes fixed on the misshapen heap

in the road that used to be Davis. The blood was spreading out from the body in a thick, dark pool. So much of it. A man ran from a shop and stood over him. 'Fucking hell,' he said, then turned to the group of women who were cautiously approaching. 'Don't come any closer! He's a gonner.'

Turning away from the scene, Ken began to run down the lane, past the workshops and the school and the men with their enamel mugs, picking up speed until he was running faster than he'd ever done in his life. Through the tunnel and out into the streets beyond, he couldn't stop himself. He had to keep running – had to get as far away from what he'd seen as possible.

* * *

At the far end of the street a brick wall collapsed and a bulldozer reversed out of the cloud of dust it threw up. He stopped running. The bulldozer drove forward again, its caterpillar tracks clattering against the cobbles, thumped into another wall, bringing it down too. He bent double, hands on his knees, gasping and panting as he tried to get his breath. He had run alone through street after deserted street for what seemed like an age. He straightened up, still breathing heavily. Every part of him was trembling. Men with sledgehammers and pickaxes moved like ghosts through the haze up ahead. He made his way to a terrace of boarded up houses and slumped down on a doorstep.

What he'd seen kept repeating in his head. Every thump of the bulldozer into a wall echoed the sound of the truck hitting Davis, his skull cracking open, his body flying up into the air. He suddenly heaved and threw up, lurching forward, just managing to avoid getting it over himself.

The whole thing had been a trap – but for Davis, not him: The man in the car, calling out to distract Davis; the truck smashing into him at maybe fifty or sixty. They'd really wanted Davis dead. It had to be Baldwin. There was nobody else it could be. Davis was the thorn in his side, the one who could still be dangerous to him. But why hadn't they grabbed Ken? He was right there, with pages of the diary in his pocket. He thought back over the conversation with Davis on the phone. Neither of them had mentioned the name of the place they were meeting. So how did they know where to find Davis – where to lay the trap? It could only be that they'd staked him out. They knew where Davis lived, so it would have been easy to follow him and radio ahead to set it up. But they didn't know Davis was heading to meet him. They'd missed him – didn't even know he was there. It was luck, pure and simple.

But his world was coming apart, bulldozed like these streets. Everywhere he turned a building was coming down on him; Maggie, Charlie, now Davis.

Because now Davis was dead that left only him. He was the only one who knew where the diary was. If they got him, it was all over. Baldwin could tell any lie he wanted and sleep easy in his bed. That story in the paper would become the only truth there was. He still had the copy of the Herald in his pocket. He pulled it out and looked at it again. The story was getting bigger every day. The more attention it got, the more pressure there was on Baldwin for some kind of result. The newspapers were already asking about arrests. He'd had to come up with something to feed them. But it was a clever one. Ian, the little no-hoper who'd fallen under Trevor's spell, had been in the wrong place at the wrong time. He fitted the bill because he was dead and buried in an anonymous grave Baldwin was in charge of. He would carry all the blame, and what happened in the home would be swept away and forgotten about because there was nobody alive who would say any different. Baldwin had it all covered – all except the diary. And that was his lifeline. Anything that contradicted this careful telling was going to be lethal to Baldwin. If the diary popped up now, it left him nowhere to go. He'd committed himself to his story. Not so long ago the diary could have been dismissed as the fantasy of some kid with a chip on his shoulder. But now there were too many bodies coming out of the ground and the diary said one of them was Ian.

* * *

The Daily Herald offices in Fleet Street were smaller than most of the others papers. In his imagination Ken pictured a suspicious commissionaire at the door who he would have to talk round before he was allowed into some grand lobby. There was no commissionaire, or anybody else outside the door to the run-down office block that housed dozens of different businesses. It helped. He needed to keep his cool in this strange world, not let himself be treated like some doormat for them to wipe their feet on.

A spotty kid at the desk inside barely looked up from his comic as he told him to take the lift to the second floor. He pulled the gate across, pressed the button and felt the lift first lurch downwards then rise slowly with a groan.

Sliding the gate open, he found himself in a big open office scattered with wooden desks, each with a typewriter and telephone, and each with one of those rotating office chairs Ken had seen in films about newspaper offices. The difference between this office and those in the films was this one was completely empty apart from a girl with bleached blonde hair and heavy eye makeup sitting at the nearest desk, nail file poised. She was wearing a very tight white roll neck sweater that emphasised the size of her breasts and she was eyeing him with interest. Ken knew he was on friendly territory.

'Well, and who have we got here?' Her voice was a little squeaky and her accent was East End.

'I'm a man with a story,' said Ken.

'Men have always got stories. What's yours?'

'I'd love to tell you but it's kind of complicated.'

'They're always complicated too – usually involving a wife. You got one of those?'

'No, no wife, just a story.'

'What's your name?'

Ken thought for a second. 'José,' he said, pronouncing the 'J'.

'Oo, foreign then are you?

'Spanish.'

'I've just been to Spain – all inclusive. Met a Juan there. Didn't like the food. Got a lovely tan, though. Look.' She drew up the sleeve of her sweater to expose her forearm.

Ken studied it with polite interest. 'Very nice. Where is everyone?'

'Down the bar of course. You don't expect them to be working this time of day do you?'

There were three clocks on the wall behind her, telling the time in New York, London and Moscow. The one for London said eleven thirty.

'Can I see someone?'

The girl slid her sleeve back down, put on a pair of glasses and assumed a more business-like air.

'Crime, politics, sport or human interest?'

'Crime.'

She looked up at him. 'You involved?'

'No. Someone I know.'

Her expression changed – suddenly soft and serious. 'Be careful sweetie, money isn't everything.' She turned to a calendar on the wall beside her. 'Crime desk's Brian today,' she said. She glanced up at Ken, the sparkle back in her eyes. 'That's Brian Sedgeworth. He'll be in El Vino's, just down the street. They won't let you in,' she added meaningfully, looking him over again. 'Ask at the door. Tell them Karen sent you. That usually does the trick. Take care.'

Ken smiled and turned back to the lift.

'Oh, and José,' she called, 'if you're ever feeling lonely in this big foreign city, you know where to find me.'

* * *

Judging by the noise from the wine bar, there was a crowded session in full swing. As Ken arrived at the door, a pimply kid in a cheap suit, tie askew, was stepping out.

'Excuse me, I'm looking for Brian Sedgeworth.'

The kid cast an inebriated eye over him. 'What for?'

Ken smiled his best smile. 'Business. Karen sent me.'

The youth raised his eyebrows. 'Karen,' he said fondly.

'She said I needed to talk to Brian.'

The youth focussed. 'Ok.' He pushed open the door. 'Sedge!' he bawled. The hubbub inside dropped for a second. 'He'll be along. I've got to go.' The young man turned away. He made slow, unsteady progress into the alley beside the bar and began to throw up.

The door opened again and a middle-aged man with a big, heavily veined nose appeared.

'I'm Brian Sedgeworth,' he drawled, his fancy accent like those of the men he met in Regents Park. 'What do you want?' There was alcohol and cigarette smoke on his breath.

'I got a story.'

Sedgeworth looked him up and down, taking in his appearance and the cuts on his hands. 'If it's police violence, I'm not interested. They're ten a penny.'

'It's not.'

'We're a national newspaper. Is your story likely to be of national interest?'

'It's that kid's home. It's on your front page.'

Sedgeworth seemed to sober up.

'What about it?'

'I got information – stuff no-one else knows.'

'How did you get it?' He spoke deliberately and slowly. Ken wasn't sure whether it was the drink or the way public school types always talked to people like him.

'I was there when I was a kid.'

Sedgeworth studied him. 'And have you given the police a statement?'

'No.'

'What have you got?'

'A diary.'

'Yours?'

'No, someone else's – someone who was there too and knows what went on.'

'And you want to sell this, do you?

'That's right.'

'How much do you want?'

'Eight hundred.'

Sedgeworth burst into fake laughter. 'Impossible. We wouldn't pay that for Christine Keeler's diary, never mind that.'

'What then?'

'We could possibly manage a couple of hundred at most – if

it's any use to us.'

'Forget it.' Ken, heart beating, turned and began to walk. One, two, three, four, five, six steps.

'Wait,' called Sedgeworth. 'Let's go back to the office and have a proper look.'

* * *

They had been gone a long time. He was sitting in a little room gazing out through the glass at the office as it gradually came to life. The paper's Editor, Bill Faraday, a tall, bald rangy man of about sixty, had come in long enough to examine the diary, read a few excerpts and finish off the haggling. Ken had been nervous talking to these men, who bought and sold the stuff of people's lives every day, and he felt the breathlessness of a fish out of water as he did his best to hold up against their pretend indifference and puffed out cheeks. But he'd done his share of horse-trading too, out there on the park benches and in the arcades.

Once they'd understood what they were looking at, and realised he understood too, he got his price up to six fifty. It had to be more than they owed Tommy or it was a waste of time. He was here to get himself and Maggie off the hook – buy their freedom once and for all. And Baldwin was going to find out what it was like to be on the receiving end. Sedgeworth had taken careful notes about who was who in the diary. When they got to Lord Percy, Sedgeworth and Faraday exchanged a look.

The sight of Faraday handling the diary had made him

strangely sick. What was in it hadn't really hit him until he saw someone else reading it. The kids he'd known at the home, they were just strangers to this man. Not even that, faceless ghosts. Sitting in this office, watching him read about the things that happened to them made it all the more real. For most of those buried in the garden this diary might be the only thing that said they'd ever lived.

It was back in his inside pocket now and he felt better having it where he could protect it. Soon he would be handing it over for cash and it would be gone, lost to him forever. But it felt good – fantastic, in fact. He'd see quotes from it in the paper when they published the story. He imagined the shock, the angry voices calling for arrests. Baldwin was trapped. The story he'd invented would sink him. The truth was going to come out, not just about the home, but about Davis too. And he, Ken, was going to spring Maggie free from the Krays at the same time. The burden was lifting. His head was light with the thought of it all – the relief that this terrible time was nearly over. Life could start again. Maybe him and Maggie – . No. One day at a time.

He got up and wandered out into the office, hoping to pass the time with a little more flirting with Karen. It was busier now, with at least half a dozen people sitting at their desks, a gentle tapping of typewriters in the air. There was a different, middle-aged woman sitting at the reception desk, cigarette wedged in the corner of her mouth, hammering the keys of her typewriter as if she had a grudge against them.

Karen had disappeared – to lunch probably. Somewhere a phone was ringing unanswered. He didn't know where the other offices were – the Editor's; the Cashier's where they said they had to fetch the money from. There didn't seem to be any other doors except the one he came in by and a fire escape. Perhaps they were on a different floor. No-one took any notice of him as he wandered through the desks. There was a window by the lift and for want of something to do he went over and stared out of it. In the building opposite two attractive girls stood at the window, chatting and smoking. He tried to catch their eye but their attention was on their conversation. He wondered when the other papers would pick up the story, why they hadn't already. Had Baldwin only talked to this one? One of the girls opposite pointed at something and they both looked down into the street. He idly followed their gaze. Below him two police cars, blue lights flashing, were screeching to a halt in front of his building. Policemen jumped out and ran towards the entrance. Seconds later the lift groaned into life. He walked over to the fire exit, pushed down the bar and fled.

CHAPTER 14

There were more police bells ringing in the street as he walked as fast as he could away from the newspaper office, his collar up, head down. The bastards had shopped him. Baldwin was everywhere, just like Davis said. That must be why they'd printed the story in the first place – they were doing it for him; getting his version out there.

It was lunchtime now, the pavements busy with business types in suits, secretaries in office clothes. It helped, but only a bit. The bobbing sea of faces in front of him didn't have a single black or brown one amongst them. Fleet Street was white man's territory. A cop car sped towards him and he quickly turned and looked into a shop window as it passed. The window was full of hats. He could use one, and even if he couldn't afford one of these expensive-looking things, he could at least get off the street for a few minutes. He pushed open the door, setting off the bell that dangled from a coiled spring at the top of it.

The place was fitted out in dark wood panelling that looked as if it had been around for a hundred years. As the peal of the bell died away, a deep silence replaced it. There was thick pile carpet under his feet as he moved further into the shop. Hats were perched on faceless wooden heads scattered around on counters and stands, with more in little cubbyholes in the wood panelling. There were Deerstalkers and Bowlers, the kind of ridiculous things only toffs could wear. An ancient clock ticked behind the counter. He felt like he'd fallen down a rabbit hole. He seemed to be alone.

'Can I be of assistance?'

A small, thin man in his forties wearing a tightly tailored pinstripe suit seemed to glide towards him from the back of the shop.

'I was thinking about a hat,' said Ken.

'Well,' said the man, sweeping his arms around in a theatrical gesture, 'we have some.'

'You do,' said Ken, watching the man closely. His face seemed familiar.

'Does sir have anything particular in mind?' There was something theatrical in the voice too.

Ken cast his eye around. 'What do you think would suit me?'

'Hmm,' said the man. He began to walk around Ken, inspecting him, his hands pressed together like he was praying, the tips of his fingers tapping together. 'You're not really the bowler type, I think. Is sir wishing to impress on the dance floor, or seeking something more practical?'

'Something to help me fit in around here.'

'Of course.' The man wandered off to the shelves at the back. 'More of a fedora than a homburg I should imagine, then.'

'A wider brim sounds good, yes.'

'Always a good choice.' The man stretched a thin hand up and ran it along the brim of an olive hat. 'A Ferret Catcher?

Perhaps not – a little too jaunty.' He moved along and picked a darker felt one off a wooden head. 'A classic fedora. A serious hat. Perfect for keeping the prying eyes at bay,' he said, returning and presenting the hat to Ken with a small bow. 'Just right for when you're sitting on a park bench waiting for a discrete liaison.' He was smiling at Ken.

Of course.

Ken tried on the hat. The man wheeled a full length mirror over and they both stared at Ken's reflection in it.

'Very nice,' said Ken.

'Very. Pull that down over those dark eyes and you'll fit in anywhere.'

'I expect it's expensive, isn't it?'

'It is rather,'

'Are there any discounts available?'

'For valued customers, yes.'

'Maybe I could become one.'

'I don't see how.'

'Then maybe I could offer a discount of my own.'

'Well, nice to see the haggling come from the other side for a change.'

'What do you reckon?'

'I'll just put the closed sign on the door.'

* * *

Rollo, as the shop manager insisted Ken call him, had been generous, throwing in an umbrella as well against the heavy rain that had started falling. Ken, fedora pulled low, held the umbrella over himself as he ran across the street in time to hop onto the platform of a bus that was just pulling away. He closed the dripping umbrella, went upstairs and found a seat. There were more people sitting upstairs than down, all of them smoking, creating a thick warm fug that Ken felt safe inside. The rain steamed up the windows too, so it was impossible for any cop to see him from the street.

He was going to be late. Ernie would have called for Maggie by now. They'd be on their way to see Tommy. He'd have to catch up with them at the snooker hall. But he knew now what he had to do with the diary. There was no other choice. And he also knew it was far more valuable than any debt they owed.

* * *

The rain was heavier as he got off the bus. His hat and umbrella were no defence against the soaking his feet and trousers were getting. The wind was picking up as well, and he held the wavering umbrella tighter as he walked along Burdett Road towards Eric Street where the snooker club stood. Coming towards him in the distance was a woman, her own umbrella raised, and he knew immediately it was Maggie. She was alone.

When she saw him, she stopped, waiting for him to reach her.

'Ernie didn't come,' she said.

They stared at each other. Ken slowly shook his head. 'Done a runner?'

'I wouldn't blame him, but I'd thought better of him,' she said.

He did his best to keep his face neutral for Maggie, but he felt uneasy. If they couldn't rely on Ernie's connection with the Krays, what sort of reception were they in for?

Taking the diary from his pocket he held it up. 'I've got something to trade,' he said. They stood close together, their umbrellas forming an intimate shelter from the rain.

Her eyes were on him, uncomprehending. 'What is it?'

He realised there was so much to tell; Baldwin; the home; Davis's involvement. He'd kept so much from her. 'It's a diary Charlie kept while he was in the home. Everything that happened to him is in it.' He watched her as she took his words in.

'Everything?' she said.

He nodded. 'And every name. There's a big shot cop in charge of the case now – Baldwin. He's in here too. Maggie, they killed some of those kids in that home. Charlie was lucky to get out of there alive.'

She stared at the diary, mesmerized by it. 'Then you can't just give it away.'

'You remember that cop, Davis?' he said. 'I was going to hand it over to him this morning but he was run down by a truck.' An involuntarily tremor ran through him as the image of the impact flashed back across his mind.

'An accident?'

Ken shook his head. 'Deliberate. Someone wanted him dead.'

'What have you got yourself into, Ken?'

'I tried taking it to a newspaper. They just called Baldwin – handed me over to him on a plate.' He could see her working to take it all in. 'He knows I've got it. He'll kill again to get his hands on it,' he said. 'So I'm going to give it to Tommy. It'll pay the debt. It's worth a lot more than six hundred quid.'

'What good will that do?' she said. 'Charlie, those children, they'll get no justice that way.'

'It's the only justice they'll ever get,' he said. 'The Krays can use it against the people in here, Baldwin included.'

'There's got to be a better way,' she said.

'Baldwin's got himself in charge of the case. He's already put out a story laying the blame on somebody else. They're all going to get away with it.'

She looked at him then, one of those odd looks of hers, as if weighing up his worth.

He tried again. 'Charlie wrote all that stuff down because he wanted to protect himself from the filthy animals that turned him into the man you knew. The Krays, they can use this information. For them, this diary is as good as a hand on those bastards' throats – better. They'll make them get down on their knees and beg for mercy. There's no-one else to go to, Maggie, no-one else to help. They're all we've got.'

She looked away, pondering what he'd said, her mouth still set in a thin line and he knew what she was thinking. The shebeen. This way, she wasn't going to get it back.

'You owe it to Charlie,' he said, and realised he'd made a mistake.

She looked back at him, eyes blazing. 'I don't owe Charlie anything.'

'He suffered, Maggie. If you put a dog in a cage, torture him, beat him, teach him to bite, he'll bite. He couldn't help himself. We have to take the only chance we've got for him.'

She looked at the ground. Rain streamed off their umbrellas and onto the pavement, joining the flow of water across the pavement, down to the gutter and away on a rippling, bubbling river overflowing the edge of the road. She was thinking about the man she'd loved and the man she'd killed.

'Ok,' she said. 'But I'll get that shebeen back if it kills me. That was Charlie's too.'

Ken grimaced to himself. Right now, coming out of this alive was good enough for him, getting back at Baldwin a bonus.

'Maggie,' he said. 'It'll trap you. You'll be their prisoner.'

'I know.'

'You'll never get away from them.'

'Fine,' she said. That air of finality. He knew it so well now.

'Why do you want it so bad?'

"If you want it, take it.' Isn't that what he said? Well, I'm going to take it.'

He sighed. 'Revenge? Some things ain't worth the fight, Maggie.'

She looked at him, her eyes flashing again. 'I was born fighting and I'll die fighting,' she said.

* * *

The same man in the flat cap and sheepskin jacket stood sheltering inside the door of the snooker hall, still reading the

'Sporting Life'. He surveyed them and without a word, jerked his head, sending them up the stairs. They were expected.

Four of the snooker tables were occupied, their bright lights casting everything else into shadow. At one, Ken's previous pick-up straightened up and caught his eye, then seeing Maggie, threw his hands out in surprise. Ken, walking behind, just shrugged. The man rubbed his eyes with his fists to imitate crying and went back to his game.

Tommy lounged in the office chair behind the desk, back to the door, phone in his ear.

'...fucking made a hundred and fifty G's each out of that train robbery, didn't they? So where's our fuckin' cut he says. South of the river, I says. Well go and fuckin' get it, he says.'

Ken knocked on the glass of the door. Without looking round Tommy held up the splayed fingers of one hand.

'...so me and Davey tool up and drive over – can't find the fuckin' place. Didn't bring a fuckin' map did we? Might as well be in fuckin' Timbuktu.'

Ken stepped away. He didn't want to overhear anything around here. It could be dangerous.

They hung about listening to the sound of snooker balls striking until the call was over. Tommy spun round in his chair and faced them as they came in.

'Well, well, look who's here.'

Maggie sat down opposite him while Ken stood behind. Tommy looked Maggie over appreciatively. She returned a cold look.

'So where's my fucking money, then?' said Tommy.

'You know we haven't got it – Ernie told you,' said Maggie.

'Ernie?' Tommy made a pretence of trying to remember. 'That old shithead. Haven't seen him about.'

'He was here yesterday,' she said.

'Was he? I'll have to ask Chas on the door. Might have turned him away.'

'Why the game?' said Ken.

Tommy glared up at him. 'Who asked you, nig-nog? But since you have asked,' he said leaning back in the chair, 'then let's talk about games. That old tosser comes in here and starts pulling my pisser with some cobblers about giving me an empty lock-up instead of my money. Now that's what I call a game. And I don't fuckin' like it.' He got up from his seat and stepped round the desk. 'You're the only ones playing games round here. So now you're going to see where it gets you.' He put his head out the door. 'Ray! Get your arse in here.'

It was Ken's pick-up who came over.

'They want to know what's happened to the old geezer. Take 'em and show 'em.'

Ken's heart took a leap and started racing. Ray turned and strolled over to the stairs at the back of the hall that he and Ken had used on his last visit. Maggie looked at Ken, her face suddenly anxious. At the bottom of the stairs Ray turned down more steps to a cellar. In the small space at the bottom, the air smelt of something stale, something rotting. Ray struggled with a rusting padlock then smiled at them before throwing open the door. The stomach-churning smell billowed out at them. They both hesitated.

'Don't worry,' said Ray, 'it's not your turn yet. You're just here to look.'

Ken stepped in, Maggie following. He felt a dread rise inside him. The stench hit the back of his throat, nauseating and rancid. It was dark, and it took a minute for his eyes to adjust. There were low beams to dodge, and the floor underfoot was wet and sticky. But he could hear a snuffling noise ahead of him, like an animal in a pen. As he got used to the gloom, he began to make out a figure on the floor in the corner.

'Ernie!' he said. 'For Christ's sake.'

He was lying on his side, hands tied behind his back, feet bound together, a bloodied gag tight across his mouth, making him give out the strange grunting noises they were hearing.

They rushed over to him.

'Don't touch!' commanded Ray. 'Leave him alone.'

Ernie's face was barely visible beneath the encrusted blood. Only his eyes gleamed in the light from the door. He made a whimpering noise, then choked with the effort.

Maggie turned to Ray. 'For God's sake let him up. He's an old man.'

Ray just smiled grimly.

Ken looked at Ernie where he lay, his feet moving slowly backwards and forwards in a slick of blood and piss. He was barely alive. He must have been here since yesterday.

'Time up,' said Ray. 'Out you go.'

Maggie turned back to Ernie. 'We'll get you out Ernie. We'll sort this out.'

Then Ray's hands were on their shoulders, pulling them out of the room.

* * *

Ken made his way to a chair in the corner of Tommy's office and sat down. He needed its support after the sight of Ernie. His legs trembled and no amount of effort would keep them still. Maggie took the battered armchair.

'So, now you know,' said Tommy. 'You don't fuck with us. I don't know why it took so much to get that through to the old twat.'

'You're a bunch of bastards,' said Maggie quietly. Ken could see she was seething.

'Yeah, 'course we are. What did you think? We're some kind of fucking charity?' Tommy drew a cigarette from a pack, tapped it on his desk and lit it. 'So I'll ask the question again. Where's my fucking money?'

Ken got to his feet and stepped forward. He drew a breath. 'I got something.'

Tommy looked up at him. From his pocket Ken pulled the few pages he'd torn from the diary for Davis and placed them one by one carefully on the desk. The big man gazed at them for several seconds then picked one up and read both sides of it. He put it back on the desk.

'What am I looking at?'

'Pages from a diary.'

'Why would I be interested in it?'

'You read the papers? About that home in Forest Gate?'

Tommy nodded.

'The diary's the inside story – who was there; who the men were.'

'So?'

'There's some big names. One of them's the big shot cop at Scotland Yard leadin' the case.'

Tommy leant back in his chair, attentive now. 'Who's that, then?'

'He's called Baldwin.'

'Jack Baldwin?'

'Yeah, that's him,' said Ken.

Tommy seemed to stare through him, eyes focussed on something beyond him. 'Well I never,' he said quietly. Picking up the other pages, he read short passages from each. 'Dirty fucking bastards.' He glanced up at Ken. 'Who're these others?'

'A local councillor. A lord.'

Tommy raised his eyebrows.

'It's worth a lot to someone like your bosses.'

'What d'you know about my bosses?'

'They've been in the papers – meeting film stars. They're taking over places up West, getting to be big men.' Tommy looked impressed at this small piece of knowledge, so Ken pressed on. 'Might want a bit more influence to help things along.'

Tommy smiled. 'You're not as thick as you look, are you?'

'Got to be worth more than we owe.'

Tommy inclined his head noncommittally. 'If you're not feeding me a load of bollocks.'

'You know I'm not. You've seen what's in there. There's a lot more – years of it.' Ken could feel the diary in his inside pocket, next to his chest. He wasn't about to produce it.

Tommy stared at the pages in his hand, weighing up what he'd got. 'If I take it, I want all of it. Nothing held back for a rainy day.' He gathered the pages, folded them neatly and tucked them into his inside pocket. He glanced back up at Ken. 'That's the deal.'

Ken tried not to let the relief he felt show on his face. It was over.

'There's something else,' said Maggie sharply.

Ken sighed inwardly. Why couldn't she just let it go? He'd solved the problem.

Tommy grimaced. 'Women,' he said, raising his eyebrows at Ken. 'There's always something else.' He looked at Maggie. 'What?'

'First, let Ernie go. He'll die down there.'

Tommy pondered, then shrugged. 'OK. I don't need him anymore.'

'And I want my shebeen back.'

Ken's heart sank in his chest.

Tommy rolled his eyes. 'Don't start taking the piss. That place is your problem.'

'It's on your patch,' said Maggie.

'So what?'

'Oh, that's good, isn't it?' Maggie stood up, and Ken saw with alarm that she was winding herself up. 'So it's just women and old men you kick around, is it?' she said, her voice rising. 'No balls when you're up against someone who can put up a fight.'

Ken watched, his anxiety growing. Why was she doing this? 'Maggie,' he said, putting out a hand to calm her. 'Please.'

But Tommy looked like he'd been stung. He lifted a thick finger and jabbed it at her. 'Don't you start mouthing off in here, girl, or I'll give you a fucking slap!'

'A slap?' She gave a sharp laugh and took a step closer to the desk. 'It'd feel like a kiss from a poof like you!'

It was quiet. The rain had stopped. No-one seemed to be potting any balls at the snooker tables.

When Tommy spoke again it was slow and quiet and dangerous. 'What did you say?'

Ken felt like his heart had stopped beating. He wanted to grab her and run – run away as fast as they could. But Maggie wasn't reading any of the signals, wasn't giving any ground.

'There's a bunch of Jamaicans running my club in your territory and all you want to do is sit on your arse and count your bloody money,' she said scornfully, 'Some hard man you are.'

For several long seconds Tommy glared at Maggie. Ken wondered if the sky was falling, or maybe he was falling. Then Tommy said: 'Get rid of the old tosser and we'll adjourn to the board room.'

CHAPTER 15

Ken took off the overcoat that was Maggie's gift to him and threw it around Ernie's shoulders. He had no choice if they were to protect themselves from the blood and the shit that smeared his body and clothes. They supported him up the stairs of the cellar, out into the street. He was in a bad way, muttering and babbling, and barely able to lift his feet. They walked him as far as the nearest corner and let him down onto the pavement. Maggie stayed with him while Ken found a phone box and called an ambulance.

They watched the ambulance disappear into the distance, blue light flashing and bell ringing, and turned to make their way back to Tommy. Ken wondered how much damage Ernie had suffered, how much a man of his age could recover after a beating like that.

'Did you see the way his eyes lit up when you mentioned that Baldwin,' said Maggie, her thoughts already back to the matter in hand. 'He knows what he's got there.'

Ken focussed. 'Yeah, I told you, they'll make all those bastards squirm.'

'You did it, Ken.'

'And you nearly blew it.' He glanced at her. 'The shebeen.'

'No I didn't, Ken. I grew up with hard men. I know how

to handle them.'

He blinked away his surprise. A few Irishmen having a punch-up on a Saturday night was nothing like these men who could kill just because they felt like it. 'You sure about that?'

'So far.'

'Well maybe you should take it easy. The deal's not done yet.'

She turned and gave him a cold look. 'Don't tell me what to do. You got what you wanted. It's my turn now.'

* * *

They left the snooker hall and went down the road to a little Italian cafe. On the short walk Tommy and Maggie strolled side by side, with Ken following. He watched them. Tommy made some remark about growing up round here. Maggie asked him a question and Tommy replied, the hand with the cigarette curving through the air to emphasise some point. To a passing stranger, they might have been old friends, even a married couple. The big man held the door for her as they entered the cafe, pulled out a chair, a hand lightly on her back, helping her into it. Maggie was right. She'd won herself something back there in the office.

The cafe was empty and the three of them were squeezed around a small table that smelt of dirty dishcloth. The old woman behind the counter served them milky coffees in glass cups and saucers before disappearing into the back, leaving them alone.

Tommy spooned three sugars into his coffee and stirred. 'I

met him once,' he said, glancing up at Maggie. 'Charlie – sound enough bloke.'

Ken and Maggie exchanged a look.

'He can't help me now,' said Maggie.

Tommy nodded. 'Tell me about the business. What's the take?'

Maggie outlined the figures to him. Ken watched Tommy stifle his surprise on hearing just how much money flowed through the place.

'And Ernie had an idea about making even more out of it,' continued Maggie.

Tommy sighed. 'Don't talk to me about him. He talks a load of shit. I don't know why Reggie ever put up with him.'

'Say what you like about him, he's got a good eye for business,' said Maggie. 'Those Jamaicans had more stock in that place than you'd shift in three months. Ernie worked out why.'

Tommy's spoon hovered above his coffee as he waited for Maggie to speak.

'Stolen. Lorry-loads of it.'

Tommy's head went back at this revelation. 'So they're the fuckers pulling those hijacks?' he said quietly.

Ken got it straight away. Screw Face and his gang had been treading on toes without even realising it. 'Looks like they're pretty successful,' he said, rubbing it in. He wanted to help, but he still couldn't work out why Maggie was handing herself over to Tommy like this.

Tommy nodded. Sitting here at the table with them, he was more businessman than thug, and Ken watched him mentally calculating the value of what was on offer, just as he had back in the office with the diary. It felt like they were bargaining on equal terms, or as equal as it could ever get. But the news that Screw Face had been hijacking lorries on his territory brought a dangerous gleam back to Tommy's eye. He was a man never far from violence.

'They've got to be put out of business,' said Maggie fiercely.

Tommy raised a mollifying hand. 'You can take that as read,' he said. 'This is our turf. We own it.'

'So what are you going to do about it?' Maggie's tone was still demanding, still ready to quarrel.

'I can put a couple of lads on it,' said Tommy.

'Could take more than a couple,' said Ken. He stroked the sticking plaster over his missing earlobe. 'A bullet took that out.'

'Did it now?' Tommy rubbed his chin thoughtfully. 'Well that makes it more interesting then, don't it? We'll have enough horsepower for the job, don't you worry. But let's just get one thing straight. If that diary's any good, you've wiped the slate clean on what you owe. If we do this, then you owe us again. We'll start something new, a partnership. And when we go into business with partners it's for good. You got that?'

That was exactly what Ken was afraid of.

CHAPTER 16

They walked through the dark streets of Limehouse on their way to the shebeen. It was foggy again, but not as thick as that first night they'd made their way down these lanes by the railway arches together. Maggie had been distant since they'd made their pact with Tommy. She seemed keen to get tonight's action over with. Over the last couple of days she'd taken to complaining the little room they shared was too cramped, even suggesting it was time for him to find his own place again, and spending more time away somewhere. He tried to take it all in his stride, used to her constantly changing moods by now. But this new deal with the Krays, the events still to come, still had to be worked through. Once she had the shebeen back, maybe she'd be happier. He'd hoped the secret she'd shared with him – that she'd killed Charlie – would bring them closer together, and maybe in time, it would. But he wasn't sure about anything, and a feeling had been growing that something had changed.

At the top of the lane they stopped and waited. It was cold. Ken had only a jacket since he'd lost his coat to Ernie, and he shoved his hands into his pockets to keep them warm. Maggie was in her new overcoat and had treated herself to a smart new pair of leather gloves. She looked like a secret agent.

They looked round at the sound of a car engine purring softly towards them. A big Rover coasted to a halt, Tommy behind the wheel.

The doors opened and three thickset men in long overcoats got out. One he recognised as Ray. Tommy wound up the window and got out too. Ken had the impression there was still someone in the back of the car. Tommy was at the boot opening it. The others gathered round and Tommy began handing out pick-axe handles before finally pulling out a sawn-off shotgun. He cracked it open and loaded it, shoving two more cartridges into his overcoat pocket.

All this looked like regular business for Tommy and his three sidekicks, but the sight of the shotgun sent a chill through Ken. Since Charlie died, he'd been shot at, beaten, burnt and seen Davis run down and killed. But he hadn't started any of it. He'd been in the wrong place at the wrong time. He could claim no innocence tonight. He was involved. And it could get vicious. He remembered the fight with Mr Elegant – the pitiless look in the man's eyes. What was he even doing here? It wasn't his scene – he didn't want to end up in prison. The reason, of course, was Maggie. He glanced over at her. She looked as if she was born to it – completely composed. There was a steely glint in her eye. This was her moment, when she would repay the taunt from Shiny Head: 'If you want it, take it – if you can.'

'Right, gather round,' said Tommy. 'You two,' he jabbed a finger at Maggie and Ken, 'you're going to follow us down and stay outside by the door there.' He pointed down the lane. 'We'll see to the bouncer and go in and do the business. When we're done, you – ,' he said, indicating Maggie, ' – come in when I tell you. Not before.' He gave each of them a hard stare. 'Understood?'

They nodded at him, a small smile on Maggie's lips.

'You got the locks, Ray?' Ray produced two big padlocks from his pockets. 'Great. Should be a piece of piss. Let's go, then.'

Tommy led his men down the lane, Ken and Maggie following a little way behind. As they got closer, the men hid their weapons under their coats. Tommy put a hand up to stop Ken and Maggie going any further.

Outside the club, a lone doorman stood smoking. It was the same youth Ken had seen the last time they'd been there, and in between drags he was picking his teeth again. Tommy strode up and began talking to him. One of his men stepped smartly behind the kid and grabbed his neck with both hands, swinging him hard against the wall. The sound of his head hitting it reminded Ken of Maggie with the bolt-cutters – the heavy 'thunk' cutting through the misty air. As the boy bounced off the wall, a second man produced his pick-axe handle and struck the still-moving head with it, like a cricketer hitting a six. The boy dropped, out cold before he hit the ground.

Tommy pushed open the door and all four disappeared inside. Ken expected instant pandemonium, but instead it remained quiet apart from the gentle sound of 'Healing in the Barnyard' from Prince Buster. Seconds went by and became minutes with nothing happening.

'I'm going in,' said Maggie.

Ken reached out. 'No, Maggie. There's at least one gun in there.'

She brushed his hand away and went inside. Ken sighed and stepped through the door after her.

On the dance floor a few couples smooched. A young DJ sorted through his records by the speakers. In a corner three black men in trilbies and dark glasses shared a reefer. There was no-one behind the bar. Tommy and his men were nowhere to be seen. Maggie was making her way behind the bar. Ken went to follow her.

A shout and the brown curtain flew open, the scar-faced barman crashing through it, panic on his face. Behind him, one of Tommy's men, axe-handle raised, charged him and smashed it down on his head. Screams went up from the dancers. Scar-face stumbled into Maggie, trying to grab her for support. She stepped aside and let him fall. Tommy's man stood over him swinging the axe-handle. Down it came again, and again, and again. There were more screams. The music stopped and everyone made a run for the door.

Maggie moved on, pulling back the curtain and heading towards the desk where Screw Face and Shiny Head had mocked her. It was crazy. It was dangerous. Ken hesitated, but only for a second. He had to be with her. Maggie needed protecting, if only from herself.

Behind the curtain Ken made his way towards the light from the office desk. Up ahead he could hear Tommy's raised voice.

'I'm going to shoot your fucking balls off!'

As he reached the scene, a vision of hell opened up before him. Blood was spattered across the walls and ceiling. Face down on the floor sprawled the half-naked figure of Mr Elegant, his trousers round his ankles, bleeding from a long gash across his back. His face was a battered red mess lying in a spreading pool of blood, white islands of broken teeth sprinkled across it. There was more blood springing from puncture wounds across his legs. With an intake of breath, Ken saw that the pick-axe handle Tommy's man held had a nail through the end of it.

In Screw Face's armchair lay Shiny Head, also bleeding from a cut on his face, one of Tommy's powerful hands squeezing his throat, the barrel of the shotgun pressed between his legs. His hands were raised, either in surrender or a too-late attempt to defend himself. He was panting heavily, trying to get his breath as Tommy wrung his throat tighter.

In the middle of all this stood Maggie, calmly gazing down at Shiny Head.

'One twitch of my finger and they're all over the floor,' Tommy's growling voice continued. 'What're you going to do to stop me?'

Shiny Head struggled to get some words out. 'What d'you want?'

'I want your fucking boss. I want Screw Face so I can screw his fucking face to the wall.'

'He's not here,' gasped Shiny Head.

Tommy put his face closer. 'Well where the fuck is he

then?' he yelled.

'I don't know, man.'

'He don't fucking know, Mrs Ward,' said Tommy, suddenly addressing Maggie. He drew back from Shiny Head, releasing his hold on his throat, then smashed the butt of the shotgun hard into his face. Then he did it again, harder, the crack of breaking teeth making Ken wince.

'Well that's a message for him when you see him. And tell him this as well.' He pointed at Maggie. 'You see this Irish bird here?' Shiny Head's eyes flicked in her direction, his tongue running over his lips. Tommy smashed the butt into his face again. 'Are you paying attention? DO – YOU – SEE – THIS – IRISH – BIRD – HERE?'

'I see her.'

'She's called Maggie Ward. This is her club. She's under my protection. Even more important than that, she's under my bosses' protection. My bosses are the biggest bastards who ever lived. Even I'm frightened of 'em. They are going to be very upset when they find out I haven't tortured you to death. And if you and your boss don't catch the first fucking banana boat out of here that's exactly what's coming to you.'

Ken kept his eyes on Maggie. She had the same small smile on her lips, enjoying it all, the power she had over Shiny Head and his gang. But it wasn't her power. It belonged to Tommy and the world he lived in. What his thugs were doing to these small-time Jamaican gangsters they could just as easily be doing to Maggie – or him – if the whim took them. What had

Maggie gained from doing this deal? She was getting the club back. But at what price? Her own life could be in danger if she crossed these people, maybe even if she didn't.

As he watched, she reached into her bag, still smiling at Shiny Head, and drew something out. It took him a second too long to realise what it was. By that time she was pointing the revolver at the Jamaican's head.

'Maggie - !' he yelled.

For a frozen moment Ken, Tommy, and Shiny Head all stared at the gun, as if unable to comprehend its existence. Then came the flash from the muzzle and the deafening blast, and the shiny head exploded, fragments and blood spraying across Tommy, Ken, everywhere.

As the smoke cleared, she dropped her arm to her side, revolver still in her hand, and stood looking at the spattered body.

Tommy finally found words. 'What the fuck did you do that for?' It came out shocked and innocent, like a surprised schoolboy.

'You killed him,' said Ken, the words sounding stupid.

She looked at him. There it was in her eyes, unadorned and undisguised, the look he'd seen that first night after Charlie's death. The cold, deadly gaze, unforgiving and relentless. 'Yes,' she said simply, 'I've killed him.'

'Fuckin' hell!' said Tommy. 'We got to get this mess cleared up and get out of here.' He turned to Maggie, wagging a finger in her face. 'I'll sort you out later.'

He was on his feet, giving orders. They tore down the brown curtain, spread it out on the ground and began rolling the body into it.

Maggie stood watching calmly for a while before turning and walking away. Ken went to her, seeking contact, his arm reaching out for her. Without looking at him she pushed it away and kept on walking. He stared after her for a second or two as she receded into the gloom. She was somewhere else, somewhere unreachable, as she had been so often since he'd known her.

* * *

The sight of it all sickened him. The broken bodies, the blood, the pulpy mess of Shiny Head's face – he had to get out. He turned and left it behind, back through the bar and the dance floor, a hiss filling the air where the DJ left the last record rotating on the turntable, and out into the darkness of the cobbled lane. He stopped, steadying himself against a wall, gratefully drawing down lungfuls of the cold, clean night air.

He was in the company of animals, savages. He had no place here – wanted no part of this rotten, stinking world of theirs. It filled him with nausea. And Maggie? He drew a hand across his face and found it slick with sweat. She was worse than any of them. That gun – she must have picked it up the night she'd saved him from Mr Elegant, hidden it away somewhere. She'd used him, used them – got what she wanted and left them to it. He needed to go after her – confront her.

Find out how much of a game she'd been playing all along.

As he went to move off he felt a hand on his shoulder. Looking round he found Ray staring at him.

'Someone wants to meet you.'

Ken shook his head. 'Not now.'

Ray grabbed his arm – tightly, and shook his head in turn. 'You don't say 'no'.'

Ray steered him to the Rover and opened the rear door. Ken could make out a bulky form inside. Ray jerked his head for Ken to get in, closing the door behind him as he slid into the seat.

'Hello Ken,' said the man next to him. 'I hear you're a bit of a shirt-lifter, just like me.' He reached a big, manicured hand across for Ken to take. 'I'm Ronnie Kray.'

CHAPTER 17

The statue of the Virgin Mary was gone. The Christmas lights glowed around the empty space. Ken went to the battered wardrobe and opened it. Only his own clothes hung there. He stood for a moment, fazed.

He had a sudden sense of sinking into quicksand. He sat down on the bed and put his hands to his temples to try and stop his head spinning. Time seemed to slow down, each second taking an age to pass. He could feel nothing but an ache in his chest. He didn't know what to do next, so he stood up again and looked around the room, as if seeking more evidence of her absence. And that evidence filled the room. No coat, no shoes, no stockings. No Maggie.

On the dresser stood the vase with the bunch of flowers he'd bought her, withered and lifeless now, and beneath, propped up against it, the photo of the two of them, standing in the street in Roman Road market. She'd bought it for him to cheer him up. It was the only thing left of her in the room. He picked it up and studied her face, the dark hair, the smile, fresh from the joke they'd just shared, her eyes, laughter lines around them, clear and beguiling, looking straight into the camera. He pulled out his wallet and picked another photograph from it; his mother. He put the two pictures side by side. They didn't look that much alike after all, except for the smile. That was the same. But the look in their eyes was different. His mother's was so warm – fresh and honest, maybe even a little young and naive. Maggie's drew you in, complicit, inviting, dangerous.

He knew without even going there she wouldn't be at the old flat in Stifford House – knew already he would never see her again. The bullet into Shiny Head's face had been a final act for her. She'd walked away forever, leaving behind him, Ernie, the gangsters, the police – everybody. And the strangest thing was she could have done it any time. But she'd stuck around long enough to face them all down, make sure she'd won every fight. What had she gained? She didn't want the shebeen back, she wanted revenge. For what? They'd taken the place away from her and rubbed her nose in it – humiliated her. That was all. But there was a well of vengeance in her that ran deeper than he could ever have imagined. 'I won't let you beat me,' she'd once said, and she'd been true to her word. He saw it now, how she'd never given an inch to anyone – the bloody-mindedness of her. He wondered what really happened between her and Charlie, how much of what she'd told him was the truth. She'd made a fool of him, fools of them all, especially the gangsters, leaving them behind to clear up the mess. They had no choice. She never gave anybody a choice.

CHAPTER 18

He didn't really know what drew him to the place. But it had featured in the newspapers so much recently, it had been a constant reminder of his past. Whatever secrets it was yielding up, it was where he came from. Grey clouds hung in a darkening sky. The rain had stopped, so the two coppers who had been sheltering inside the big porch came out and went back to their guard duty outside it again. The front door was the same shade of green he remembered, except the paint was fresher. The curtains were drawn on all the windows, but there was a light just visible through a gap on the first floor.

The papers said that all the kids had been removed to other homes, so the place must be empty now apart from the police. They continued digging in the back garden, but hadn't turned up anything new for a week. There were still the four bodies. Just the four. And he knew the two they'd named so far – Sheila and Cliff. No Sally. Speculation as to who the other two were was dying down. Sheila and Cliff's names and photos had made the headlines. Ian's photo too had featured on the front pages, along with pictures of his mother's house in Norwich. A reward was offered for information, Interpol were on the case. But the story was already getting old. The international manhunt would run on until everyone forgot about it. Eventually it wouldn't matter anymore. They were just some kids without parents anyway. Or if they did exist, they were bad parents. How else would the kids have ended up here? Parents like that wouldn't bother themselves with the fate of children they'd wanted rid of. No-one was going to mourn for them.

What if he'd been one of those bodies in the ground? Would his mother come looking? He hadn't even thought of that before. Maybe she had. Two of the bodies hadn't been identified yet, though he knew one was Ian, but if there was anyone out there interested in what happened to their kid, there must be something. There must be somewhere to go and ask, to 'make enquiries' as people say. The home was run by the Council. So somewhere in an office a pen-pusher would have a list.

The surge of excitement made him dizzy – this sudden possibility. He had to do something about it – follow it up. He'd get on it first thing tomorrow. But there was no point getting too carried away. It was only a long shot. He needed to stay ready for the disappointment. After all, he didn't know anything about his mother. She might even be dead herself. And the dead don't rise from the grave – except in the back garden of his old home.

His thoughts were interrupted by a man arriving at the gate to the home, opening it and walking up the path to where the two coppers stood. His heart bounced in his chest. Without even consciously realising it, he knew he was looking at Trevor.

He was greyer, unshaven and shabbily dressed, but not in the down-at-heel way Davis had been. This was more like a man on holiday, at his ease, and even now starting a friendly conversation with the cops.

Trevor told some story, and Ken watched as they all laughed at the end of it, Trevor loudest of all. Then Trevor turned, put his key in the front door and made a final cheery comment before disappearing inside.

He struggled to know how to react to what he'd seen. Trevor, carrying on life at the home while men dug bodies out of the ground in the garden behind him – bodies he'd been responsible for putting there. How could it be? Surely at the very least he was a suspect. Even if he wasn't, why was he in the house? Is that what the Council did when they had a murder investigation in one of their homes – let the boss carry on life as if nothing's happened – give him a holiday until it's all blown over?

But then Trevor wasn't just any boss. He got away with it because he was surrounded by powerful friends – friends he could blackmail when he needed to. Councillor Harshaw wasn't it, as well as Baldwin? Others too. With Baldwin still in charge of the investigation, Councillor Harshaw was probably turning up to work just the same as Trevor. But sooner or later Baldwin would be getting a phone call and asked a favour that he wasn't going to be able to refuse; the same with the Councillor, and Lord Percy too. Ronnie Kray had expressed his thanks and wondered if Ken might like to attend a little get-together he was having. Ken knew he'd handed him and his brother a weapon that would help them become far more powerful than they already were. But Trevor – he was still the spider in the middle of the web. If you wanted someone to cater to your sadistic sexual appetites, he would be only too happy to oblige. That was his value. Lust and perversion could take people down some very dark alleys. Waiting at the end, in the darkest place, was Trevor. And the men who had the diary now would see in him a man ready to help them find their own special kind of fulfilment whenever they needed it.

Ken could see now that he might have got some kind of justice with Baldwin, and maybe the Councillor and Lord Percy as well, but Trevor wasn't going to be paying any price. He was too useful. The investigation would be over soon, the blame laid at the door of the insignificant Ian. The ripples on the pond would settle and everything would go back to normal. And, after a decent interval, Trevor would start again.

* * *

THE END

FROM THE AUTHOR

Hello, I'm Gerry Duffy and 'Charlie's Little Secret' is my first attempt at a self-published novel. I've been writing for several years – short stories and other novels – and belong to a group of writers called the Bristol Novelists. Their help in reading and giving me feedback has been invaluable in producing this final version of the story.

Like all writers, what matters most to me is that people get to read my work. So I'm taking a bit of an unusual path to help make this happen. You may have come across this novel on the Amazon website, or you might have found a copy I left in one of those old phone boxes converted into libraries, or maybe in a charity shop. If you're really lucky you'll be one of a very small number of people who have had one delivered directly to your home. I like the idea of sprinkling things randomly and seeing what happens.

But however you come across the novel, I really hope you enjoy reading it.

If you do, it would be great if you could tell the world via a review on Amazon or Goodreads. And if you'd like to buy lots of copies for your friends and relatives, you can find both digital and paperback versions on the Amazon website.

Finally, if you would like to find out more about me and read/hear more of my work, take a look at my website: writergerry.wixsite.com/gerryduffy.